Still Life, Still Dead

by

Sydney Abrams

An Arts and Crafts Mystery

Still Life, Still Dead

Cover Art by *Tina Lynn Stout*

The Wild Rose Press, Inc.
PO Box 708
Adams Basin, NY 14410-0708
Visit us at www.thewildrosepress.com

Publishing History
First Edition, 2025
Trade Paperback ISBN 978-1-5092-6023-2
Digital ISBN 978-1-5092-6024-9

An Arts and Crafts Mystery
Published in the United States of America

Dedication

This book would not have been possible without my partners in crime—the friends, family, and my art group, who propelled me into this journey and gave me invaluable feedback. I might have given up on the absurd notion that I could do this, but my husband's endless humor and unwavering support kept me moving forward. I am profoundly grateful to Bryn Donovan, whose editing and coaching transformed my writing from a hobby into a craft, and to Eilidh MacKenzie, my incredible editor at The Wild Rose Press, whose guidance has been instrumental in helping me reach the finish line.

Flat Rock Falls is a fictional town, and The Creative Workshop and all the characters in this book are derived from my overactive imagination. Any mistakes with procedures or techniques are mine, and mine alone.

Chapter 1

Friday

I was walking at a good clip but slowed my pace as I passed the darkened storefronts along Main Street. The vintage streetlights cast a soft glow and illuminated the window displays filled with pumpkins, fall leaves, and corn husks, officially ushering in my favorite time of year. It had been dark when I left my apartment this morning, but by now, the faint predawn light was beginning to contrast with the hills that surrounded our town, and I took a deep breath of the cool crisp air as I welcomed the new day.

Okay, that sounded corny even to me, but as those who knew me could attest, I just really liked fall. I frequently noted how the air felt different here in Flat Rock Falls, and I have, on occasion, spontaneously shouted, "I feel alive!" during the transition from summer to fall.

Although I no longer had to get up this early, I often did because I loved the stillness of this hour. Back in Philly, the golden hour was also when the best brainstorming took place, so when a thought struck me, I didn't hesitate before pulling out my phone to call Maggie, my assistant manager.

After a number of rings, a sleepy voice answered, "Alex, is the building on fire?"

"No! Of course not."

"Okay then. You've just forgotten, again, that most of us aren't up with the first chirp of the birds."

I came to a halt and inwardly groaned. "Omigosh, Maggie, I'm so sorry—Go back to sleep," I added in a hoarse whisper, as if lowering my voice would lessen the aggravation of the wake-up call.

"You might as well tell me why you called." Her voice sounded farther away now, as if she had put me on speakerphone and buried her head under the pillow.

"Never mind, it's not urgent. Go back to sleep."

"Mmm," she mumbled. "I'll text you when I get there."

"Yeah, sure, I'll…" She disconnected the call before I could say anything further. It's difficult to kick oneself while walking, but I tried.

And then, as if Maggie had sent a message to the universe, the skies opened up, and I was caught in a driving rain. I ducked under the awning outside the Sugar Rush bakery, which, sadly, wasn't open yet, and as I stared at the enticing signage for coffee and pastries, I couldn't help but think this was a special kind of karma.

It didn't take long for the rain to let up, and I was debating whether to continue walking or head back to my apartment when I noticed the silhouette of a lone figure across the street. It was dark where they stood, but I could tell they were facing my direction, and it was a little creepy how motionless they were.

Were they watching me? Maybe someone would join them, pick them up, or they would move on. I waited a few minutes, pretending to read a poster in the bakery window, but when no one came, and the figure still hadn't moved, I felt a tingling sensation on my arms and neck that I recognized as fear. This made the decision for me, and I headed straight home with a purposeful stride.

I looked over my shoulder a couple of times but didn't see anyone following me, and by the time I reached my building, I felt silly. This was, after all, Flat Rock Falls. Nothing ever happened here.

After changing into what had become my staple wardrobe of paint-stained jeans, an oversized men's button-down shirt, and work boots, I impatiently waited while the coffee machine went through its grinding, brewing, and milk frothing. I considered making some toast, but even through the bag, I could see dots of mold on the bread.

I hadn't quite gotten the hang of small-town domesticity, which meant my larder was frequently bare or in a state that looked like a science experiment. So, instead, I grabbed my coffee and a handful of candy-coated chocolates from the bowl on the counter and went into my home office to wake up my sleeping laptop. Time to get to work.

I now owned and managed the Creative Workshop, a collective for artists. We currently had over a dozen professional artists renting studios, and we had become a community hub for classes in every art and craft form imaginable. This was my new chapter, and even at the age of forty-seven, I occasionally felt like a kid fresh out of school embarking on their first professional adventure. Everything was new and exciting.

Next week the Workshop was hosting an artist retreat, Palette and Pencil: The Art of Making Art. This was our first event with participants from out of town, and it could take our business to the next level, so I really wanted things to be buttoned up. Spencer Wells, one of our resident artists, was leading it, and Niko Romano, a prominent painter coming from New York City, was the main attraction.

I had lost myself in a sea of details when my phone pinged with a text from Maggie.

—*I'm here.*—

—*Be right down.*— I texted back.

When renovating the building, I had included an apartment for myself on the second floor, so all I had to do was grab my worn leather satchel, a third cup of coffee for me, and an apology macchiato for Maggie and walk across the landing to take the wide center staircase down to the lobby and front desk.

"Mornin'. I come with a peace offering!" I called out, making my descent.

"I will gladly accept your offering, but no worries, I'm almost getting used to those random early calls. So what was it this time?" Maggie asked, tucking her pencil above her right ear. Today, her sandy-blonde hair had vibrant streaks of blue, and she had chosen a pair of multi-colored cat-eye glasses from her vast collection. She looked younger than her thirty-one years, but she was sharp as a tack, and we'd devised a mutually beneficial arrangement where I gave her studio space for her photography in trade for helping me manage the Workshop.

"I had another idea for our winter roster. A Paint and Sip series," I said.

"Oh yeah, I've heard about those. It's more like a social mixer, but people paint while having a little wine and cheese. They're also great for birthday or bridal parties."

"Exactly, and we could incorporate other arts and crafts ideas, like pottery painting. Anyway, it was just rolling around in my head, and we can talk more about it later. Any messages this morning?"

"Dustin from the Thunderbird Lodge called to say he got your message, and yes, they are all set for the opening reception on Sunday. He also confirmed the names of the class members staying there but noted Niko called to cancel the reservation we made for him."

"What?" I asked, in a panic. "What does that mean? Is Niko pulling out?"

"I don't know. Dustin just said he canceled. Surely, he would have contacted you or Spencer if he wasn't going to come."

"Right. Let me text Spencer, and if he doesn't know anything, I'll call Niko." I pulled out my phone and fired off a quick text to Spencer. "Anything else?" I asked, while waiting to hear back.

Maggie stood on her tiptoes, leaned forward on the reception desk, and lowered her voice. "I was going through the receipts and noticed Ari is behind again on her fees. I'm assuming that conversation would be better coming from you."

I nodded. "I'll try and catch her while she's here today."

Back to a normal voice, she said, "Otherwise, it's all good. As of this morning, our fall classes are full, and I've already been getting inquiries about the winter lineup since we put out the announcement on social media."

"That's great," I said distractedly, since my phone had dinged with a text from Spencer. "Okay, we're fine," I said, with relief. "Niko wants to stay at the Danbys' B&B instead of the Lodge."

"The rest of the class are staying there, right?"

"Yep, except JJ and Bitsy." They were locals, and friends of ours. "I just hope they have a room available." I skirted the front desk to drop my things in the office, and said, "Spencer's already here, so after I call the Danbys, I'm gonna check in with him. I'll stop by your studio later to update you."

"Cool," she answered, as she put her earbuds in and bopped in time to whatever tune was playing.

I sat at the desk and counted to ten. In my old job as a political consultant and strategist, I had to problem-solve constantly, and I rarely showed stress, but that didn't mean it wasn't rolling around like a tsunami on the inside.

Once I had collected myself, I placed the call, and after a few minutes wrangling with Brenda Danby, we got it sorted out. No, Niko had not called. Yes, she had a room available, and since he was the guest of honor at our retreat, she assigned him the best room of the house. She was thrilled; I was relieved.

I went down the hall to the large classroom where Spencer had set up shop for the retreat. Spencer was a well-known painter who had moved from New York to settle in Flat Rock Falls soon after the Workshop opened its doors. His deep brown eyes radiated warmth and intelligence, and his quick wit kept us laughing.

"Hey, Spence!" I said, walking through the open door.

"Hi," he huffed, shoving one of the large easels into place. Once finished, he put his hands on his hips and said, "Damn, these are unwieldy. I could pick up and move my first car—my old Mini, named Mimi, by the way—more easily."

"Ahem, that was what, over twenty-five years ago?" I asked, and grinned.

He looked at me sideways. "Smart-ass."

Spencer was well over six feet tall with broad shoulders, large hands, long fingers, and a buzz haircut. His physique could make you think he made big, bold pieces of art, but he was a master at trompe l'oeil and was known for his small vignettes that looked so perfectly three-dimensional you might think you could pick something up off the canvas.

"So I got Niko's accommodations squared away at the B&B," I said. "That gave me quite a jolt this morning. For a hair-raising minute I thought he had pulled out of the retreat."

"Sorry about that. I assumed he took care of it himself, and would have let you know."

"Yeah, it seems he only took care of half of it, and it happened to be the cancelling half." I assessed the easels, paints, canvases, brushes, sketching materials, and task lights at each work station. "It looks like you're all set here. Could I take a look at the schedule?"

"Sure." He crossed the room in a couple of strides to pull some papers from a hodgepodge of stuff piled high on the desk and handed me the outline and class schedule.

I wiped some unidentifiable schmutz from the paper. "Geez, clean much?"

"Ha-ha," he said with sarcasm.

At that moment, Ryan, a professional sculptor, and my other part-time staffer, ambled into the room.

"Morning!" he said, with a twinkle in his green

eyes. He was working his way through a doughnut, which meant he also had an impishly happy grin, powdered sugar on his chin, and a little smeared in his tousled brown hair due to his habit of running his fingers through it to brush it back from his eyes. "It's Friday, so I stopped by the Donut Hut!"

"Oh man, you're the best," I said enthusiastically. Doughnuts had a special place on my personal food pyramid.

"I knew you'd be happy about that."

"How's the sculpture going?" Spencer asked.

"Pretty good, but I'm at a crossroads with what direction to go in next, so I'm taking a break to let it simmer a bit and thought I'd stop in to see if you've nailed down the field trip to the falls."

Spencer answered, "The weather still looks good on Tuesday, so we'll take off first thing that morning and be back for lunch."

Ryan nodded and gave a thumbs-up while swallowing the last of his doughnut. "I'll be here early to help load the van before shuttling you guys."

"Thanks, Ryan," I said. Sometimes, dealing with creative personalities was like herding cats, so I was incredibly grateful I didn't have to micro-manage my crew.

"Sure, but we're going to need to get the van jumped before then."

"What?" I squeaked. So much for not having to micro-manage.

Chapter 2

"What's wrong with the van?"

"I think the battery is dead."

There was no point wasting time asking him how long he had known the battery was dead or why he hadn't told me before now. I just pulled my glasses down from the top of my head and pulled my phone out of my pocket.

"I'm texting you the contact for the auto shop. We're not going to jump it. They will come to us. Find out when they can get here, and I'll leave the credit card with you if I'm going to be out."

"Okay, I'm on it."

I quickly flipped through the pages Spencer had handed me. "I'm going to borrow this to update the online calendar. Is there anything else I can do? Have I forgotten anything?" After the morning I'd had, I was questioning everything.

"Nope. I'm actually ahead of schedule with the prep work, and I'll go over everything again with Niko before the reception on Sunday."

"You're sure he has a good grasp of who is coming to this retreat?" I asked with a hint of doubt in my voice. Niko was fairly well-known in art circles, and at forty, he was on the hot list for collectors who wanted to buy from a younger, but established, artist. I still couldn't quite grasp why he wanted to come to our small-town art retreat.

"Yes. I've known Niko for years, and while he can be a bit arrogant, he was open to working with both professionals and amateurs."

"I'll have to take your word for it. The couple of times I've talked to him he's been pleasant enough, but I must admit, I did sense some condescension. He better not pull any of that crap while he's here."

Laughter bubbled up from Ryan. "Uh-oh, I know you won't have patience with that. You'll squash him flat if he acts like a jerk," he said, smacking a fist into the palm of his hand.

"Mmm, with an invited guest, I think I would practice restraint first," I mused.

"Too bad." He grinned. "I would buy tickets to see you take him down."

Spencer let out a breath, and said, "Ryan, don't egg her on. And aren't you supposed to be calling the auto shop?"

"I'm going right now," Ryan said, with a two-finger salute, before jogging out of the room.

Spencer looked at me with an amused expression. "You're going to get Mount Everest-sized grooves in your forehead from scrunching your brow. Don't worry, I've got this under control."

I laughed and used my finger to smooth the spot in between my brows. "Yeah, yeah, I know. I just want this to go well. It could really set us up for future events."

"Don't forget, this ain't my first rodeo—as they say. And it's a walk in the park compared to what you used to do." He came over and turned me around to face the door. "So get out of here and let me finish setting up."

"Yeah, fine, I'm going." Once out the door, I couldn't help calling back over my shoulder. "Just clean up that desk before everyone gets here on Monday." I could hear him cackling from halfway down the hall.

****

Even though we didn't need someone to be at the front desk all the time, I liked to visit with people coming in for classes. It kept me connected with the community and made them feel more connected to the Workshop.

It also made time fly, and it was well after noon when I went to see if Ari was in her studio so I could talk to her about the rental fees and check that task off my list. She wasn't in yet, but across the hall, the photography studio was brightly lit, and Maggie was working at her computer.

"Hi," I said, entering her domain. "The retreat schedule is updated online so you can plot out getting some photos. And did I see you're going to be the live model for the portrait segment?"

"You did! Wait till you see my outfit. I've been working on it for a week." When she turned from the computer to face me, her smile dropped and she scrunched her nose. "Oh, you have that look."

"What look?"

"The one when your head is about to burst from all the stuff in it." Maggie used her hands to mimic an exploding head.

I couldn't help but laugh, then said, "I hoped it wouldn't show."

"It doesn't. I'm just finely tuned to your every

nuance."

"What a crock."

I walked around the room to look at what she was working on and breathed deeply to take in the smell of the photography chemicals—developer, stop bath, and fixer. Probably not appealing to most people, but for me, it brought back memories of my childhood when my mom turned one of our bathrooms into a darkroom and we learned to develop film. And just like the old bluish-purple mimeograph ink from early school days, it was an aroma that could be conjured up even if not in its presence.

"These are gorgeous," I said, pointing at a set of nature shots Maggie had mounted on wood boards. "Did you take them in the area around the falls?"

"Yes, and thanks! I'm planning to do a really large-format landscape when we get to peak fall colors. It will be *huuuuge*." She grinned and opened her arms wide.

"I can't wait to see it. So how long are you here today?" I asked.

"I've got some freelance work I'm in the middle of, but I'll be heading home at about six to get ready for a date," she said coyly, but then scrunched her face. "Of course, it's a blind date set up by my old roommate, so I'm not too hopeful. I'm thinking of adding some purple to my hair to see if he's got the staying power. Anyhoo, I'll likely be back here tomorrow morning. I want to get this job off my plate so I can get back to my own work."

"Well, have fun tonight, and I look forward to hearing about it." Her dating stories always made me laugh and at the same time incredibly grateful I didn't have time for the dating scene. I turned to leave, almost running smack into my friend Annie.

Annie and I had been friends since college, and after she settled in Flat Rock Falls, she ended up dating, then marrying, my cousin Jack. She had helped me develop the plan for the Workshop, and she also happened to be an incredible photorealism painter.

We shuffled back into the hall and I said, "I'm heading over to the Café for a late lunch. Wanna come?"

"You bet, let's go!" Annie said. "I'm having a serious hankering for Claudia's fried chicken!

****

The Main Street Café was really a diner, with a long counter and stools, booths lining the exterior walls, and tables in the center, covered with red-checkered plastic tablecloths. My aunt Claudia had owned the Café for as long as I could remember. She was on the short side and pleasantly plump, with quick-witted bright eyes. Her hair was always up in a bun clip, and she often had the additional accessory of a pen tucked into it. She was an open book, and her laugh could be heard across the room, but you could also sense her displeasure from the same distance.

"Hi, Aunt Claudia," I called over to where she was sorting order slips at the counter.

"Hi, girls," she sang back. "Grab a seat and I'll be over in a minute."

Annie and I looked around and saw our friends Bitsy and JJ having coffee, so we weaved our way over to their table.

"Hey! Can we join you?" Annie asked.

"Of course!" they chorused.

Annie and I scooted into each side of the booth and grabbed a menu, even though we didn't need to since we knew everything on it.

Aunt Claudia came over with a big smile, two glasses of water, and her order pad. "All right, girls, what's it going to be?" After we put in our order, she peered over her glasses at me and said, "You look a little puny. Add a side salad."

"Oh, okay!" I mock-grumbled back. After my mom passed away, Aunt Claudia enthusiastically embraced the mantle of a mother figure. I might gripe about it at times and sometimes felt like I was twelve years old again, but I cherished her for it because it helped lessen the sting I still felt at the loss.

I sat back in the booth and felt myself relax with the animated chatter of my friends surrounding me like a warm blanket. Bitsy, a semi-retired therapist, was married to our town's sole attorney. She had an effortlessly polished look, her laugh was infectious, and her personality lit up a room. She had a predilection for including birds in her art, which she had recently expanded to include unique hats and fascinators. Today, she had on a meticulously crafted pillbox hat with a bird perching on a nest, nestled in a pillow of veil netting. Somehow, she made it seem perfectly normal to have a bird on her head.

JJ, a retired symphony musician, had the poised demeanor and good posture performers often have. She was a voracious reader and super smart, but she also had the whiff of a free spirit. She told us her divorce allowed her to explore life to its fullest, which included picking up and moving to Flat Rock Falls. She was into crystals, meditation, and organic everything. She had also dabbled in an array of eclectic hobbies since retiring. She learned how to play the accordion, wrote poetry, gardened, and made her own soap. Her art was boldly creative, and she liked to break the rules of tradition and think outside the box. Sometimes we had to rein her in and keep her from straying too far, but her creative freedom was a breath of fresh air.

Later, after popping the last deliciously golden fry in my mouth, I shoved my plate back and asked, "So I'm going to see you guys at the meet-and-greet reception Sunday evening, right?"

"Definitely!" Bitsy said. "We can't wait to meet the other classmates, and of course, Niko. It will be so inspiring to see some of his techniques in person."

"Yeah," JJ agreed. "I've been working a lot on my painting skills, so I think I'm as ready as I can be."

Annie, who was leading some of the class segments, said, "Trust me, you guys will fit in just fine." Looking toward the door, she suddenly smiled from ear to ear. "Oh look, Jack's here." She caught his eye and waved him over.

Jack leaned down to kiss Annie on the cheek, then pulled a chair from a nearby table over to the end of the booth and plopped down to join us.

"Well, it looks like you've had quite the feast," he observed.

"Oh yeah, this now qualifies as 'linner' for me," I said.

When Bitsy gave a questioning look, Jack rolled his eyes. "You haven't heard this one before? *Linner*," he said, using air quotes, "is what she calls it when she's eaten late enough to combine lunch and dinner. This way she doesn't have to think about more than one real meal."

Annie nodded, then added, "She did that back when we were in college, too."

"Hello, I'm right here," I said, indignantly. "You can poke fun, but it's tedious and time-consuming to come up with three squares a day. Don't you agree?" I asked my tablemates.

"I'm staying out of this one," JJ said, chuckling.

Jack and I were more like siblings than cousins. I spent many summer holidays here in Flat Rock, and since childhood, we'd bickered and teased, but there was a deep bond between us. He was a few years older than me, with gray starting to tinge his sandy, short-cut hair. He was of medium height and stocky in the hard muscle way, although not from working out at the gym. It's more just how he was built.

He was mild-mannered, except when giving me a hard time, but always alert and observing, with a powerful energy percolating just under the surface. This demeanor served him well since he was the police chief of our little hamlet.

Since moving here, I occasionally did some office work for Jack. He called it tapping into my old skills. I called it free labor, since I always volunteered my time. Not much happened in Flat Rock, but once he'd cleared me as a consultant through the official channels, this relationship had served two purposes. It kept my hand in the research, data crunching, and strategy game I had left behind. And it helped Jack out because he was chronically short-handed, he knew I was fast, and he could trust me as a sounding board. Both of our dads had been in law enforcement, so it was sort of a family thing.

After indulging in the impossible-to-resist desserts, Annie and I headed out. We walked with a little less urgency than when walking *toward* the food. Now it was more of a stroll, and the late afternoon sun warmed us as the fall leaves crunched under our feet. I was feeling pretty good until I got a call from Spencer.

"So, we lost someone for the retreat. They have the flu and aren't going to be well in time to travel."

"Oh no, that's too bad."

"But I have a last-minute addition," he said, with enthusiasm, "so it's a wash."

"Wait, it's a little late to be adding someone, isn't it?" I asked.

"Look, it's no problem on my end. I know a little about her, and she's a pretty good artist. We can just swap out names for the room at the Thunderbird."

"Okay, text me her contact info so I can get her squared away, and also the name of the dropout for when I call the Thunderbird."

"Will do, and I almost forgot, Niko emailed a list of food and drink he likes to have on hand."

I turned toward Annie and mouthed *unbelievable*, then asked, "Does he think he's a rock star? He actually has a rider? Don't tell me, he wants a can of mixed nuts, but we have to remove all the pecans," I said sarcastically.

"It's not really a rider. Just a specific brand of water and energy drink, and he wants almonds, fruit, yogurt, and dark chocolate on site, if possible." When I didn't say anything, Spencer interpreted my lack of response as me tempering my aggravation, and added, "Um, do you want me to handle some of this?"

I breathed out a sigh. "No worries, I'll take care of

it."

After we hung up, I relayed the recent hiccups, and said, "I knew this day was going to be a mess."

"Let's just hope this is the end of it, and the rest of the retreat is clear sailing."

Back in the office, I contacted the new class member. She quickly sent me the information I needed for her enrollment, and I secured her a room at the Thunderbird and then emailed her the retreat details. Ryan stopped in with the receipt from the auto shop for the battery replacement, so that was done.

Tomorrow, I would hit the Bushel Basket market to fulfill Niko's wish list, but for now, I was determined to go off-duty for a while. I went to my art studio to work on a piece of stained glass I had started a few weeks earlier.

My studio was more of a glorified craft room. Having grown up with a mom who dabbled in an endless stream of arts and crafts, this truly felt like home. During my childhood, along with the bathroom becoming a photo lab, it had seemed perfectly normal when I came home from school one day and found a weaving loom set up in the living room, or the dining room table covered with a large wooden board for making stained glass, or the arrival of a kiln on the back patio. Just like my mom, I dabbled in multiple arts and crafts, and it was a dream come true to have a dedicated workspace where I could have a variety of projects going at once.

As I folded the copper foil over the edge of a piece of glass, I thought about how much she would have loved this place, and I often felt she was with me as I dived into one project or another. I used to tease her about starting something new before finishing what she was working on, so I chuckled in salute to her as I surveyed the room scattered with my partially completed projects.

During the remainder of the afternoon, I periodically drifted up and down the hallways. This afternoon Shelby was holding her weekly drawing class for teens, and I liked to stop in to soak up their youthful creativity. Moving farther down the hall, I saw light coming from Ari's studio and decided it was a good opportunity to talk to her about the studio fees.

I knocked on the frame of her open door. "Hi, Ari, how's it going? Boy, that is exquisite work." Her overhead light was off, and a task light illuminated a beautiful still life painting of flowers scattered on a table.

"Oh, thank you."

Even in the soft light, she looked tired, and her ordinarily beautiful olive skin was chalky. "Are you okay?" I asked.

"I'm doing fine. Really. I just need some sleep," she said, brushing her dark hair off her forehead. "Um, I know I'm behind on the monthly fees. If you could please give me a little more time, I'll be able to settle up. Is that all right with you?"

"I was going to talk to you about that." I leaned my shoulder against the door frame. "Don't worry, I can wait a bit longer. Just don't let things get too far behind, and keep me updated. I'd rather you come to me rather than me having to seek you out about it."

"Of course, and I do apologize." She breathed a sigh of relief. "Thank you, Alex. I know I've been a little out of it, but everything's going to be fine soon."

"You're welcome. You just take care of yourself."

"I will," Ari said. She curtailed any further conversation by turning back to her work.

Ari's slight frame seemed even smaller today. Clearly, something was weighing on her, but I didn't feel I should probe further. I returned to my studio, put on a podcast, and tried to lose myself in my glasswork until Annie popped in to say goodnight.

After another half hour of cleanup, I made the final round of the now-empty building, then climbed the stairs to my apartment. Normally I didn't even think twice about rambling around here alone, but tonight, the stillness hung heavily in the air, as if the building itself was holding its breath.

Chapter 3

Sundays were for taking it easy, working in my studio, and, if things were in a desperate state, a few household chores. I wasn't terribly consistent with housekeeping, but I was good at what I called deceptive tidiness. However, the opening reception for the retreat was tonight, so after the run to the Bushel Basket to fulfill Niko's snack and drink order, I cut out the chores and indulged in a short nap before getting ready.

Sometimes my old wardrobe came in handy, and I plucked an appropriately professional outfit from my closet: black slacks and a silk blouse with a bold abstract pattern in green and black, finished off with black low-heeled slingbacks.

While having yet another cup of coffee, I applied a more comprehensive cosmetic routine of eyeshadow, mascara, and some brow definition. Other than knocking into my coffee mug, which required a three-tissue mop-up, and sneezing as I applied my mascara, which resulted in an extra raccoon ring of black under my eyes, this was a seamless process. I brushed my unruly, long brown hair back into a manageable mane, put my glasses on my head, and took one last look in the mirror. "It's showtime," I said to my reflection, with some jazz hands thrown in.

****

The Thunderbird Lodge had a woodsy theme, with

a post-and-beam A-frame lobby flanked by two wings of rooms. The restaurant and lounge faced the densely forested back of the property with large windows overlooking an outdoor patio. It had a homey feel, particularly in the fall and winter, with the enormous fireplace in the lounge creating an inviting atmosphere for visitors and locals alike. It was the perfect place to host the opening reception for the retreat.

Dustin, the owner, was working the front desk and greeted me as I entered the lobby. "Hi, Alex. Your gang's already in the lounge."

I had arrived early, but it appeared the others had too. "Thanks, Dustin," I said, and quickened my pace. "I'll be back later to settle up."

Upon entering the lounge, I had the opportunity to survey the group because Annie and Spencer already had things well in hand. Reading a room was a valuable tool from the toolbox of my old job, and I learned a lot by simply watching people's body language and how they interacted with others. Early in my career, it had proven invaluable, but now it was simply a fascinating study of human nature.

JJ caught my eye, so I headed to the group she was with first. "Hello, I'm Alex Montgomery from the Creative Workshop. Welcome to the retreat. I hope you've settled in and are ready for a fun week!"

A chorus of "hellos" came from the group.

Bitsy took the lead and introduced everyone, with the bright red cardinal on her fascinator bobbing happily as she spoke. "Alex, this is Monica Sewell, Laura Mason, and Edgar Childs."

I shook hands with each as Edgar said, "Bitsy's been telling us a little about the Workshop. It sounds like an incredible place."

Edgar looked in his early sixties, with silver hair and a friendly face to match his outgoing and affable disposition. His blue button-down shirt highlighted his blue eyes, which were nicely framed by character-filled laugh lines. I could tell he was the one everyone would like to be around.

"Thank you, we are very proud of what we've accomplished in just two years."

"I'm an architect by trade, so I'm looking forward to seeing what you've done to make an old building work for you. Bitsy said it's an early twentieth-century brick school building, so I'm guessing gabled roofs, stone arches, and lots of big windows."

"You're spot on, and I'd be happy to show you around," I said, with genuine enthusiasm.

I then shifted the conversation away from me and listened while they chatted about the week ahead. I guessed Monica to be in her late twenties or early thirties, definitely the youngest of the group, and I sensed an insecurity in her. Her shoulders were drawn slightly inward, and her eyes cast shy glances around the room. She had on beautiful silver earrings and a delicate silver charm bracelet. The earrings were unique, and I wondered if she had crafted them herself and made a mental note to ask her.

Laura, our last-minute addition to the retreat, was in her late thirties, and from what Spencer told me, she was talented but hadn't broken through yet to be widely recognized. She had artfully tousled her dark brown hair and wore black jeans, a form-fitting hemp T-shirt, a tooled leather belt latched low around her hips, and knee-high boots. Normally, she would be considered quite attractive. However, her eyes reflected a self-absorbed personality, possibly diminishing her allure.

She was talking at, not with, the group. "Frankly, I wasn't sure I would have the time to come to this retreat because I need to finish a painting for a gallery show I've been invited to be in." When no one responded to her satisfaction, she added, "Believe me, it's a really big deal. But when Niko told me he was coming, I decided it would be a kick to see what goes on here in Flat Rock Falls." She looked at JJ and Bitsy and added, "I would never have imagined someone of Spencer's caliber would end up living here."

Bitsy tilted her head and asked, "Why do you say that?"

"I mean, why on earth would you leave New York City to come here?" she asked.

Bitsy looked nonplussed, and JJ had raised her eyebrow, which I knew meant she was close to firing off a snappy retort, so I stepped in. "Well, I left Philadelphia to come here, and it's been a good fit. This area seems to attract creative people, but I can see how it might be hard to imagine if you are fully invested in city life."

"Mmm," she muttered. "And, of course, Niko and I travel in the same circles, so I figured if he was going to be here, I might as well come too." Laura scanned the room, as if looking for Niko.

Monica and Edgar were politely nodding, and her lofty tone had started to rankle me, so I decided to cut this conversation short. "Well, we shall strive to live up to, and maybe even surpass, your expectation of it being a *kick* to be here." Laura narrowed her eyes, as if trying to determine if I was being folksy or sarcastic, so

I rewarded her with a big smile to further confound her, then turned back to Edgar. "So Edgar, tell us about your art journey."

He smiled. "I've always felt drawn to art but have only been able to really work at it since my career has settled and I can carve out more time for it."

Bitsy easily engaged with him. "Architects have a creative eye and are usually good at drawing, right?"

"To a certain degree, yes, but I definitely have a lot to learn. I'm a widower now, so I spend my vacations traveling to museums and galleries to soak up as much as I can."

"Oh yes," Monica said in a quiet but confident voice. "That's how I like to spend my vacations, too."

He smiled at her, and said, "This is my first retreat, and I feel like a kid because I'm both nervous and excited. It's such a thrill to be around so many talented people."

"Is this your first retreat, Monica?" I asked.

"No. My sister and I attended one in our hometown. Both of us wanted to major in art, but my parents thought we should get *practical* degrees instead," she said, with a youthful petulance. "Mine is in accounting. So, I spend my days crunching numbers and can only paint in my spare time."

Edgar turned on his avuncular charm. "That's a shame, but I think most parents want their children to have the financial security of a job that pays the bills. The good thing is you're young, and you have time to change your career direction if you so choose."

She beamed at Edgar's encouragement. "My dream is to go back to school to get my art degree, and then after I get in a gallery, I could teach."

Annie, who'd joined our group, said, "Oh, what a great idea. We can explore some degree programs while you're here."

"Have you all met Annie?" I asked. "She's one of our resident artists, and she'll be leading some of the class segments this week."

Once the introductions had been made, I took the opportunity to excuse myself and moved toward Ryan.

"Hey! Your ears must have been burning. I was just talking about you," Ryan said. "Peter, this is Alex Montgomery. As I was just telling you, she's in charge of the Workshop. Alex, this is Peter Bigsby."

"Hello," I said and gave what would become my standard intro.

As we shook hands, I felt like I had seen him before but couldn't place him. He was probably in his mid-fifties, and his facial features were slightly off-balance, which made him intriguingly attractive. He also quietly oozed self-confidence. He was clearly well-heeled, even though he was trying to downplay it; I knew an expensive watch when I saw it, and his leather loafers were top drawer, possibly custom-made. The rest of the package was more understated; pressed jeans with a white Oxford cloth button-down shirt and a business-exec-type haircut.

"What brings you to the retreat, Peter?" I asked.

"Well, I'm a modest collector of art, and about five years ago, a colleague prompted me to try my hand at painting. I think it was intended as a joke, but it turns out I have a modicum of talent, so I find it to be a relaxing outlet. Plus, I simply enjoy the process of learning something new."

"What do you do then for your day job? And

forgive me for asking, but have we met before? You look familiar to me."

"Oh, I don't think so. I've been told I have that kind of face. As for my work, I'm in business. Fairly boring stuff, which is why this is such a nice change of pace."

He clearly didn't want to elaborate on his job, so I let it drop.

"Peter was just asking me about the history of the Workshop and the area," Ryan added.

I laid my hand on Ryan's arm. "Well, you have a good resource here. Ryan's from Flat Rock Falls, and he's been involved with the Workshop since the beginning."

"I'm curious about the whole concept," Peter said, with interest.

"I can answer that from my perspective," Ryan said. "For many of us artists, finding a place to do our work is difficult. I mean, I can't exactly carve stone or do metal work in my apartment. It's messy, it can be loud, and, I need a lot of room. So having a designated studio space is invaluable."

"That makes sense," Peter said.

Ryan continued. "The bonus is the community we have here. Most of the time, our work is solitary. So having a place where we can hang out with other people when we want to is awesome."

I nodded in agreement. "Under one roof, artists can rent space at a fraction of the cost. We have over a dozen full and part-time artists, including painters, pottery and textile artists, and everything in between. We also offer a wide variety of classes, and now we've added the retreat aspect to the mix, which is why we are excited about this week and having you all here."

"That's fairly impressive. How has it been to change careers in such a drastic way, Alex?" he asked, turning his gaze toward me.

How did he know about that? Ryan looked surprised by the question, so I knew he hadn't told him about my past.

"You've done your homework," I said, matching his unblinking stare.

His smile was faint, but I read a hint of mischief in his eyes, and when I didn't further elaborate, he added, "The worlds of politics and art don't usually go hand in hand."

Something about this guy made me know he could throw me off my game if I wasn't careful. "Well, I've done the big city thing. And rubbing shoulders with the elite sounds more exciting than it actually is. Besides, I minored in art history at college and grew up around the arts, so this is like coming home. I'm much happier living this life."

Ryan gestured toward me. "Yeah, don't let these nice clothes fool you. She doesn't usually look like this. Most of the time she's got paint, dried clay, or stained-glass stuff on her."

Peter looked amused, and I shrugged with good humor but did a mental eye-roll at Ryan's youthful exuberance and lack of tact. Once he transitioned back to talking about the town, I took the opportunity to meander over to the bar.

Bitsy walked up and asked, "What are you having?"

"A cranberry mocktail." I learned a long time ago that drinking on the job, even in a reception like this, was just asking for trouble, but I do like to have a prop in my hand. "What do you think of your classmates?" I asked.

"So far, everyone is really nice, and it's an interesting group. I love learning about people and their experiences." She put her back to the bar and locked around the room. "Laura is a little off-putting, but I'm sure she'll relax once we get started. You handled her like a pro, by the way. Have you met everyone? Has Niko arrived?"

"I haven't seen him yet, but I know he's here somewhere. And I've met everyone except the group talking to Spencer."

"Oh, you're going to love Marie. She's a hoot."

"Is she the one with all the jangly jewelry?"

Bitsy laughed. "Yes! She's fabulous."

I picked up my drink and said, "Okay, off I go."

As I approached, I could hear Marie saying. "I brought a picture of my precious pooch, Pookie, and am hoping Niko will give me pointers on doing her portrait."

Spencer smiled. "You'll be happy to know we'll be focusing on portraits during one of the first classes. Oh, here she is...Everyone, this is Alex, the owner of the Creative Workshop. Alex, this is Marie Wheaton, her sister Paula, and Charles Sandling."

"Welcome," I said enthusiastically.

Marie clapped her hands together. "Paula and I are thrilled to be part of this group. I've just been telling Spencer and Charles how we participate in all of the art classes at our local community center and just love painting. We were going to take a holiday trip with the senior center but decided this would be much more fun!"

Charles looked like he was in the presence of a seriously contagious disease. His angular face became quite pinched as he looked down his nose, and he emitted a barely audible snort of disdain. He tried to catch Spencer's eye in an attempt to share the touch of superciliousness in his own, but Spencer was carefully avoiding his gaze, and exhibited nothing but generosity toward the sisters.

Charles appeared to be in his early forties, with dark stringy hair hanging just below his chin. He wore designer jeans over high-top sneakers, and a collarless white shirt under a brown blazer with the sleeves pushed up on his arms. His thin frame and gaunt face under the patchy five o'clock shadow made me want to offer him a sandwich, but I refrained.

Standing next to him, Marie and Paula were quite colorful, with matching pantsuits, Marie in lavender, Paula in blue. Marie was bigger than life, with a fully made-up face and colorful jewelry that jingled when she moved. It was evident she had no insecurities talking to anyone. Paula was more understated, with a quiet demeanor. I instantly liked them both.

"So tell me about yourself, Charles," I said, wanting to bring him into the conversation.

"Well, I've been painting abstracts for about ten years now and have just been invited to do a one-man show in Santa Fe next spring, so I'm working to finish up that series."

"That's exciting. I look forward to seeing some of your work. What will your focus be while here?"

"Well, Niko has some great techniques for using acrylic washes, and I am always looking for ways to expand my repertoire of tricks of the trade. Anything to knock 'em out faster, you know. Plus, it's just good to get a change of scenery and get out of the city." Looking down his nose at Marie and Paula, he added, "I'm sure with Spencer and Niko at the helm, it will prove to be worth my while."

Charles had started out pleasant enough, but I didn't care for his attitude toward Paula and Marie. I found it challenging to make nice with another prima donna personality, so I excused myself, knowing a five-minute recess would significantly increase my tolerance level.

I was coming out of the restroom when I saw Ari nearing the hotel's front doors. She was tightly clutching the straps of her shoulder bag, and her face had the telltale signs of holding back tears. I called out to her, but she didn't hear me and was out the door in one quick stride.

What was going on with her? What was she doing here? Ari was young and had no family in town that I knew of, so I felt compelled to look after her and made a mental note to check in on her more regularly.

Soon after I returned to the lounge, Niko walked in from the patio area. A lot of heads turned when he entered the room; some gave him curious looks because he was the celebrity guest, but Monica and Laura openly stared at him. My lip curled slightly, thinking about how easily he must reel them in.

He was quite handsome, but he was just not my type. His were more textbook good looks. He got all the best bits of his heritage, with an olive complexion, a graceful slender face fit for a sculptor, gorgeous shoulder-length wavy dark-brown hair, and a lithe physique. He was dressed in slim-cut charcoal dress slacks with a crisp white button-down shirt, and Italian dress shoes...the slick kind, that come to a point at the toe.

I walked over to greet him. "Hello, Niko, I'm Alex. It's so good to meet you."

"Helloooo, what a pleasure it is to meet you," he said, with just a touch of leer in his voice, while he appraised me up and down. Instinctively, I took a step back, and after a brief pause, he made the connection and realized who I was. "Ah, of course, Alex, we spoke on the phone. Spencer has told me so much about you."

"Yes, he's been a big part of the Workshop and was so pleased you were interested in participating in our retreat."

Spencer walked up as Niko said, "Well, we used to run into each other all the time in New York, but then he suddenly up and moved to this, um, quaint little town. I couldn't fathom what had made him turn tail and run to the boonies."

Spencer responded to the ribbing in good humor. "Yup, I realized I was not into the glitz and glam of the pretentious art scene. I just want to paint, breathe some fresh air, and take in the natural beauty around me. It's amazing how much work I get done without the distractions of the city. Come down off that high horse, Niko, and you'll see how much small-town life has to offer."

"Touché," said Niko, with a mock bow. "In all seriousness, I *am* happy to be here. I have a work commitment in Chicago, and this seemed to be a good stop along the way. Every time I talk to Spencer he speaks with such enthusiasm about the Workshop, so I look forward to having the week here to see first-hand what he's been raving about."

"Well, we are fortunate you were free to come, and we're excited about the week ahead. I'm sure you guys have some catching up to do, so I'll leave you to it."

I spent the rest of the evening making the rounds, and after the official reception was over, I settled up with Dustin, then made my way outside to where a group had congregated on the patio.

"I'm calling it a night," I announced, pulling my keys out of my purse.

Niko got up, reached for my hand, and mock-purred. "What? You're not going to stay and party with us?"

"Down, boy," Spencer jokingly chided. "One, she's the boss, and two, that's Alex. Let me tell ya, you don't mess with Alex. She may be small, but she's got moxie."

Thankfully, Spencer could make almost anything funny, so I laughed along with the others, and gave Niko the *I'm watching you* v-sign with my hand. "Enjoy your evening, and I'll see you all in the morning."

Joke or not, Niko was a piece of work. This was going to be an interesting week.

Chapter 4

Monday

Everyone arrived the next morning with an air of excitement for the first day of class. I played the role of greeter and directed them to the classroom where Spencer was already at the helm, and Annie was on hand to help them get settled. Niko was last to arrive. While immaculately put together, his languid manner told me he could use some coffee.

"Good morning, Niko."

He mumbled, "Morning. Ugh, morning."

"Not an early riser, hunh?"

"No, I'm not. I always do my best work at night." Somehow, even in his tired state, he managed to make it a smarmy comment and looked at me sideways with a wink.

I ignored it. "Coffee?"

"I've already had some. I'll be fine once we are underway."

I led him down the hall to the classroom. "Here we are," I said, extending my arm to usher him in. "Spencer can point you in the right direction if you need anything."

The next couple of hours were a blur. I got the lounge area set up for the morning coffee break, the weekly scrapbook class arrived, and a good number of our artists were working in their studios.

Midmorning, I stopped in to observe the retreat before they took a break. The group was engrossed in the drawing class. They were working on portraits, and I was happy to see Marie using the photo of her pooch for hers. Niko was standing over her, looking like he was going to hyperventilate. She was oblivious and kept enthusiastically asking him questions.

Peter piped up and said, "That's fabulous, Marie! You're in league with Manet and Hockney, who also did dog portraits."

Niko turned and scowled at him, so Peter swiveled back to return to his work. Although, he discreetly looked at Paula first, and they shared a mischievous grin.

Most of the group used the live model, Maggie, for inspiration. She was lounging in an armchair with her legs casually crossed at the ankle, dressed in a chic outfit of black-and-white-striped wide slacks, a white scoop-neck tee, and a black slim-cut blazer with white stitching. A sleek hairstyle and a fedora tilted over one eye completed the look.

Monica timidly raised her hand. "Um, Niko, would you please take a look at this?"

He stood next to her, studying her work. "It's your shading that's off. Work on it some more. I don't want to spoon-feed you the solution."

While he was talking, she stared at him as if willing him to look at her instead of her drawing. "Okay, I'll try."

Niko made the rounds to each person. When he talked to Laura, I noticed he put his hand on her shoulder, and she brusquely shrugged it off. Mmm, from the way she talked at the reception I assumed they were friends. Maybe they were, but like me, she didn't like his smarmy side. He leaned down to whisper something and she shot him a look, which made him laugh. Interesting dynamic there.

He reached JJ's easel, looked at her drawing and said, "You have some gaps in your technique. Maybe I can salvage this." He made swift movements with the drawing pencil.

JJ's face had fallen at the criticism, but then lit up when she saw the difference he made. "Oh! That was such a simple fix, but it made it so much better!"

"Sometimes that's all it takes," he said, and moved to Peter's station.

Monica leaned over toward JJ and whispered, "Why did he help you and not me?"

JJ chuckled. "Be thankful. It probably means you have more talent than me."

Everything seemed to be under control, so I went back to the lounge and had just set the thermal coffee carafe on the table when I heard voices out in the hallway.

"Hey! Having fun?" I asked, as JJ and Bitsy wandered in.

"Absolutely," Bitsy replied. "Maggie is such a marvelous model, and Spencer and Niko are giving nuggets of wisdom to those of us who need help on sketching a portrait. Then this afternoon, Niko's going to talk about color theory and give tips for the first layers of painting after sketching."

"It's an action-packed first day, that's for sure," JJ said, grabbing an apple. "And I love scoping out what the others are doing. I was a little nervous, but it looks like all of us nonprofessionals are at about the same level."

Maggie sauntered into the lounge, and her face broke into a big smile as she approached us.

"What do you think?" she asked, taking a quick twirl.

"It's fantastic! You look like the heroine from a nineteen-forties film noir," I replied. Before turning to leave, I quietly said to the threesome, "Don't forget, after class, we're going to have happy-appies out in the courtyard." Happy-appy was our slang for happy hour plus appetizers.

"Wouldn't miss it," JJ said, while Bitsy and Maggie gave me a thumbs-up.

Walking back to the front desk, I saw Charles outside talking on his phone, taking a smoke break, and out of the corner of my eye, I caught Peter coming down the center staircase. What was he doing up there? I went over to meet him as he reached the bottom step.

"Can I help you find something?"

"Oh, hi, Alex. Thank you, but no, I'm just looking around," he said, putting his hands in his pockets and rocking back on his heels.

"I'm afraid there's not much to see upstairs at the moment. The exhibit hall is closed unless an event is taking place. You'll see it later in the week when the works from the class are exhibited. There's also a large storage area behind the exhibit hall, but that's off limits to the public because our artists keep some of their pieces up there. And the other side is my apartment."

"Oh, of course, that makes sense. I noticed all the private entry signage, and now I know where that elevator goes," he said, pointing to the far end of the hall. "It certainly is a beautiful building. Maybe you can give me a tour later." He looked at his watch. "If you'll excuse me, I'll just wander down to get some coffee before we start back." He walked toward the lounge, stopping to look in each studio along the way.

Hmmm. He was a curious sort—in every sense of the word.

****

Everyone had already grabbed their boxed lunches and were eating al fresco at the tables in the courtyard when Niko strolled into the lounge. After going to the kitchen to get one of the super expensive energy drinks he had asked for, he looked at the lunch offerings, twitched his nose in condescension, and ambled outside.

I saw Monica stand up and invite him to join her table, but he politely declined and went to talk with Spencer and Annie. *Oh, don't get smitten, kitten. You deserve better...there you go, good girl,* I thought to myself, seeing her face fall but quickly recover before rejoining the happy chatter with her table mates.

I scanned the rest of the courtyard, and at face value, spirits were high. So far, so good, or at least good enough, I thought, grabbing a cookie as I walked by the table on my way outside.

When everyone made their way back to the classroom, Niko remained outside on his phone. He appeared agitated, abruptly swiping his phone to end the call before stomping toward the lounge door. Upon seeing me, he quickly recovered and was his normal smooth self.

"What a pleasure to see you again, Alex," he said, reaching out to stroke my upper arm.

I sidestepped him. "Cool it, Niko, I'm not buying what you're selling," I snapped. Professional courtesy only went so far.

He put his hands up in resignation and grinned at me. "Sorry, can't help it. It's my default mode. But I promise it won't happen again."

"Good. I'll hold you to it. Now, in an effort to have a normal adult conversation, do you feel good about how everything's going so far?"

He let out a laugh. "Spencer was right, you do have moxie. And to answer your question, yes, it's okay. You have a nice thing going here, Alex. I can see why your artists love it so much."

"Thank you."

"Plus, it's great to be able to spend time with Spencer again, so I'm glad it worked out to come. I saw some of Annie's work, and she's actually quite talented, too."

Finally, I was able to have a normal conversation with him. "Yes, she certainly is. Don't let her angelic look fool you. She's wicked good with a paintbrush in her hands."

"The three of us are going to dinner at the Lodge tomorrow night after class. There will be lots of entertaining stories, if you want to join us."

"I'm kept pretty busy here, but I'll think about it. No doubt, those two will have you laughing all night."

"I'm sure." He looked at his watch. "Well, it's time for class." He switched gears back to his more arrogant personality, and said, "I do like people who are eager to learn from me. Although dealing with amateurs tests my patience, so we'll see how the afternoon goes." He gave me the merest hint of a bow and then sauntered out of the lounge.

I rolled my eyes and shook my head as I watched him leave. What a twerp.

****

Later in the day, I stepped in the doorway to monitor their progress, and it appeared I had arrived just as a controversy was brewing. A discussion had ensued about whether artists should blend pigments to create their own black paint. It wasn't a topic that should be all that controversial, but Niko and Laura seemed to be in a standoff.

"I simply believe a serious artist will mix their own black instead of using a commercially mixed product," Niko stated.

Laura poked her finger at him. "That's a pretentious attitude with no merit."

"Think what you like. I'm just saying any artist worth their salt is going to blend their own."

Laura crossed her arms and squinted her eyes at him in defiance, and he put his hands on his hips and stared back at her.

Charles stepped in. "Well, I've done it both ways, and I can see value in both opinions."

"Spineless," Laura snapped at him.

Marie turned toward Edward and Paula. "Oh my, this is above my head. Do you understand what the big deal is?"

"Type-A personalities clashing," Paula whispered.

Edgar put his hand to his mouth to smother a laugh.

Spencer had let this go on long enough and introduced a new topic, which split the class into subgroups. Charles was more at ease with Niko and conferred with him on a professional level. Laura just ignored him now. Monica seemed to shy away from him and avoided too much direct interaction, but she observed him while he was working with the others. She was probably a little intimidated, unlike Edgar and Marie who were eager to soak up everything Niko had to offer.

Spencer came over to stand next to me, and I whispered, "I don't think I could handle his approach, but how do you feel he's doing with this group?"

"Unfortunately you popped in during a tense moment. It was going smoothly earlier, but now I'm having to intervene more than I'd like. I plan on pulling him aside later to tell him to tone it down."

"Mmm, good idea."

After class, the out-of-towners left together to walk to the Lodge for dinner, and the gang congregated outside in the courtyard. I pulled out leftovers from lunch, and we whiled away the hours with lots of laughter and storytelling from the day. By the end of the evening, I truly felt like the rest of the week would be smooth sailing.

****

Tuesday

The next morning, the class congregated out front to head up to Flat Rock Falls State Park to sketch at the falls. The morning air was cool and crisp, and I could already tell it would be a beautiful day, with blue skies and a few high wispy clouds.

Marie's jewelry was a little less prolific today, with only a set of silver bangles clanging merrily on her wrists, and I noticed Bitsy had also toned things down and wore a simple beret with a solitary painted enamel cardinal pinned to the side. She probably feared a bird might attempt to nest on her head if she did anything more elaborate.

I enjoyed eavesdropping on the animated chatter coming from the group, but Laura seemed in her own head, holding her to-go coffee cup in both hands as she leaned against the building, staring at nothing.

"Are you doing okay this morning?" I asked her.

She looked at me and actually graced me with a small smile. "I am. I'm just a little stressed about how much I have on my plate, so I didn't sleep great."

"Well, maybe being in the great outdoors will refresh you," I said, encouragingly.

"Doubtful," she said, off-handedly.

I lightly clasped her upper arm, then moved on. From experience, I knew there was no point in expending energy trying to change someone who was hellbent on having a glass half-empty attitude.

After Ryan and Spencer finished loading the van and Spencer's car with the supplies for the field trip, Ryan hopped in the van's driver's seat while Spencer wrangled the group.

"All right, everybody," Spencer called out, "let's hit the road!" He then turned to me. "We'll see you back here for lunch, Alex."

After the class left, I enjoyed a few hours of normalcy, and even had time to stop in and chat with Annie. I knocked lightly before entering her studio and couldn't help but laugh when she turned toward me, because the magnifying visor she wore for detailed painting made her blue eyes the size of saucers. Annie was a photorealism painter, which meant she spent hundreds of hours meticulously working on a painting that would look exactly like a photograph.

"Hey, there," she sang, with a hint of the southern accent that lingered from her childhood.

"I noticed you got here early this morning," I said.

She pulled the visor up to perch on her head. "I have *got* to get this done by this weekend, so I made myself set an alarm. The tiny detail on this painting might do me in. Why did I pick so many props for this? I'm ready to throw something across the room."

"You'll get it done—you always do," I said.

"So what have you been up to this morning?" she asked, setting down her paintbrush to pick up her giant neon-green thermal mug with a built-in straw. Her cheeks puckered and her eyes opened wide as she took a deep sip of her smoothie.

"The class is up at the falls, so I'm just holding down the fort."

"If I wasn't on such a tight schedule, I would have gone along just for the fun of it. It's a beautiful morning to be up there."

I walked over to her easel. "It is, but hey, this is looking great."

"Thanks. Once I get this section finished, I'm going to tweak my notes for the retreat."

"I hope the talk about the class dynamic last night hasn't given you any reservations." During our hang in the courtyard there had been a lot of discussion about the various personalities in the class.

"No, not really. I'm doing a short segment on thinking outside the box—like finding paint brushes in unlikely places, such as this cheap blinged-out makeup brush I use for blending edges." She laughed, picking up a brush with swirling glitter in the acrylic handle. "Niko will dismiss me as a dingbat if he's there, but I can't worry about that."

"Right," I said. "You do what you want to do and don't worry about him or anyone else."

Annie had a set of floor-to-ceiling bookshelves in her studio that housed all her painting props, everything from troll dolls and old-fashioned toys to worn leather suitcases and rusty metal tools. A new collection of Pez dispensers caught my eye.

"What are you going to use these for?" I picked up a Bugs Bunny Pez, and used my thumb to gently open and close his spring-loaded head and ears.

Her eyes widened with excitement. "I found those on eBay! Some are vintage. I think I'm going to paint a Pez chorale, with all the characters lined up in a semi-circle like a choral concert. The reflection is fantastic if I put them on a shiny black lacquer floor."

"What a fun idea." There were candies in the Pez, so I popped one out and ate it.

"Alex!" Annie exclaimed in horror. "Those were in the Pez when I got them. They've probably been in there for years, and who knows where they've been!"

I paused for a few seconds, mid-crunch, then shrugged my shoulders. "No worries, they seem okay."

"Oh good Lord, you are hopeless."

I reluctantly put Bugs back on the shelf and headed to the door. "I have some phone calls to make, so I better scoot. I'll see ya at lunch."

"You betcha!" Annie said, with a smile.

****

I had cleared a pile of work from my desk when I heard animated voices coming through the front door.

"Hello!" I called out, as the rosy-cheeked group came bustling in. I joined their procession down to the lounge for lunch.

"What a *wonderful* morning!" Edgar said, in a joyful, booming voice.

"Oh, we had such a great time out there," JJ exclaimed, draping her jacket over the back of a chair. "The weather was gorgeous, and it was so nice to breathe the fresh air. I felt one with nature!"

"And the falls were perfect," added Bitsy. "The recent rain has them flowing nice and full."

"Where's Monica?" I asked, looking around the room.

"Her boots got muddy, so she's popped over to the hotel to change. She'll be right back," said Bitsy.

Marie and Paula were also divesting themselves of their jackets and were animatedly talking with Peter. Even Charles looked happy. The morning out in the great outdoors had done wonders for his pallor and disposition. He was attempting to engage with Laura. She was a little lukewarm toward him but allowed him to chatter on as they took their boxed lunches to one of the outside tables.

Monica came bustling in, breathing deeply to catch her breath. "Sorry I'm late! Is it too late to grab something to eat? I'm not really hungry, I just want some fruit or a small bite."

"Of course not! You have plenty of time. Spencer and Ryan haven't even gotten here yet. So how did you like it at the falls?"

"You are so lucky to have such a beautiful park this close to town. I'm afraid I didn't do my best work with the sketching assignment because I was so distracted by the scenery."

I smiled. "I'm sure you did just fine. Go on, get

yourself some lunch."

Spencer and Ryan were the last to enter, having finished the task of unloading the van.

"Has Niko been in yet?" Spencer asked.

"No, I haven't seen him. Didn't he join you at the falls?"

"He did, but I thought he left before us. I'm sure he's around here somewhere. Maybe he stopped at the B&B first to change his clothes. You know he prefers his city slicker wardrobe." Spencer laughed.

"I can well imagine he does. I'll keep an eye out, but in the meantime, grab some lunch while the grabbing is good. Aunt Claudia sent barbecue."

"Yum!" Ryan said, making a quick dash to grab a boxed lunch.

After the meal, I was wiping down the tables when Spencer came into the lounge and looked around the room with his lips tightly pressed together.

"Do you need something?" I asked.

"Do you have anything pressing at the moment?"

"Nope, what's going on?"

"Niko hasn't gotten here yet. I left him a message earlier, and I called again just now, but he's not picking up."

"Did you give the Danbys a call at the B&B?"

"Yeah, but no one answered. Brenda and Lyle must be out. I didn't actually see him leave the falls, but he said he was heading back to town."

Strange. "Maybe he went back there and fell asleep?" I suggested.

Clearly miffed, Spencer said, "I can't believe we have to track him down. It's so unprofessional."

"Look, no problem. I can go over there to check."

"Thanks so much, Alex. I'll cover the class until he gets here. Annie is around too, so I can always have her come in to talk about photorealism and what she's working on; sort of a show-and-tell segment that will fill some time."

"That's a good idea. I'll be back with Niko in tow in short order."

****

The Danbys' B&B was only a few blocks away on a quiet, tree-lined street. I checked the small parking area and saw a couple of cars with in-state plates, so I had my doubts, but I parked anyway and took the sidewalk around to the front steps of the old Victorian house. The heavy oak door was open to let the fresh air in, and I called out a hello as I pulled open the screened door.

Brenda Danby walked into the living room from the kitchen, drying her hands on a towel. "Hi, Alex! What brings you here?"

"I'm looking for Niko. Is he here, by any chance?"

"No, I don't think so, but I've been working out in the garden. He left this morning around ten to go to the falls. Is his car here? He drives one of those fancy small SUVs. Silver, I think."

"Mmm, no, I didn't see an SUV in the lot." I stood for a moment, then made up my mind. "I think I'll go over and check at the falls to see if he's lost track of time. If he comes back here, could you please ask him to give me a call?"

"Will do. See ya later," she singsonged, bustling back to the kitchen.

I hopped back in my car and made a quick pass through the Café parking lot in case he got sidetracked by a piece of pie. I knew that had happened to me before. Nope, no sign of his car, so I kept going and made the short drive to the state park. Fifteen minutes later, I pulled into the main parking area. At the end of the lot, somewhat obscured by the restrooms, was a silver SUV with New York plates. At least I'd found his car.

"Great. Now I've got to wander around looking for him," I muttered under my breath.

I threw on my light jacket and was grateful I had on my work boots as I started making my way up to the falls. As I got closer to the top, I called his name a few times, but got no response. The woods were thick here, but the trail was wide and well maintained. There was no way he could get lost unless he strayed off it, which I didn't imagine he was the type to do, but I scanned the woods just in case.

I finally reached the area where glimpses of the falls could be seen through clearings in the woods. There were multiple paths off the main trail in this area where people could get good views of the falls and the river below. I started with the first and took them one by one. There were times when the silence of the woods soothed the soul, with only the water and the birds as a soundtrack. Today, however, because I was growing irritated with Niko for losing track of time, the silence felt a little tense.

Eventually, I wound my way to a clearing where the ground was scuffed, with little divots in the soil. It looked to me like this was the beginning of the area where the class had been working, and the marks were from the easel and stool legs. The clearings were small, so the class would have been spread out across multiple arms off the trail.

I scanned the cliff's edge to see how far it was to the top and it didn't look like I had much farther to go, so I allowed myself a moment to take in the beautiful scenery and then dropped my eyes down to the river.

What was that dark patch? I moved a little closer to the edge and suddenly the hair stood up on the back of my neck and my skin felt prickly. Below, on the riverbank, Niko's face was partially submerged, and his arms and legs were bent in an awkward and unnatural way. The only movement came from his hair gently floating on the water. Niko was dead.

My mouth went dry, and I could hear the blood pounding in my ears. I stepped back and tried to catch my breath, scanning the landscape around me, looking for someone to call out to for help. I pulled my phone out of my pocket, but my hands shook so badly I dropped it, and then it took three fumbled attempts to pull up my favorites list and tap the number I wanted.

"Jack, I'm up at the falls. I need you here now."

Chapter 5

After I hung up with Jack, I called 911 and the park ranger station, then moved back to the main trail to wait. I felt every muscle tighten from the shock, and knew I needed to do something proactive.

Get it together, Alex. I pulled out my phone again to text Spencer. —*Please step out and call me asap.—*

What would I tell him? What if I was mistaken and Niko was still alive? I was sure he wasn't, but I should only relay the bare minimum at this point. A moment later my phone rang, and Spencer asked without preamble, "What's wrong, Alex?"

"There's been an accident. Just tell the class that, and I'll be back later to fill you in."

"Uh, okay…is Niko all right?"

"No, he's not. I'm sorry, Spencer, I just don't want to say more until Jack and the paramedics get here. I'll fill you in when I have more information, and I don't want to freak everyone out, so keep your cool."

"Okay, but—"

"I'm really sorry, I gotta go." I disconnected the call before he could ask me any more questions. Within minutes, the park ranger arrived, and after I pointed out Niko's body, he told me to go back to the parking lot to wait. I was happy to oblige.

I was leaning against my car when Jack and the ambulance arrived. As Jack walked over to me, I could hear the leather of his holster rubbing against his belt. His face was all business.

After I described the part of the trail where I saw Niko, he said matter-of-factly, "I'm heading up to take a look. Are you okay?"

"I'm pretty shaken up, but I'll be all right." A sudden movement caught my eye and I pointed to a big fluffy face in the back of his car. "Um, Jack? Who's that?"

Jack looked over his shoulder. "That's Baxter, Frank Pasco's dog. You know he hasn't been getting around so well lately, and he's moving into the retirement village where he can get some extra assistance. No pets are allowed."

"Oh no! Frank is such a sweet old guy. So why do you have Baxter?"

"Frank asked me to take him to the humane society. Unfortunately, none of Frank's poker buddies can adopt him, and he just couldn't bring himself to do it."

Baxter's tail wagged with excitement. "He's so adorable. Can I bring him out?"

"I guess so," he said, walking away. "He's a big boy, though, so keep a good hold of the lead. I'll be back as soon as I can. And please don't leave until we talk." He turned back, and asked, "You're sure it's Niko?"

"Not a doubt."

Time seemed to stand still. I alternated between sitting on the hood of my car, holding Baxter's leash, and pacing the parking lot with him, as if I was trying to run away from my thoughts. Images kept popping into my head: Niko's hair floating effortlessly in the water, his hands bobbing on the surface, and the unnatural position of his legs on the muddy earth above the water line with the crushed vegetation beneath his body.

Finally, Jack came down the hill and strode over to the car. "The paramedics are down at the river. It appears at face value to be an accident."

"Of course it was an accident. What else would it be?" I asked.

Jack raised an eyebrow and matched my tone. "We have to rule out foul play—like that he wasn't *helped* off the edge of the cliff. So to cover the bases, the team is documenting the site down there, and up top, where we think he went over."

"Oh." I started pacing again.

"Now, what can you tell me?"

Having something constructive to focus on was helpful. "The retreat class was working up there this morning from about eight thirty to noon. From what Brenda said, Niko left the B&B around ten a.m. Spencer talked to him up at the falls, and Niko said he was planning to head back to town before the rest of the group."

"So he wasn't teaching this part of the class? Was Annie up here?" he asked, with some urgency.

"No, she wasn't. And Niko was taking the afternoon segment. He just wanted to come up here to assess what everyone was doing."

"Were you here at all during that time?"

"No, I stayed at the office to get work done. Ryan drove the van, and Spencer took his car. Maggie went separately to take some pics, and she got back around eleven a.m. or so…I didn't really pay attention. Other than that, it was just the class."

"Okay. I will want to talk to everyone. Let's see, it's almost four thirty. What time does the class finish up today?"

I couldn't believe how many hours had passed since I left in search of Niko. "They wrap it up at five thirty. Do you want me to head over and have them wait till you get there?"

"Let me talk to Travis for a minute. He can hold down the fort here, and I'll follow you back."

I watched Jack walk over to Travis, one of his deputies, and after loading Baxter back into the car, I pulled out my phone to let Spencer know we were on the way.

****

Spencer was waiting for us outside when we arrived.

"So what happened?" he asked.

Before Jack could answer, I asked Spencer, "Do you need me to go tend to the class?"

His head swiveled as he looked back and forth between me and Jack. "Annie's handling things with the class. What the hell is going on? You guys are freaking me out."

When Jack gave him the news of Niko's death, Spencer froze in place and stared unblinking at Jack.

"I'm so sorry, Spencer." I leaned in to give him a hug, but he pulled away and looked at me sharply.

"He's dead? Alex, you didn't say you were up at the falls when you called me." His voice became agitated. "What happened? How did this happen? We were all up there!"

I had never seen Spencer like this, but Jack had

years of experience dealing with the fallout from an unexpected death. He remained calm and looked him square in the eyes. "Yes, Niko took a fatal fall up where the class was this morning. We are working to figure out what happened and when, but it's going to take a little time. I know this comes as a shock. Take some time if you need it, but I have to talk to the retreat class before they break for dinner. Do you want to remain out here?"

Spencer held his gaze and then scrubbed his face with his hands. "Sorry. I lost it for a moment. No, I'll come in with you. I have a responsibility to represent the Workshop alongside Alex."

I squeezed his arm and quietly said, "We'll get through this, Spence."

Jack nodded. "Okay, let's go."

We were walking toward the door when I stopped. "Wait. Let me put Baxter in the office. I don't want him left out here in the car."

As I went to get him, Spencer asked Jack, "Who the hell is Baxter?"

Understandably, Jack was impatient, wanting to get on with the more important matter of Niko's death, so I tried to be quick about it but failed miserably. I became tangled in Baxter's lead when he bounded out of the car, and then he dragged me over to the grass to sniff around. I looked sheepishly at Jack but then felt vindicated when he found a spot to piddle.

After securing Baxter in my office, the three of us walked down the hall to the classroom. Everyone looked at us anxiously as Jack stepped forward.

"Hello, my name is Jack Maddox, chief of police here in Flat Rock Falls. I regret to inform you that earlier today Niko Romano took a fatal fall from the area where you were working this morning."

There were audible gasps around the room. Laura looked up sharply at Jack, with one eyebrow cocked. Marie's hand flew to her mouth, and she looked at Paula, who was intently watching Jack. Peter, on the other hand, was watching me. Monica's hands were clasped tightly in her lap, and she looked down at the floor.

"I know this news comes as a shock, and you probably have questions, but at this point we don't have a lot of details to pass along to you. It appears to have been an accident, but until our medical examiner can do his part, we won't know exactly what happened. I need to ask each of you some questions right now, and then you'll be free to go about your business for the evening. Alex, it would probably be more comfortable to use the lounge. Is that okay?"

"Of course," I said.

Over the next hour and a half, Jack talked with everyone in the class, plus Spencer, Maggie, and Ryan. The subdued out-of-towners left to go to the Lodge for a much-needed drink before dinner, and the rest of us decided to wait in the courtyard while Jack checked in with Travis.

I brought Baxter out for a quick walk, and after everyone had been introduced to him, he settled quietly next to my chair. Understandably, he was a little clingy with all the changes in his life, and I had to admit, after the shock of Niko's death, he provided comfort for me.

"I just can't believe it," Annie said, in a subdued voice.

JJ was slumped in her chair, picking at a thread on

her sleeve. "I know. Poor Niko. He must have gotten too close to the edge, don't you think?"

"It's just awful," Bitsy added, trying to busy herself by putting out some of the leftovers from lunch.

I said, "We'll just have to see what Jack comes back with, but in the meantime, what did Jack ask you?"

Bitsy answered. "He basically wanted to know when we saw Niko, and if we had seen him leave or wander off onto the trails."

I could feel my brow scrunch. "Clearly, if he took a tumble during the class, someone would have noticed, right?"

"I only saw him for a few minutes when he came by to observe me and Edgar, and I'm afraid I was so absorbed in my own work I didn't notice much. I did go around at one point to see what everyone else was doing, but I didn't run across him again. What about you, JJ?"

"Same as you." She looked at me and explained, "We were spread out because each spoke off the main trail only had room for one or two of us to set up with the easels and stools. I was with Paula, and we saw Niko when he stopped by to observe, and another time I saw him talking to Charles out closer to the path. I thought maybe he was getting ready to head back to town."

Spencer was quiet, staring at nothing in particular, deep in his own mind.

"Are you okay, Spence?" I asked.

"I feel responsible. I was the one who brought him here to do this retreat. If he hadn't been here, this wouldn't have happened. I should have been paying closer attention, but I was busy going from person to person, and I didn't keep track of him."

Bitsy, being a therapist, had all the right things to say. "Spencer, you're not responsible for this. He was a fit, level-headed adult, and there was no need for you to have paid closer attention to him. There are things in life that are outside of our control, and an accident is one of those things. I know that deep down you know this. Work toward acknowledging that, and allow yourself the time you need to come to terms with it."

"She's absolutely right," Annie said, reaching over to grab his hand.

Jack came out through the lounge doors and pulled up a chair. "I just talked to Travis. They've taken Niko to the medical examiners over in Eaton, and I should get a report some time tomorrow morning."

"I just can't fathom what happened," Spencer said, looking at Jack. "Niko's not the type to go hiking through the woods. So how did he fall? And we thought he had left, so had he gone off wandering around? It just doesn't make sense."

Jack looked at him and said, "Even experienced hikers don't always realize how precarious it is at the edge of the cliff, so accidents happen, and they can happen in the blink of an eye. Just hang tight and try and get some rest tonight. We'll do our best to get some answers for you." He then got up and leaned down next to Annie. "I'm afraid I have to head back to the office to file the report. Are you going to be all right getting home?"

"I'll be fine. Don't worry about me. I'll grab some dinner with Alex, and then head home."

"Um, Jack?" I inserted. "Why don't you just leave

Baxter with me for the night? I can pop out and get some food for him, and he'll be fine here."

Jack and Annie gave each other a look that said, *Yeah, we know where this is going,* but Jack simply said, "Sure, if you want. The humane society is closed by now, so it would be a help if he could stay here with you."

Spencer, Maggie, and Ryan followed Jack to the parking lot. Annie, Bitsy, JJ, and I decided to go to the Café for dinner, so I took Baxter back to the office, filled a bowl with some water, and told him I'd be back soon.

News had traveled fast, and after a round of hugs, Aunt Claudia led us to a booth and quickly returned with hot water for tea and a napkin-lined basket with warm bread and butter.

"I think you could use some nice soup to warm your souls, yes?" she asked.

"That sounds like just what the doctor ordered," I answered, while my three friends nodded in agreement.

After our plates had been cleared, Annie sat back, and said in a tired voice, "I guess I better make some notes tonight on ideas to help with the class tomorrow. I don't want Spencer to have to cope with all of it, or even any of it, if he would prefer to take the day off. He knew Niko better than the rest of us."

"That's really nice of you. I know he'll appreciate it," I said.

JJ sat up straight. "Oh wow, it's going to be kind of weird to go to class in the morning. Do you think we'll be able to clear our heads enough to carry on?"

Annie answered. "It feels callous to just go on like nothing happened, but, at the same time, we're all still here, and nothing we do, or don't do, will change the situation, so we might as well carry on."

"Maybe we should have a cleansing ceremony." JJ suggested.

We all knew better than to even ask what a cleansing ceremony involved.

Bitsy said, "I think we should just take it one step at a time. The first step is to show up, and we'll see where it goes from there."

I thought about that and came up with an idea. "Why don't we have everyone come to the lounge in the morning and have an orange juice toast to Niko. Then you can move on to start the class."

"That's a great idea, Alex," said Annie.

****

After a quick stop at the market, I hauled in the bag of dog food, water and food bowls, a play toy, and orange juice for the morning. I dropped the OJ in the kitchen behind the lounge and took Baxter out to do his business before going upstairs. Upon entering the apartment, he made a beeline for the couch. I put out food and water and then plopped down next to him. Within minutes, his head was resting on my lap, and as I petted his soft fur, I could feel my blood pressure lower a notch. I had grown up around animals since my mom had taken in every stray that came her way, and I hadn't realized how much I had missed the companionship of a dog. After a while, I gave him a kiss on his nose and went to bed.

I tossed and turned throughout the night, dreaming of falling or of standing on a precipice in the dark and catching myself just before taking the step into a bottomless pit.

****

Wednesday

When I woke up the next morning, something felt different. Warmth emanated from the left side of the bed, and I rolled over to find myself nose to nose with Baxter. From head to toe, he was almost as long as I was, and he looked utterly adorable as his tail thumped a couple of times to indicate he thought this was a great sleeping arrangement. I reached out to pet his head and looking into his big soulful brown eyes, I thought, *Uh-oh. Game over. This dog isn't going anywhere.*

The group arrived in a somber mood, and I guided them to the lounge, where a table was set with wine glasses filled with orange juice.

"Good morning," I said. "I know we have all been blindsided by what happened yesterday. While it's difficult to feel closure after a sudden death, let's have a moment of silence, and then we'll raise a glass in honor of Niko."

Everyone observed the moment of silence, then I raised my glass and said, "To Niko, may he rest in peace."

"To Niko," chorused the group.

Afterward, the class talked among themselves in hushed tones, and I noticed the common thread with all of them was a visible lack of sleep. The bright eyes and energy I had seen the day before had been replaced with dark circles and fatigue.

After a respectful amount of time, Annie took the lead. "Okay, everyone, while we can't overlook this tragedy, and I know we're all reeling a bit from it, let's get started with our day. I'll be handling the class this morning, and I think we should try and make the most of our time here."

I went to the office and tried to busy myself with mundane work, but my mind kept churning about Niko's accident—not only how it could have happened, but the more clinical side of what it could mean for the Workshop. I made a note to call my insurance company to ask what our policy covered when it came to liability.

****

Spencer arrived around noon, and I asked, "Are you sure you want to be here?"

"Yeah. I'm just sitting at home staring at the walls, so I figured being here with friends and working with the class would help me more."

"Good. I know everyone will be glad to see you."

During lunch, the chatter was not as boisterous, but it seemed the class was finding their way, and I hoped some of the good cheer would eventually bubble back to the surface.

After lunch, Maggie stopped in the office and plonked down in the chair next to my desk. She let out a sigh and asked, "So, what do you think?"

I leaned forward and rested my forearms on my knees. "Honestly? I don't know. It seems like we might be able to get everything back on track. But Spencer, Laura, and Charles knew Niko. Will that affect how this week goes? I'm not sure."

"Spencer seems to be managing as well as can be expected, don't you think?"

"I do. But I've not seen much reaction from Laura and Charles, yet. At some point, I would imagine emotions might surface, and they will have to deal with them. And…" I trailed off, not wanting to voice my thought.

"What?"

"Well, let's face it. This could be bad for us. What if people start thinking we were somehow negligent—that our negligence caused Niko's death? It could ruin us."

I heard a sharp intake of breath from Maggie. "Oh, Alex, I hadn't even thought about that."

"I don't expect you to worry about such things. That's my job." I felt guilty for thinking in such a calculated way, but the truth was, until we knew what happened to Niko, I was going to stew about these things.

Maggie stood up. "What can I do?"

"Nothing at this point. Let's just hope there is a simple explanation for Niko's terrible accident, and that it's proven, without a doubt, the Workshop had no culpability. In the meantime, I'm going to put my head down and get some work done."

A little later, I heard a soft knock at my office door. I turned and found Ari standing in the open doorway.

"Um, sorry to disturb you, Alex, but I wanted to drop this off. It's all here, and I've included an advance of my fees." She awkwardly reached out to hand me a wrinkled white envelope.

I was surprised at having an envelope full of cash handed to me, but tried not to show it, particularly as I counted the total for the months of back fees plus three additional months of studio rental. I entered the information on the laptop and printed out a receipt.

"I'm so glad you got things sorted out. I'm worried about you, you know."

"Thank you. That means a lot to me. I'm okay, and

everything is going to be fine." Ari had one foot out the door but paused and added, "All of you here at the Workshop are so wonderful. I can't tell you how much I love it here. I know I'm not good at expressing it, but I really want to be a part of this community, and I think things are going to be better now."

"I'm so glad, Ari. If you ever need an ear, I'm here. Listen, come join us out in the courtyard sometime when we're hanging out after work..." I hesitated, then added, "I'm not sure if you've heard, but right now we're a little off kilter because of the death of our visiting artist Niko Romano. But when things are back to normal, I know everyone would love to get to know you better."

For a split second, Ari's eyes clouded, but then cleared, and she said, "I heard about that. It must be incredibly stressful for you, and I'm so sorry. And yes, I'll join you guys sometime, I promise."

"Good."

As Ari walked back out around the front desk, I thought something looked different about her. Her eyes still carried deep pockets of fatigue, but her body language was more relaxed, like maybe she was pulling herself out of a difficult time. I hoped that was the case. I hated to see someone so young look like they were carrying the weight of the world on their shoulders.

After taking Baxter out for a quick walk, I was back in my office catching up on some emails when Jack appeared and sat heavily in the chair next to my desk. He looked way too serious to have just come by for a casual update.

"What's up?" I asked. "Is there news about Niko?"

"Yeah. I just came from talking to the medical

examiner. Good thing you're already sitting down, because it appears Niko's death was not an accident."

Chapter 6

I let out a gasp. "What?"

Jack said, "We're calling it a suspicious death, but I feel in my gut it was murder."

My heart started racing. "Are you kidding me?"

"I'm afraid not. The medical examiner found faint perimortem bruising on Niko's back that indicates he was pushed with some force at the time of his death." Jack pantomimed a quick hard push with both hands outstretched.

"I cannot believe this! And what do you mean, suspicious death?"

"*Suspicious* is a broad category when it's an unexplained or unattended death. It covers a variety of things such as medical conditions, suicide, accidental, criminal—as in someone was with him, there was a scuffle, and he accidentally went over—or murder. Personally, I think someone intentionally pushed him, intending to send him over the edge, which makes it murder."

My hand flew up to my mouth. "Oh my gosh. When? Why? Who would do this?"

"That's what we have to figure out, Alex. I was over at the B&B early this morning, hoping to find Niko's phone to get a contact for family notification. Fortunately, I asked Brenda to keep the room locked and leave it as is. Now we'll need to go over all of his stuff with a fine-tooth comb. First, though, I want to ask you a couple of questions."

"I'm not sure I can think clearly enough yet to be of any help, but I'll try."

"I didn't find his phone, which didn't surprise me. It probably ended up in the river. And he didn't have an address or date book that might have an emergency contact. Do you know if he has any family?"

"I have no idea. Spencer might know."

"Okay, I'll ask him. Next…sooner or later I'm going to have to eliminate you from our inquiries, so let's get that out of the way now."

I started to balk, but before I could, Jack put his hands up and said, "This is standard procedure, so just relax. I have to do this by the book. You know that." He then pulled a small notebook and portable recorder out of his jacket pocket. "Go over with me what you did Tuesday morning between ten a.m. and when you found Niko."

"As I told you, I was here the whole time working. I didn't go to the falls."

"I know, but did you see anyone or talk on the phone during that timeframe?"

I knew what he was doing. He needed me to establish an alibi to prove I didn't have the opportunity to leave the Workshop, kill Niko, and then slip back in. I took a moment to think, then sat back and answered. "Let's see…yes. Ryan came back with the van shortly after nine, and he worked in his studio until he left again to make the pick-up around noon. I made the rounds while the quilting class was going on. That had to have been a little before ten thirty. I stuck my head in to say hi to everyone, and you can confirm that with

Shelby. I was at the front desk when they left at eleven. I visited with Annie, and I saw Maggie when she came back from the falls, and we talked briefly before she headed to the photo lab. I'm not sure what time that was, but you can ask her. I also saw Jeff from the Café when he delivered the lunches."

"Think. Who else?"

"Um…who else did I see…Elaine. She was here painting in her studio. I stopped in to see her after the quilters. I fielded a few phone calls in between all that other stuff. Is that enough? Do you need to see my phone?"

He took my phone, made a screen shot of the call history, then handed it back to me. "Thank you. I will have Travis verify all of this," he said, clicking off the recorder. "And once we do, it will sufficiently eliminate you, and then I can ask you for some help. For now, I want to ask you some questions off the record."

"You know, Jack, I am really trying not to freak out here. I feel like I'm on a spinning carnival ride. Just seeing Niko dead was hard enough. But now…"

"Now with it being a murder, that compounds it, right?"

I nodded. "The thought of a murder taking place with my people up there—well, it's too much to wrap my head around."

He leaned over and squeezed my knee. "That's understandable, but try and go into your problem-solving mode. It will keep your mind from overloading. You'll also have to sort out how to manage the retreat folks while the investigation is going on, so dig deep. You can fall apart later."

I knew he was right. "I'll try," I said, starting to

chew on my left thumbnail, an old habit I thought I had kicked. "What do you need to know?"

"How much do you know about these people? The ones here for the retreat, that is."

"Not a whole lot," I said. "It's not like I did background checks on them. Of course, JJ and Bitsy are in the class, and we know Spencer and Annie wouldn't be involved in this. I'm sure you'll have to officially check them out, but we can eliminate them for our own purposes, right?"

"They have to be cleared like everyone else. But off the record, I'm pretty certain they're not part of this. I mean, hell, Annie's my wife. I think I'd know if something was out of the ordinary. But I'll need to have Travis question her so there's no conflict of interest. And we'll have to thoroughly look at Spencer. He knew Niko, and he brought him here."

"Oh, come on. Spencer? His shock was genuine when you told him Niko was dead."

"It seemed to be, but I can't discount him just because you and I like him and he appeared genuine. So that leaves what, seven other people in the class?"

"Yes."

"How were his interactions with them? Did anything stand out to you?"

"Well, Niko was not an easy person. He even got under my skin, and I snapped at him. And I saw some tension in the room on Monday. But enough to warrant murder? I honestly don't think so."

"Let's hope that's the case. I know you have the software to do research and background checks from when you did campaign work. My boys will be spread really thin, so would you be willing to do some work for me once I get you cleared?"

I hesitated before answering, "Sure, I can do it, but this is not like what I've done for you before. This involves investigating my own people, and the retreat folks. I can't imagine any of them being involved. Isn't it more likely it was a random attack?"

"Realistically, random violence is not common. You know that. It's usually someone the victim knew. Plus, due to the water temperature, the ME can't tighten up the time of death, and the window of time includes when the class was up there working."

"I don't like it, but I see what you mean."

"Of course, our net will be wider than the class, and we'll need to delve into Niko's personal and professional history. However, the circumstances are fairly unique to this group of people—the time and the place."

"I'll help out in any way I can. This happened on my turf, so I want to resolve this as quickly as possible." I suddenly felt the little surge of adrenaline I used to get when digging around in my old job. "And maybe I can ask some questions and get people talking."

Jack looked at me sharply. "Uh, no. You are background only. Got it?"

"Yessir," I replied, but my mind was already churning, thinking about how I could maybe get people to open up. Being proactive would help me cope. "So what now? Do you want to talk to everyone again here?"

"Yes, I have Travis coming to meet me. There's no need to haul everyone down to the station at this point. Right now, we need to get as much information out of them as we can to create a timeline and see if there are any discrepancies. And hopefully, we can eliminate some people." He pushed himself up from the chair and said, "I want to tell Spencer and Annie first. Why don't you pull them out, and we'll talk in the hall."

I let out a long sigh. "Okay."

The four of us huddled in the hall while Jack gave the update.

Spencer whispered, "I'm not sure if I'm just in a constant state of shock or if I actually feel some relief."

"What on earth…?" Annie asked, looking at him sharply. "How could you be relieved?"

"I've been carrying around this burden of feeling responsible for Niko's accident. If someone else was involved, then it was outside of my control."

Spencer had echoed my earlier concerns, and I said, "I get it. It felt like we were somehow negligent, which we now know we weren't. But now we have to make sure no one in the class was involved."

Annie couldn't stand still and was looking wildly at us. "How can you be so calm about this? If he was murdered, that means there's a *murderer*!"

Her whisper had become coarse, and Jack put his arm around her protectively as he leaned down and said, "It's going to be all right. You're safe here."

Travis walked up to join us, and Jack said, "This is how we're going to do this. Travis, you take a statement from Annie. Spencer, you come with me. I also need you to draw me a layout of who was working where during the time up at the falls. Alex, go to the classroom. Don't say anything, just walk around and casually observe whatever they're working on, but keep an eye on how people are acting."

"If anyone asks, I'll tell them I needed Spencer and Annie to take care of something up in the exhibit hall."

"Fine. Once we're done, I'll come in and talk to the class."

I returned to the room and found everyone focused on their work, so I meandered around looking at their progress. Fortunately, no one asked me anything, and within ten minutes Annie returned, shortly followed by Spencer.

Jack then stepped into the room and made the brief statement that there were unexplained circumstances regarding Niko's death, and it was now classified as suspicious. There was a cacophony of *Oh my! No! Are you serious?*

Peter caught my eye. I couldn't tell what he was thinking, but the intensity of his fixed stare struck a different note than what I had experienced thus far from him. It was direct and intelligent, as if he could bore through my eyes to my brain to see what I knew. I looked away first, which discomforted me. I never shied away from a good stare-off.

I recovered by observing how others were reacting. Paula was trying to quiet Marie, Laura was looking at Charles in disbelief, and JJ and Bitsy were standing next to Annie, who was talking quietly out of the side of her mouth.

Jack raised his voice above the murmurs in the room. "I'm sorry for any inconvenience this may cause, but I have to speak with all of you again. We need your assistance to determine what happened up at the falls yesterday. You might have seen something you didn't realize was important at the time. So please think back. Did you see anyone on the trails or anywhere around the falls? Maybe you will recall another time you saw Niko, which will help us narrow down the timeline." Jack paused, then added, "I'm afraid I'm also going to have to instruct you not to leave town for the time being."

Charles stood up. "We're not allowed to leave? For how long?"

"Please don't be alarmed by this. It's standard procedure. Since you're scheduled to be here through the weekend, I hope you will just continue on with the retreat as best you can. I am certain the Workshop staff will do everything possible to make your time here as comfortable as possible. Thank you again for your assistance. My deputy will come get you one at a time to speak with us in the lounge."

At first, the group was stunned into silence, but then gradually, they started talking amongst themselves about their shock and disbelief.

The news had certainly knocked the wind out of Charles' sails. I noticed he slipped a whiskey flask out of his backpack with shaking hands.

Laura leaned toward him, saying in a hushed voice, "Come on, we knew him. He liked to live life fast and loose. With his track record, his past probably caught up with him. It's got nothing to do with us."

I filed that bit of information in my head to delve into later and looked to see how Spencer was holding up. Peter was talking to him in a calming manner and looked like he was accustomed to handling a crisis. I really needed to find out what kind of business he was in.

Monica was fussing with her bracelet and speaking in hushed tones to Edgar, so I pulled a chair over and joined them.

"You guys doing okay?" I asked sympathetically.

"I don't know. I kind of want to go home," she said, with a furrowed brow.

Edgar patted her hand and spoke to her with a father-like charm. "Don't worry, dear. We'll look out for each other, right?"

"It's going to be okay, Monica," I said. "I don't have a lot of experience with these things, but I do know when there is what they call an unattended or suspicious death, the authorities have several steps to go through, so they need everyone to provide as much information as possible. And they need us all to stay put while they sort things out."

She gave me a weak smile. "I guess that makes sense."

I got up and stood by the window, looking out at the fading afternoon light. I could hear Marie's jewelry jangling across the room and turned to see her rooting through her purse. She pulled out a tissue, then put it back, then hand lotion, etc. This process repeated itself a number of times, which told me it was nervous energy.

Paula sat quietly as Marie ran through a gamut of speculations. "It must have been someone hopped up on drugs. Or maybe it was a mob hit! Surely, it's not safe for us to be here. Or maybe they don't know what they are talking about, and it really was an accident."

Paula looked at her with exasperation. "Marie, get a grip. Don't jump to conclusions, and just think about what you saw when we were out there. Maybe you can actually be of some help. And then we can go back to the Lodge and get a drink. You blustering around like this makes me want a martini, with extra olives, no less."

I turned back toward the window to stifle an inappropriate chuckle but quickly sobered when Annie came up next to me.

"This is crazy, Alex. Who would want to kill Niko?"

"I don't know. I'm still reeling from the news, myself. We can talk about it all later after everyone has gone. But for now, will you hold down the fort here with Spencer? I need to take care of some things."

"Sure. I'll text ya when we're done."

I went in search of Ryan and Maggie, brought them up to speed, and told them Jack would want to talk to them again. Back in the lobby, I stood for a moment wrapping my head around what I needed to do, and then walked to the office with a purpose. I grabbed my things and went upstairs to my apartment where I could work in privacy.

****

While brewing a cup of coffee, I turned on lights to ward off the cloudy feeling, booted up my laptop, and got out a notepad to start making a list. I still liked working with pen and paper, even though it often meant an extra step to enter things into the computer later. Once settled at the kitchen counter, I started with a list of people I needed to research.

Niko

Marie and Paula Wheaton

Edgar Childs

Monica Sewell

Charles Sandling

Laura Mason

Peter Bigsby

What about our locals?

The last in the list was unsettling. Was it possible one of them had done this? I just couldn't go there, and decided to shelve that until Jack did his interviews. I wasn't comfortable delving into the lives of the other people on the list either, but if I looked at this as a job, I could detach and get to work.

I had just gotten a checklist of search parameters organized when my phone dinged with a text from Annie. —*Wrapping it up. JJ and Bitsy coming too.*—

I texted back. —*Come on up.*—

"Coffee, tea?" I asked, when they entered the apartment and made their way to the living room.

"I have my own tea, if I can just get some hot water," JJ said, pulling a baggie out of her purse.

Here comes that whiff of the free spirit…literally. JJ likes Pu Erh tea, which to me, has an earthy pungent aroma, sort of like dirt.

"I already have a soda," said Annie, holding up her can.

"Coffee for me," chimed Bitsy, my coffee kindred spirit.

They cooed over Baxter, who seemed to enjoy the attention. He was also very curious about the robin's egg in a bird's nest fascinator Bitsy wore, and he kept trying to get a good sniff or have it for a snack, I wasn't sure which.

JJ pulled me aside. "Do you meditate, Alex?"

"Um, no, not really." I've tried to meditate before, but all I ended up doing was having a verbal sparring match with myself in my head, which went something like this: *Breathe deeply and clear your mind…wait, I need to think about this...no, clear your mind...okay, I'm not going to think about x, y, or z, which means I'm actually thinking about x, y, or z...dang it, clear your mind!...okay, okay!...I wonder what I should have for dinner?...oh look, a butterfly!...times up. Wasn't that calming?*

"You're going to be under a lot of stress, so let's try a quickie. Close your eyes and breathe deeply," she instructed.

I did as she said.

"Now, it's impossible not to acknowledge what's happening, but instead of thinking about things, I want you to simply focus on your breathing," she intoned, in a soft, song-like voice. "In, out, in, out..." She breathed with me. After a few minutes, she said, "Good, now open your eyes."

I actually felt fairly calm. "Well, I'll be damned, that worked!"

"Of course it did!" she said cheerfully. "Now, let's get you some of my healthy tea."

"Uh, no thanks." No liquid dirt for me. I grabbed a cup of coffee instead.

We had congregated in the kitchen, and Bitsy said, "Alex, I know this isn't the same as what happened in Philadelphia, but have you thought about how that experience may compound things for you?" My friends knew about the shooting at a campaign rally in Philly, which had prompted my move to Flat Rock Falls.

"I haven't had time to think too much, but you're right. Thankfully, no one died that day, but seeing one of my volunteers on the ground seriously injured from violence has left an indelible mark. So some things might resurface, like the nightmares."

"Niko's death is definitely a trigger, so being aware of your emotional stress is important. And just know we are here if you need us."

"Thanks." I looked at my three friends with gratitude. "I am so lucky to have you guys."

JJ picked up her tea and moved to the living room. "Okay, let's put our heads together about Niko."

"I just cannot believe it," Annie said, after we had settled in. "What in the world happened? Wrong place, wrong time? I mean, why would someone want to kill him? And poor Spencer. He's reeling from this."

JJ said, "We're all going to have to help Spencer realize this was not his fault." She cocked her head and said, "I think I'll bring in a rose quartz healing crystal for him."

Bitsy, accustomed to JJ's meanderings, simply said, "How thoughtful of you." Then she addressed me. "What do you think, Alex? You don't really think it was someone from the class, do you?"

"I sure hope not."

"He was arrogant and condescending at times, but that doesn't qualify as a reason to kill him," Annie said.

Jack might not approve, but I knew I could trust this circle of friends. "What I'm going to tell you is in the vault, right? Jack won't want me blabbing things."

They all nodded in agreement, so I continued. "The medical examiner found bruising on Niko's back, indicating he was shoved. Why is that significant? It tells me he turned his back on whoever pushed him."

JJ was quick to pick up on the indication. "So that means he either knew the person and didn't feel threatened…"

"Or if it was a stranger, he thought they were

harmless," Bitsy added.

Annie's eyes widened. "There could have been a psychopath in the woods lying in wait as you worked, which means any one of you could have been in danger. That's a scary thought! Oooo, I can feel their eyes watching us while we're blissfully ignorant."

I gently cleared my throat and said, "I honestly don't think we're living a teen slasher film here. We simply don't know much about Niko and what was going on in his life."

"That's true," JJ said.

"Perhaps he arranged to meet someone there, and he doubled back after the class left. It could be *that* kind of stranger. Let's be methodical and ask ourselves the five W's of journalism: who, what, where, when, why."

"We know the *where*," Annie said.

I tapped my chin with the pen. "And the *who* is connected to the *why*. Once we know one, we'll be able to determine the other."

Bitsy said, "And the *when* depends on the timeline, which we don't know. So that isn't helping us narrow things down at all. Let's think about motives. There's the typical one of revenge."

"And money," JJ added.

"Jealousy," Annie contributed. "The art world is pretty cut-throat. Who gains from his death?"

That was a good question. I jotted it down to discuss with Jack.

"Love," Bitsy mused. "Love and hate are often closely linked. Both are intense emotions, and sometimes they collide if love is unrequited or if there's a deep betrayal."

I looked up from my scribbling. "That's more a

crime of passion, which would indicate a more complex relationship than anyone here had with him."

"True," she agreed. "But it does put a tick in the column for being an outsider, which I like."

"Hopefully he circled back after the class left. Otherwise, we have the looming question of how this could have happened when you all were up there."

Everyone fell silent while contemplating that very real prospect. A text ding from my phone broke the spell. Jack was coming up to talk, which was the cue for JJ and Bitsy to head home.

"All right, we'll see what tomorrow brings," JJ said. She took the mugs to the kitchen and gave Baxter a pat on the head. "I'm going to meditate on this tonight and see if anything comes to the surface."

"I'll walk out with you guys," Annie said. "I'm gonna work a little on my painting while Alex and Jack talk."

I thought about my friends going their separate ways and didn't want to downplay the possibility the murderer was someone in the class.

"Hey, a word of caution. I know we're avoiding the elephant in the room—that it's possible we have a murderer in this group. Let's not lose sight of that. Keep your eyes and ears open, but more importantly, please be careful. I would feel better if you always stay with, or within reach, of someone you trust. Don't go off on your own with any of these folks until we know more."

Annie raised her chin and said, "Then we need to quickly figure out who did it, don't we?"

Chapter 7

Jack arrived just as the group was walking out. After they made the rounds of hellos and goodbyes, and he had a brief word with Annie, I extended my arm and said, "Come on in and take a load off."

"Thanks," he said, flopping on the couch, where Baxter promptly joined him. "It's been a long day."

"Did the interviews help at all?"

"You'll be happy to know we've been able to clear your friends. It's a good thing they're such social people, because based on the interviews, none of them were alone or out of sight at any point up at the falls. And, by the way, Travis was able to corroborate your movements. So you're in the clear."

"Well, that's a relief. What about the others? Did the interviews eliminate any of them?"

"Unfortunately, no. Since the area is new to them, most wandered off at different times for a quick stroll in the woods or along the cliff, or to go to the restroom, which means they don't have an alibi for the entire time up there. A little more of the timeline was filled in, but not enough to point us toward a specific person. There's a loophole somewhere, but I just don't see it yet."

"How did each of them handle the questioning? Any surprises?" Jack knew that from childhood I found human nature a fascinating topic.

He opened his notebook. "Nope, just your garden

variety of personalities in a crisis. Marie was quite theatrical and had some wild ideas. Paula was reserved and very controlled. She gave a lot of careful consideration to each question. She saw a couple of hikers on the path, and we've noted it, but it was before Niko even got there. Edgar was open and tried to be helpful. He recalled an additional time he had seen Niko walking down the path. Laura was a little haughty, and her statement felt rehearsed. She put forth ideas about revenge or money."

"I heard her talking to Charles about Niko's past catching up to him. That he liked to live life fast and loose."

"That's what she said. Unlike Laura, Charles seemed insecure and nervous, and he smelled a little of booze, but he wasn't at all inebriated. He didn't have anything more to contribute, but I couldn't tell if he was actually thinking clearly enough to pinpoint anything."

"I would imagine the same would go for Monica. She's young, and she wasn't handling it well."

"Yeah, she wants to go home. But she remembered she saw someone hiking out on the path at one point during the late morning when she came back from the restroom. She gave us a clear description of a male, medium-build, dark hair, maybe in his thirties, and she described what he was wearing."

"That's encouraging."

"It is. She said he seemed a little overly curious about what the group was doing. So, we'll be looking into that. Then the last one was Peter. He handled it like a pro. Very succinct and composed. He had nothing more to add to the timeline."

"Not surprising. He seems like a thorough sort who

would have recalled everything the first time around. Have the park rangers been questioning people on the trails?"

"They've stopped hikers to take names and check their whereabouts and to see if they heard or saw anything. We'll get this description over to them."

"Well, none of these folks seem like master manipulators, nor strong enough, for that matter, to overpower Niko."

Jack challenged my statement. "Age, gender, and size don't play into it. Any of these people could have shoved him off the cliff. Plus, a couple of them were working on their own in the smaller clearings, so there were gaps when they were absent or not visible. Someone leaves their station, and someone else could slip in."

"Well, that's frustrating. It leaves too many loopholes for an outsider or someone in the class."

"Right. And the odd thing is if Niko was alive and well when the class left, they would have seen him, and he would have gone with them. So either he strayed from the area and went back after the class, or something happened while everyone was up there, and it happened right under their noses."

"I thought about that, and it's a creepy prospect." I shuddered. "Plus, Niko turned his back on whoever shoved him, so clearly, he didn't feel threatened. Either scenario is quite unsettling."

"Yes, that was my concern when the ME relayed the info about the bruising. And it's why I want you to do any work you are doing on this quietly. Very quietly."

"No kidding. You don't have to tell me twice."

"Okay then, tell me what you've found so far."

"I'm just getting started. Do you want to relax and have something to eat while I finish sorting through the first batch of info?"

"Sure, I'll get it. You get busy. And thank you. It's been a fourteen-hour day so far, and on top of the Niko investigation, there was a three-car accident earlier up at the junction and a petty theft report, so my guys are tapped."

This was one reason I didn't mind helping out. I was more reluctant to admit I actually liked the investigative aspect because I feared Jack would bench me if he knew this new interest was blossoming.

I brought my laptop to the living room and sat on the floor in front of the coffee table. After about an hour, Jack had dozed off with his arm draped over Baxter.

I had already accumulated a lot of professional info on Niko, wading through magazine articles and gallery posts, his website, Facebook, Twitter, and Instagram, etc. So, I took a break from him and picked a few easy ones to do next—Marie, Paula, and Edgar. Then I went back to Niko to do a more in-depth records search.

"Oh my gosh!" I exclaimed, waking Jack.

"What?" he asked with a groggy voice, rubbing his eyes.

"It looks like Niko got married when he was in his early twenties, and I don't see any divorce record, which means he's still married."

"So?"

"I just did a cross reference, and I don't believe this, Jack—it appears he's married to Ari. Our Ari!"

Jack let out a whistle and looked at his watch. "I

can talk to her tonight. Can you get me her contact info, please?"

"Yes, but, oh Jack, it makes me feel horrible to do this, but I need to tell you a couple of things first." I then recapped everything to do with Ari over the past few days: the late rental fees, her leaving the Lodge in tears, the haunted look, and then the envelope full of cash. "Surely that has nothing to do with what happened to Niko. And she probably still thinks his death was an accident. Of course, everyone will know quickly—it's a small town—but Ari's been keeping to herself, even more than usual. So please, handle her with care, okay?"

"You know I will. But you also understand I have to question her. This is a solid lead."

"I know, I know," I said, leaning back against the couch. "Before you go, do you want to know about the others I've researched?"

"A quick rundown, yes. Anything critical?"

"Unfortunately, nothing significant, so I can just give you the nutshell version. Marie is exactly what she seems. Lots of Facebook pics of her community center friends, art projects, grandkids, pets. No Instagram or Twitter. No outstanding warrants or past criminal activity. Paula is absent on social media. I will have to dig around more on her. The last in this batch is Edgar."

"I'm assuming similarly benign."

"Yes. He's listed with a photo on his architectural firm's website. He has a modest Facebook page with just close friends and family, and pics from past vacations, which supports what he's told us. He follows the local humane society along with a couple of environmental groups that promote clean air and oceans. No criminal record, and only a minor traffic accident from a couple of years ago. That's as far as I've gotten aside from Niko's professional profile. I'll keep going and have another report for you some time tomorrow, okay?"

"Okay. It's a start. Thank you. Text me if anything unusual pops up. I'm assuming class is going on as scheduled?"

"Right. Both Annie and Spencer are covering things tomorrow."

Jack got up off the couch and yawned. "I want to walk Annie to her car, so I'll see if she's ready to go home before I head out. Are you coming down or staying up here?"

I texted Ari's contact info to Jack's phone before answering, "I'm staying here. Tell Annie I'll talk to her in the morning."

Jack paused with his hand on the doorknob and asked, "And, um, Alex, from the looks of it, I'm assuming there won't be any need to take Baxter to the humane society?"

I smiled as I looked at Baxter stretched out on the couch. "I think he's happy here. And besides, Frank will be so relieved to know he has a good home. Maybe I can even take him over for a visit."

"Yeah, that's what I thought you'd say."

After Jack left, I sat back down on the floor and tried to keep the sick feeling in my stomach at bay. Surely Ari had nothing to do with this. *There has to be a simple explanation,* I told myself, but I couldn't concentrate because my brain kept spinning around her odd behavior. I realized I had mentioned Niko's death to Ari, but she'd kept quiet about her past with him.

That was concerning.

I didn't have an appetite, so I just grabbed a yogurt and a banana, and on impulse the bag of cheese curls, and tried to watch some TV to distract my mind a little before getting back to work. While eating, I texted Ryan to see if he would be willing to build a fence for Baxter at the bottom of my exterior staircase. He got back right away with a thumbs-up emoji.

Thirty minutes later, after washing the orange cheese dust off my fingers, I was ready to resume my research when Annie called.

"What's up?" I asked, putting her on speaker phone.

"Nothing, I'm just bored. I came on home when Jack finished with you, but he had to go back to the office and won't be home for a while. How about you?" she asked.

"Doing background on the retreat folks for Jack."

"Oh, anything interesting?"

Normally, I would not discuss work I was doing for Jack, but this was Annie, and since she was married to Jack, it meant she was not only my oldest friend, she was also family. I did draw the line at talking about Ari, but this was now an opportunity to have company while I did the more mundane work, and we talked as I tapped my way around the computer keyboard.

"I've already done a little on Marie, Paula, and Edgar. And I'm now finding Monica's online presence seems to be as benign as theirs. She has Facebook posts with lot of pictures with her sister, parents, her cat, and get-togethers with friends. Some memes, but no political posts, and the groups she follows are innocuous."

"That's what I would expect. She's kind of milquetoast—and I don't mean that in a snarky way. She's not bland, just unassertive, like she doesn't want to rock the boat, which means she's not going to put anything on social media other than happy, feel-good things."

"Don't worry, I know what you mean. I'm finding the pics with her sister uncanny; they look like identical twins. Her sister dresses a little more casually and styles her hair differently, but otherwise she's the spitting image."

"Oh yeah, she's talked about her sister. Bianca, isn't it? And yes, they are twins. Having a twin would be so cool."

I thought about this, then said, "Jack is like a brother to me, but we're not even remotely like twins."

"That's for sure," she said with a laugh.

"At any rate, she's listed on her company website, and everything seems on the up and up."

While Annie rambled on about Monica's apparent talent as a painter, I did a quick criminal check. If I had found something, which I didn't, I wouldn't have said anything to Annie, but I would have made a note for Jack. Once I checked Monica off the list, I moved back to Paula.

"Okay, Paula, let's see what else I can find on you. She graduated from William and Mary with a double degree in statistics and global studies. That would explain her quiet intelligence."

"Yeah, she's one cool customer. I really like her."

"I haven't found anything on her employment. Has she talked about what she did before retiring?"

"Not much. She might have said something about

being a market researcher or an insurance broker."

"Those aren't remotely related fields, Annie."

"No, but they are equally uninteresting to me, so I wasn't remembering similar professions, just similar vibes."

"Oh, okay," I said, with a laugh.

The time passed quickly talking to Annie, but I could feel my crossed legs starting to ache, so I got up off the floor, stretched, then said, "Hang on, getting more coffee."

The aroma alone gave me a spurt of renewed energy to keep working.

"Who's next?" she asked, after I returned from the kitchen.

"Let's do Charles."

"His should be easy. That guy posts his every move."

"He sure does. He's been in a number of gallery shows around the country. He's got over five thousand followers and lots of photos with other artists, but I don't see anything personal," I said.

"For him, the social media thing is solely for networking. Has he posted since Niko's death?"

"Interestingly enough, no. He posted some pictures from Monday, and hey, here's one with you! But nothing after that."

"I think that's a good thing. I don't like it when people rush to lay out a tragedy on social media. Later, fine, if that gives you comfort, but immediately? I find it weird."

"Agreed." I came across a photo of Charles, Laura, and Niko at a gallery opening. So, they did run into each other occasionally. I took a closer look at the image. Niko had his arm around Laura in a way that indicated a familiarity: his thumb hooked in her belt loop with his hand partially in her front pocket. She was leaning in toward him with her hand on his chest. It felt intimate. *Interesting.*

"Have you heard Charles or Laura talk about a personal history with Niko?"

"What do you mean?"

I described the photo of Laura and Niko. "Has she mentioned being in a relationship with him?"

"She hasn't. But that may be out of embarrassment. I could tell Niko was a player, and who wants to admit they had been one in a long line?"

"Perhaps." I made a couple notes for my report. How well did Laura know Niko? What was their history? The deeper background on Charles revealed one DUI and one speeding ticket, but both were over three years ago. He'd kept his nose clean since.

Annie said, "Let's see if there is anything deeper in Laura's photo gallery on social media. Oh, and see if she's posted anything since Monday."

I was looking for something that might substantiate a personal history with Niko. She showed up on a few gallery sites, and like Charles, she used all social media platforms for networking. I looked back through old photos she had posted and found a few more of her with Niko.

"Aha, here we go. Here's one with Niko that looks like it was taken in Italy. Maybe on holiday together? The others are from gallery openings or at restaurants with friends. Then, suddenly no more Niko. From the dates on the posts, it appears whatever their relationship had been, it lasted only a few months."

"As I thought. When was this?"

"A few years ago, from the looks of it."

"So, water under the bridge. She probably didn't think it was worth mentioning at this point." Annie let out a long yawn. "Enthralling as this has been, I think I'm going to get ready for bed."

"I don't blame you. The days feel long right now, and this is somewhat mind-numbing. Thanks for keeping me company, though" I said, before signing off.

I was getting bleary-eyed, myself, but I shifted over to Peter Bigsby before wrapping it up for the night. However, after searching all my usual sites, I found absolutely nothing on him. There were others by the same name, but they were either way off in age, deceased, or not him, based on photos. Now this was interesting, and I felt the same adrenaline rush I used to get when faced with the challenge of uncovering secrets.

Chapter 8

I looked at the time and decided it was still early enough to make a couple of phone calls about Peter's lack of identity.

Michael picked up after just a couple of rings. "Well, look what the cat dragged in. To what do I owe this pleasure?"

"Hey, Michael," I said fondly. "How's it been on your end?"

"Oh you know, busy every day in the halls of justice."

Michael was a high-powered attorney, and my ex-husband. We had met in Philadelphia and were considered to be quite the power couple. However, we soon found two ships occasionally passing in the night did not make for a great relationship. After five years, we made what we perceived to be the "mature" decision to go our separate ways; we were better as friends than as a married couple. Frankly, I think it boiled down to us both being too selfish to give an inch, which is actually quite immature. However you dissected it, it was the right decision, and we have remained good friends ever since.

"I won't keep you long. I just have a quick question for you," I said.

"Sure, what's up?"

"Let's say you were trying to find information on

someone, but that someone doesn't seem to exist. What do you do after exhausting the normal search tools?"

"Okay, back up. First, why are you looking for information on someone? You aren't getting back into the old business again, are you?"

"No way." I laughed, but then sobered. "I'm helping Jack with a case. There's been a murder here, and unfortunately, it might be linked to the retreat going on at the Workshop."

"Are you serious? You're getting involved in a murder case? What are you thinking? Who was murdered?"

"Don't worry, Michael. I'm not directly involved. I'm just doing some research for Jack. And besides, I need this to be resolved quickly because I don't want the Workshop to suffer any fallout. The victim was the guest artist for our retreat, Niko Romano. Have you heard of him?"

"No. But of course I don't really have time to keep up with the art scene. So, what were you asking? You've looked into someone who doesn't exist?"

"Yes. His name is Peter Bigsby. He's one of the retreat participants. I found a handful of others of similar age, but none are him. I've done a deeper search and found no records that match this guy. So where do I look now?"

"Hmmm. I'm assuming you don't have his social security number, right?"

"Right."

"So that means you can't do a deeper background on him. Off the top of my head, the only thing I can think of is for Jack to take his prints and run a check. But if he doesn't have a record, that's not going to reveal anything. Plus, he would have to have cause to bring him in and take his prints. It's not illegal to use a pseudonym unless the intent is to defraud."

"Okay, that's what I was afraid of. He seems kind of familiar to me, so I'm going to call Izzy and see if he rings any bells to her. I took a pic of the class on my phone, so I can text her his photo."

"That's a good idea. Look, Alex, be careful. Delving into a murder is way outside your scope of experience. Do your research and then leave it to Jack, okay?"

"That's the plan."

Michael's voice softened as he asked, "How have you been otherwise? Are you taking care of yourself? Are you sleeping okay?"

"To answer in order: things have been going great up until this, I think I take care of myself just fine, but you, like Jack, would probably disagree, and the nightmares are few and far between now, so for the most part, I sleep like a baby." I knew the additional stress would likely make my dreams more active and my sleep less restful, but I wanted to downplay that with him.

"That's all well and good, but you know I'm going to worry while you're in the middle of a murder investigation. Remember, don't have caffeine too close to bedtime, and unwind with some nice herbal tea instead. And be careful and look out for yourself, yes?"

"I will," I agreed, although, I was only agreeing to be careful, not eliminating the caffeine. "And thanks, Michael. Take care and we'll talk again soon."

I hung up and tapped Izzy's phone number. I had handled Isabelle's political campaigns, the last of which was for state Senate. We had become good friends back when she held a local commissioner position, and she was one of the few people I truly missed from my old life. She had a quick intelligence and a healthy dose of irreverent humor, which enabled her to go toe to toe with the big boys. And, like me, she had no patience for the injustices in the world.

"Hey!" Isabelle chimed when she answered. "It's been too long! How are you? How's life in the hinterlands?"

"I'll fill you in on me in a minute. How are things going for you? I try to keep up with what's happening at the state capital, but as you know, I can only stomach so much."

"Oh my gosh, Alex. The BS is never ending! I can't believe you wanted to leave all this behind for your green patch in the hills! It's so invigorating—and deliciously aggravating. But instead, you're listening to crickets."

I laughed. "Better you than me!"

After a few minutes catching up, I told her about the murder and Peter Bigsby and how he felt familiar to me. I texted her the photo from the class, which I had cropped to show him more clearly.

"Wow, Alex. Are you kidding me? What the heck are you doing involved in a murder case? I thought you left Philly to get away from the gritty realities of life! Okay, your text came through. Hold on." She put me on speaker, and after a pause said, "Hmmm, he does look familiar. I feel like I've seen him but can't place him either. Isn't that weird? That means he must be from this world. Oh geez, Alex, do you think he's somehow connected to 'that which we don't talk about anymore'?" She was referring to the shooting and subsequent trial.

"Let's not go all conspiracy theory, Izzy. Besides, if he'd been part of all that, I'm sure I would remember him, don't you think? And you would, too."

"Yeah, I guess. But maybe you should mention it to Jack, just as a precaution. And I'll quietly ask around and show the picture to a couple of my staff. They might recognize him. But listen, I know you always loved the investigative aspect of your old work, but don't get in too deep here. This isn't digging to avoid a political scandal. This is digging around in a murder."

"I know, you're right. I'll be careful."

Was she right? Could this somehow be related to what happened in Philly? That was an unsettling thought, and I would follow her advice and hash it over with Jack. As we had been talking, Baxter had started to pace back and forth at the door.

"Listen, I need to jump off and take Baxter out. I want to catch up more with you soon, though."

"Wait. Who the heck is Baxter, and why does he need you to go out?"

I laughed. "Well, I think Baxter is my new dog! He sort of looks like a Bernese mountain dog mixed with something, maybe retriever. I'm not really sure," I said, as I patted his big head.

"Oh good Lord, you've definitely lost your mind. He's probably almost as big as you are! Okay. I'll let you know if I find out anything about this guy. Hugs to you, and I guess Baxter too!" She disconnected before I could respond, which left me smiling as I put the phone in my pocket, got the leash, and took Baxter down the back stairs for a quick walk around the grounds before getting back to work.

Later, my eyes started glazing over from looking at the computer screen, and having accomplished nothing more, I decided to call it a night. After repeatedly reading the same page in my book, I eventually drifted into a fitful night of sleep.

For some reason, the vision of the lone man on Main Street, standing in the dark watching me during the rainstorm, kept looping. And then I dreamt I was standing on the edge of a cliff. I could hear the amplified voices of a campaign rally in the distance and the heavy footfall of someone running behind me. Before I could turn around, I felt the force of two hands on my back, and I was catapulted into darkness.

****

Thursday

The following morning Baxter and I were both happily crunching our food—his kibble, my granola cereal—when my phone dinged with a text from Jack.

—*You up?*—

—*Yep*— I texted back, and a moment later my phone rang.

A man of few words, Jack simply started with, "I think it might be a good idea for you to meet me at the B&B to go over Niko's room. I want you to take a look at the art stuff to see if there's anything we need to handle carefully, and you may pick up on something I'd miss."

"Good morning," I said, in an overly pleasant voice, which I knew he would take with the intended sarcasm.

"Good morning, Alex. Would you please meet me at the B&B to go through Niko's room?" he asked, with controlled patience.

"Sure, no problem," I said, with juvenile self-satisfaction. "What time?"

"Let's make it ten thirty."

"Okay. How did the interview go with Ari?"

"I can't go into that right now. I'll see ya in a bit."

I heard the beep of the disconnected call, muttered, "Twerp," to myself while tossing the phone on the counter, then went back to my cereal. I spent the rest of my breakfast in a contemplative mood, worrying over what happened with Ari and reviewing what I had found, or not found, the night before. I had some nagging questions I needed answers to. Who was Peter Bigsby? Was there more to Paula? What was the relationship between Laura and Niko? And what did Charles know about it? What had happened with Ari? Was one of these people a murderer? And was that figure of the lone man on Main Street just a manifestation of my overactive imagination?

****

It was almost nine by the time I had tended to some unavoidable chores around the apartment, called the vet to schedule a check-up for Baxter, and organized what I had so far for Jack. I shoved my notes and laptop into my bag and had just grabbed my coffee and keys when Baxter blocked my path and stared at me intently with his big brown eyes.

Oh, what the hell. "Okay, big boy, do you want to come with me for a little bit?" He responded by happily bounding over to the door.

At the bottom of the staircase, the clang of metal coming from outside caught my attention. Looking out through the courtyard doors, I said to Baxter, "Ryan is already working on your fence." Baxter wagged his tail by way of response.

I dropped my things in the office, and Baxter followed me down the hall to where Annie and Spencer were working with the class. I was curious to see how things were going this morning, but since dog hair and wet paint don't mix, I put up a hand, hoping he understood the "sit and stay" command. He seemed to get it, so I was free to stick my head in the door and observe the class. Everyone was focused on their individual still life projects, and the only sound was the quiet murmur of voices as Annie or Spencer spoke with someone to answer questions or give a tip.

Paula was calmly looking between her easel and the vignette as she delicately put her brush to the canvas. Marie's features were in constant motion—scrunched up, then enlightened when she figured out a solution, wide-eyed to furrowed brow as she worked through the process. She would never win at poker. Every emotion was displayed on her face.

Monica smacked down her brush in frustration. Her face flashed anger, and then she took a deep breath, picked up her brush, and started again. Charles and Laura were working with the professional calm of experience. Spencer looked over at me and gave me a sign to wait. He finished up with Paula, and then stepped out and motioned me down the hall.

"Everything okay?" I asked.

"Yeah, it's fine now. Everyone was a little worked up this morning, uncomfortable with having to remain here, asking questions, and clearly uneasy about things."

"I was afraid of that."

"Annie and I talked with them and explained the investigation has just begun, but the police are working hard to get this resolved quickly, and they didn't need to worry, they are safe here. I hope you don't mind, but I told them if anyone has concerns, they should feel free to talk to you, Annie, or me, and we would help in any way we can."

"That was just the right thing to say."

"Thanks. Once we got them focused on the class work, things settled down."

"How about you, are you doing all right?" I asked.

"It's not easy, but I'm holding on. I can process all of this later. Is there anything I should know at this point?"

"Not yet. Jack's doing his thing with the department, and I'm working on some research for him. I'll keep you posted if anything develops. Let's try and keep things as normal as possible for the class, but if you have any trouble, let me know and I'll handle it. In the meantime, I'm going to send Maggie down to get some candids. I like the light in there this morning."

"Sounds like a good plan. Hang in there." Spencer said.

"You too."

Baxter and I went to the opposite hallway to pop in on Maggie in the photo lab.

"Baxter!" Maggie called out, reaching down to give him a good ear rub. She looked up at me over the rims of her pink-and-green glasses. "So, I see he's still here. And I saw Ryan outside starting to work on a fence this morning. Does this mean we now have a Creative Workshop mascot?"

I laughed. "It's looking that way. We gelled so

quickly, and now I can't bring myself to let him go. I'll call Frank to let him know, and I'll take Baxter over for a visit next week."

"He will be so happy about that. And, I have to admit I'm relieved you're not rambling around in this big building by yourself at night. Particularly with what happened to Niko. Speaking of which, how's the investigation going? Any news?"

I wasn't going to mention Ari or any personal details on the participants I had researched. "Nothing yet, but Jack is interviewing everyone and looking at all the angles. I just hope this is resolved before the retreat finishes."

Maggie was smart, and she knew I had done some work for Jack before, so she looked me square in the eyes and said, "You're helping though, right? I mean, this affects the Workshop, so anything that can contribute to solving it needs to be done."

I lowered my voice and said, "Yes, I am helping, but I'm doing it quietly. I don't want these people to know I am looking into their lives. Got it?"

"Got it."

"And I'm not comfortable talking about what I find unless it has a direct bearing on the case, and it doesn't step on the toes of the investigation. It's not fair to blab about people's personal details."

"I understand. That's the right way to handle it."

"That being said, being observant and good ol' gossip could be really helpful, so keep your eyes and ears open, and let me know if anything interesting crops up."

"I'm on it," she said, with the eagerness of a junior reporter.

I held up my hand. "But be careful. While I still have hope this was unrelated to this group, I've come around to the reality that it's more likely someone we know who committed murder."

Maggie's whole body shuddered. "That's a truly scary thought. I need to believe it was someone else. It creeps me out to think of any of these people committing murder, particularly while they're all still here."

"It's going to be okay. Jack will figure this out. Besides, as far as I'm concerned, there's safety in numbers. Maybe we'll get lucky, and it will prove to be unrelated to this group, but if that's not the case, it would be better if whoever did it feels like they got away with it so they don't get backed into a corner and strike again. So just go about your business as usual, and for crying out loud, don't walk around looking spooked."

"Okay, okay," Maggie hissed.

Returning to a normal voice, I said, "I came by to let you know they're working on individual still life projects right now. The lighting in the room is really nice with the overhead lights off and the task lights on their individual vignettes at each easel, so you might want to grab a few pics."

"Cool, I'll head down there now." She swiveled around to grab her camera. While we walked together down the hall, she noted, "There are some really good shots from the first day, but it's kind of hard to know what to do about Niko's pictures for the slideshow at the closing reception. We'll have to figure out how to handle that without being too maudlin or disturbing. I'll keep working on it."

"Okay. Put together whatever you feel is best, and then I'll watch it with an objective eye and see if it hits the right tone."

We parted ways at the front desk. I had some time before I needed to leave for the B&B, so Baxter and I stepped outside to see how the fence progress was going.

"Looking good, Ryan! You got started bright and early," I called out as we approached from the courtyard.

"Thanks, Alex. Actually, it's a good distraction from thinking about Niko. I'm not feeling terribly inspired to work on my sculpture right now, and since it's not a huge area, I should be finished by later today. How do you like it, buddy?" Ryan asked Baxter, who sidled up to him for a quick rubdown.

"I think he likes it," I said, with a smile. I couldn't help but notice the absence of the carefree boyishness made Ryan look a little older. "And yes, distractions are good. You haven't seen or heard anything unusual, have you? Do you have any opinions on our visitors?"

He rubbed some dirt from his hands onto his jeans, then leaned on the handle of the shovel. "I haven't heard anything, but then again, I haven't really been around the class all that much."

"Yeah, I guess there wouldn't be much reason for you to mingle with them."

"Although, I can see people outside in the courtyard from my studio windows. I think Niko had a short fuse. I saw him outside on the phone at the end of lunch on Monday, and boy, he was barking at whoever was on the other end of the call. And after class he was outside again, just looking at his phone and, I don't know, I guess it was his body language that struck me. He stiffened, scowled, then stomped off."

"Interesting." Clearly, whoever was bothering him at lunch was still annoying him at the end of the day, too. Either that, or he had more than one tumultuous relationship going on. "Anything else?"

"I've seen Charles outside chain-smoking, but that's not unusual; he's a smoker. Otherwise, folks have just been hanging out on breaks like normal."

"I'm wondering what Niko did Monday night. I'll ask Jack if any of the interviews gave a clue to where he went after class."

"Oh, there is one other thing. I'm not sure if this qualifies as suspicious, but I've seen Peter roaming around the building, away from the rest of the group. Do you remember how he was asking a lot of questions at the opening reception? Maybe it's just curiosity, but I thought you should know."

"Mmm, yes, thank you." Dang, I needed to get to the bottom of who this Peter guy was.

"I've been thinking it might be a good idea for me to bunk down here in the guest suite until this is resolved. What do you think?"

We had a guest suite on the first floor for the occasional visiting artist who came for an extended stay, and I was touched, and a little relieved, by his suggestion.

"Well, I don't think it's necessary, but I won't lie, I would feel better having someone else in the building at night."

"Okay, I'll go home later and pick up a few things. Starting tonight, I'll be here."

"Thanks, Ryan, and I'll find you this afternoon to

settle up for the fence. Come on, Baxter, time to go back upstairs."

After getting Baxter settled, and refilling my coffee cup, I headed back down to the office to get some work done until I needed to meet Jack. I closed the office door and pulled my laptop out to review what I had found the night before. I texted Izzy to see if she had checked around about Peter, and while waiting, did a little more searching on Paula and her job, which didn't seem to have an online presence.

In this day and age, there was so much information within reach on the computer that it set off a little alarm bell when nothing was found. It didn't necessarily mean there was something hinky; it was just unusual. I was twirling around the information highway, getting nowhere, when there was a soft knock on the door. I quickly put my notes away and closed my laptop before opening the door to find Ari standing in front of me.

"Ari, come in, sit down."

"Thanks, Alex. I wanted to talk to you before you hear this from anyone else."

As she sat down, her eyes welled up, on the brink of spilling over onto her cheeks. I handed her a tissue from the box on my desk and waited until she was ready to begin.

"I feel just horrible, Alex. I've made a real mess of things."

I felt a pit in the bottom of my stomach. What was she going to tell me? That she murdered Niko?

Chapter 9

I tried to keep my eyes neutral as I looked at Ari. "Go on," I said, encouragingly.

"I've kept something from you, and I know it was wrong. I just didn't know how else to handle it. I was at the police station for hours last night and again first thing this morning."

"Why don't you start at the beginning."

She took a deep breath, then started. "I know, um, knew, Niko. We met at art school. I was nineteen, and he was twenty-three. He was so talented and confident, and I was in awe of him. We started dating, and eventually he wanted to move in with me. Everything was great. We went to gallery openings, hung out with other amazing artists, and I was in heaven being surrounded by his creativity. It sparked my own ambitions to be a better painter."

She looked at me, and I nodded in encouragement.

"Well, on a whim, we got married."

I feigned surprise because I didn't want her to know I was the one that dug up this information. "Wow!"

"I know, the stupidity of youth. That's when things went south. He started staying out all night, he ignored me, and when he wasn't ignoring me, he bullied me. It was a bad scene."

Ari took a sip from her water bottle before

continuing, "But you see, I was the one paying for everything. At the time, I used a small inheritance to cover my art school classes and the apartment. Niko wasn't a high-selling artist yet, so he was living off my money. I paid for our living expenses, his art supplies, for classes, travel, all of it. That's why he didn't want to divorce. I was his meal ticket."

"Oh my gosh, Ari, this sounds dreadful."

"Eventually, I couldn't deal with it anymore. I paid the landlord for three months of rent and told him after that I was no longer the leaseholder. I left Niko a letter explaining I was leaving and I wanted a divorce, and then I went back home."

"Good for you. I'm sure that took some guts."

"Well, he never responded to my letter, nor the divorce papers I had an attorney serve him. I heard he simply surfed from couch to couch, and girlfriend to girlfriend."

"So what did you do?"

"I took some art classes in my hometown, but it wasn't like being at a great art school. I mean, I should have been grateful I have loving parents who let me live at home while I sorted out my life, but I floundered a bit."

"Regardless of how fortunate you were, that was quite an adjustment to make at that age."

She nodded in agreement. "Anyway, after a while, I made my own way, and Niko was but a dim memory. I didn't have any contact with him for years. I would read about him in the art magazines, watching his rise in the art world, and frankly, I didn't really care. I had some bitterness about that whole scene and was just as happy not to be a part of it."

"That's understandable."

"Yes. But this past year I've had some big expenses that drained my savings. That's when I started being late with my studio fees. I thought about how much money Niko had taken from me, and I felt it was time he paid it back. Heck, I was technically still his wife. If we divorced, he would owe me a lot more because of his earnings, so I felt he might be more willing to just pay back what he owed me."

Ari sat back in the chair and rubbed her eyes. I braced myself for what was coming, but I had to ask, "Did you decide to do something about this when you found out he was coming to the retreat?"

She exhaled and said, "Yes. I heard he was the special guest artist. I mean, really, what are the odds? I couldn't believe he would come to our small town. Anyway, I waited to call him until the day he arrived. I left him a voicemail that I wanted to talk to him, but he didn't return my call. I didn't want to confront him here in person; it would have been too embarrassing to make a public scene. So, I asked Ryan when and where the opening reception was, then waited at the Lodge until I saw him walking toward the lounge. He pulled me outside to talk." She hesitated, then said, "I'll just say it didn't go well. He was not interested in paying me back and treated me like an annoying gnat."

I took that moment to interrupt. "I saw you leaving the hotel that evening, and you looked quite upset. That must have been after you spoke with him."

"Yes. I heard you call out to me, but I just couldn't face you, so I hightailed it out the door."

"What happened next?"

"I went home, and after a good cry, I decided I was

not going to let him get away with it."

"Oh Ari, what did you do? Please tell me you didn't kill Niko."

"What? Oh my gosh, Alex, no, of course not! I've told the police all of this. And I have an alibi for the entire morning Niko died."

I put my head in my hands, and said, "What a relief! You have no idea how worried I was about where this was going."

"I'm so sorry. I guess I should have led with that! I didn't think in a million years you would ever think I could have killed him...but actually, considering what I've told you, I can see how you might jump to that conclusion."

I felt myself relax, and said, "All right, let's both take a deep breath, and please continue."

Ari sat up straighter, like a load had just lifted off her shoulders. "So, that night I decided enough was enough. I called Niko the next day and told him I was going to get an attorney and re-file divorce papers immediately, and he could pay me what I asked for or he would end up losing a lot more. It was his choice."

"Was that around lunch time on Monday? I remember seeing him on the phone outside looking rather perturbed."

"Yes, it was. Believe it or not, later that evening, he came to my apartment and dropped off a rather hefty load of cash and said when he got home, he'd send an additional check because of the hassles he caused me."

"Wow. I'm so glad you got a quick resolution."

"I know. He just gave me the money, said no hard feelings. He also told me if I didn't make any further financial claim, he would sign divorce papers. He was almost flip about it, like it was no big deal. I was really surprised."

"Why do you think he gave in so quickly?"

"I think as long as I was a coward and didn't fight back, he could keep playing the game, but when I finally stood up for myself, he just paid up and the game was over."

"Well, I think you may be right. When he came in from that call, he was able to instantly shift gears and was all schmoozy with me. I think everything was a game for Niko."

"Yes. I'm a little older now, and can see he was more bluster than substance. At any rate, the end of this embarrassing story is that after he left that night, I threw together an overnight bag and drove down to my parents' house. I spent the night there and was with them until I left around noon to come back here. That's when I stopped in to give you the back fees. I'd heard about the accident and made the stupid decision to withhold my relationship with Niko from you and the police."

"I really appreciate your willingness to confide in me, Ari. Do you mind if I ask you a couple questions?"

"Sure."

"Can you think of anyone who would want to kill Niko?"

Ari shook her head. "Chief Maddox asked me the same question, and geez, I have no idea. I hadn't seen him for years, but with his track record, there's no telling how many people he crossed in one way or another. At the same time, I can't imagine anything he would do that could be so extreme as to push someone to murder him."

"What about family? Where are his parents? Any siblings?"

"Niko was an only child, and he lost both his parents in a car accident when he was nineteen. He had no other immediate family that I know of."

"Oh boy," I said. "That kind of tragic loss can have a drastic impact on someone so young."

"Yeah, I think so," Ari said, as she got up to leave. "You know, Niko had a decent side. I admit I was naïve and stupid, but I truly saw a lot of good in him. I think his ambition got the best of him. He had no guidance to give him balance, and I wasn't a strong enough personality to stand up to him."

"So what happens now?"

She leaned against the door frame and said, "Chief Maddox said he'll confirm my alibi, and then I guess I have to get an attorney to handle the estate. I'm Niko's only heir unless they find a will, which knowing Niko, is doubtful. He thought he was invincible."

"Whew!" I whistled. "Talk about a life-altering event." I then asked the question I knew was none of my business, but I was curious about, nonetheless. "If you don't mind telling me, how much cash did he give you Monday night?"

Ari smiled slightly as she said, "Over twenty thousand dollars."

I sat for a few minutes after Ari left and mulled over what she had told me. That was a lot of money. How did Niko come up with that amount of cash on short notice? And I sure hoped Jack was able to fully clear Ari. Talk about a heck of a motive; she ticked the boxes for both revenge and money. I had to assume he would not have let her go if he had not been able to substantiate her whereabouts.

So, we were still no closer to finding out what happened. What was it about the here and now that caused this? That had to be the key. I looked down at my watch and groaned. I was going to be late for my meeting with Jack.

****

Using my occasional rolling-stop method at stop signs, I arrived at the B&B in record time. Opening the screen door, I called out a hello, and Brenda emerged from one of the first-floor rooms with a vacuum cleaner in tow.

"Oh, hi, Alex, this is just horrible, isn't it?" Brenda said, with a hushed excitement. "I can't believe this happened in our little corner of the world, and Niko was staying right here at our B&B! We've had the police here asking questions, and we've had reporters calling. It's been *so* upsetting for everyone."

Brenda's generally a sweetheart, so I cut her some slack over the gleam of excitement in her eyes from the sudden swell of activity in her normally quiet life, and said, "I am sure this has been really hard. How have you and Lyle been handling it?"

"Lyle, as usual, doesn't really pay attention to what's going on around him, and just keeps tinkering in his workshop out back."

"And you?"

"Fortunately, until the weekend, our only guests are the three, not counting Niko, of course, from your retreat, so I have time to deal with all the hullabaloo."

"That's good. I hope our folks are easy guests."

"Oh yes. Edgar has been such a kind and calming presence, particularly to Marie, who has been quite worked up over it. Paula's nice, but she just sits quietly doing her needlepoint while we all talk things over."

"Well, hang in there, Brenda. I'm sure you're keeping your guests as comfortable as possible. I'm meeting Jack here. Is he in Niko's room?"

"Yes, he is. Room three, upstairs."

Sprinting up the stairs, taking them two at a time, I arrived slightly out of breath but tried to appear composed as I casually asked, "Hey, how's it going?"

Jack looked at me. "Geez, what'd you do? Run here?"

I couldn't help but laugh. "No, I just attempted some stair sprints. Maybe it's time for a little cardio exercise."

"Ya think?"

"Okay, okay. Now, what can I do to help?"

"Let's take a look at all this art stuff and see if anything needs special handling. But first," he said, pulling out a piece of paper, "sign this. It makes you a consultant on this investigation."

I scribbled my signature, then looked around. "Can we move everything art-related to one area so we don't miss anything?"

"Sure. I've already gone through his belongings again, and there's nothing out of the ordinary. His cell phone cord was plugged in on the desk. That was the only personal item left sitting out. Everything else was neatly put away."

I hadn't been past the public area of the B&B, so I took a moment to appreciate the spacious room. The king-sized bed was covered in soft cotton quilts, flanked by matching bedside tables, an antique table and chair was placed under the tall windows, and an upholstered armchair with a standing lamp was tucked in one corner. The bathroom was nicely appointed too, with a marble-topped antique vanity and a tiled walk-in shower.

Jack and I made quick work of splitting the contents of the room, putting personal items on one side of the bed and the art materials on the other. I opened his leather satchel first and made a list of what I found.

Satchel: An art book, The Craft of Old-Master Drawings*; spiral notebook with notes for the retreat, reminders, lists, etc.; promotional materials for the show in Chicago; a map of Pennsylvania; a small leather notebook with initials and dates; a week-by-week datebook; and the usual assortment of pens, pencils, and paperclips.*

Questions: Why a paper map of PA? Everyone uses GPS now. The date book had various appointments, the retreat week blocked out, nothing on the schedule two days before the retreat, and simply an asterisk on one of the days before the retreat and on the following Monday. What does that signify? What's with the notebook with dates and initials?

I put the briefcase aside and started on his art case. It was well organized and held various oil and acrylic paint tubes, a variety of brushes that had been carefully cleaned and wrapped in a rolled-up leather tote, charcoal pencils, etc. All the usual supplies an artist might take on the road.

While I was looking through the art case, Jack had opened Niko's portfolio. He let out a breathy whistle. "From what I can tell, this guy was good."

I looked over his shoulder as he flipped through the images of Niko's works. "Dang, he sure was talented."

I then pointed to the packing cases leaning against the wall. "What about these? Have you gone through them?"

"The cardboard shipping boxes have paintings in them. I haven't pulled them out because they're well-packed, and I didn't want to damage them. Do you think we should open them?"

I went over and opened the top flap of each so I could see inside. "I don't think so. The paintings in these boxes must be going to Chicago. You can call the gallery to confirm that. But this shipping case is empty."

"I assume that's also for the Chicago part of the trip or for whatever he brought here."

"That doesn't make sense. He has three paintings here to show in our exhibit, but those are in their cases in storage at the Workshop. Paintings are either shipped or transported by the artists. Either way, the case usually stays with the painting."

"So you're saying, why schlep around an empty case?"

"Right. It's not really a big deal, but we could cross-reference his datebook to see if he made a notation about dropping a piece with a buyer or if he was picking up a new piece someplace where he would need an empty case."

Jack nodded. "I'll call the gallery, but unless it becomes clear it has a bearing on the investigation, there's no point in doing a lot of unnecessary legwork. Word of mouth is going to spread fast within the art world."

"Good point."

I looked around the room one last time. "I wonder

why Niko wanted to switch his reservation and stay here instead of the Lodge. Wouldn't you think his type would want to be where the bar and restaurant are?"

"Maybe he wanted privacy, or he sleeps better in this environment. I could sleep for days in that bed."

"Yeah, it's nice in here," I agreed.

After making a detailed list of everything, I started putting things back in order. In the art case, I noticed a compartment underneath the acrylic paints. It had small, barely noticeable flip toggles; the kind that sometimes hold the back board of a picture frame. I used my fingernail to swing them open and pried up the compartment door. Inside was a cell phone.

"Jack, take a look at this. It was in a hidden compartment in his art case," I said, handing him the phone.

"Hmmm, isn't this interesting." Jack turned on the cell phone. It was immediately evident it was new, and had not yet been used. "Well, well, Niko," Jack mused to himself, "what were you up to that you needed a burner phone?"

"I wonder what that means?" I asked.

"I don't know, but we're going to find out. Nothing good can come from a hidden burner phone."

"Would it be okay to show some of these art things to Spencer and Annie?"

"Might be a good idea. I'll set something up with them."

I reached for my bag. "Do you need anything else from me before I go?"

"I don't think so. Thanks for your help. Are you heading back to the Workshop?"

"Yeah, I want to get back before they break for

lunch. By the way, Ari stopped by the office this morning and filled me in on everything. She has a tough history with Niko, but I'm assuming she's been cleared?"

"She has. We confirmed she was with her parents, and she gave us access to her phone records, computer, and bank accounts."

"Why her accounts?"

"She could have hired someone to kill him."

"Oh. Dang, that's a scary thought, and one that hadn't crossed my mind. She said she'd had some big expenses lately, and I'm assuming you tracked those, too. I just took everything she said at face value."

"We looked into everything. Her accounts, her phone and email records, and her search history. You must be off your game a little since following the money and doing the deep dive on people was something you used to do."

"Clearly, I need to get my head on straight and start realizing I don't really know these people."

"Cut yourself some slack. You've been blindsided by this murder. Anyway, she came back clean as a whistle, so maybe you do know these people. At any rate, I'm glad she told you everything. Since you work with some of the people involved, the separation of duties is important. I would have told you she was cleared but wouldn't have felt good telling you the details of her history with Niko. That's her story to tell, not mine."

I nodded. "Agreed. I think we do a pretty good job of managing that balance."

I hefted my bag onto my shoulder and walked toward the door, but turned back and said, "Oh, I saw

Niko after lunch on Monday having a phone call that seemed to make him angry. Turns out he was talking to Ari. But at the end of the day after class, Ryan saw him get an email or text that clearly threw him. Have you been able to access his phone records? And have you found out where Niko was Monday evening, other than making the money drop at Ari's?"

"It's taking time to get his phone records since we don't have the phone and have to jump through a lot of hoops. He met everyone for drinks at the Lodge on Monday evening but didn't stay for dinner. I'm still trying to track what he did and where. We know he went over to Ari's, but he didn't stay there long, and no one saw him come back to the B&B, so he must have been out late."

"Speaking of that money drop, do you know how he managed to put his hands on the money he gave to Ari so quickly? Did you find any cash here?"

"No, and I'm not sure he would have had time to go to the bank, either. It's going to take a little more time to get Niko's bank information." Jack's brow furrowed in frustration. "There's a lot of red tape even for law enforcement."

I looked around the room and noticed an air vent behind the antique armchair. I put my stuff back down and went over to look more closely. "This may sound ridiculous, but should we check this vent? I've seen them used as hiding places in movies."

"It's a little nutty, but what's the phrase—leave no stone unturned." He pulled out his pocket gizmo that seemed to have an endless supply of tools tucked into it, including a small screwdriver. "We might as well check it out. There are no room safes here, and if he had the kind of cash on hand to pay off Ari, he wouldn't leave it sitting in a drawer."

I slid the chair aside so Jack could kneel down and unscrew the vent cover.

He felt around and then looked over his shoulder at me. "Well, I'll be damned." He pulled out an envelope stuffed with cash.

"So I guess I'm not a nut, after all."

"Well, I wouldn't go that far."

Chapter 10

I looked at the envelope stuffed with money and asked, "How much do you think is there?"

"A lot, so I need you to record me while I count this out, okay?"

I used my phone and videotaped Jack meticulously counting the money. He had reached ten thousand and change when he put the last bill on the stack. Once he had stuffed the money back into the envelope and had put it in an evidence bag, I turned off the video and sat on the bed.

"Holy cow."

"You said it, sister. That's a load of walkin' around money. Including what he gave Ari, that's more than thirty grand."

"What was he up to? Maybe he was using cash to buy a painting with a questionable provenance, and that's what the empty case was for? Or he sold one and dropped it off on his way here, which was one of our scenarios for the empty case. But a cash transaction for a legit sale? That's unusual."

"I don't know. At this point, we're only guessing. Have you found anything of note in your research yet?" Jack asked.

I sat on the edge of the bed. "Not much new to report." I decided I better tell him about the guy from Main Street. "There's one thing that's probably a big nothing burger, but in light of the murder, I should tell you."

"What's that?"

"The other morning I was out walking early—it was the morning of the big rainstorm—anyway, there was this guy across the street on Main, and it's hard to describe, but he kind of creeped me out."

"What do you mean 'creeped you out'? What'd he look like?"

"It was too dark to tell. He was standing stock-still, and I don't know, I sensed he was watching me." I felt ridiculous making a mountain out of nothing. "Saying it out loud sounds so silly. I'm being all 'oooo' about a guy just standing on the street."

"You know you can always tell me anything. Maybe he was just waiting out the downpour, like you were. After all, you saw him and observed him long enough to feel like he was observing you, so maybe he felt the same thing, that you were staring at him. Or maybe he was half asleep, waiting for someone to pick him up. You haven't seen him since, right?"

"No. Okay, I feel better just mentioning it. Now maybe he won't keep popping into my head."

"It sounds to me like you would have forgotten all about it, but the murder has got you spooked."

"I bet you're right. So, back to the retreat folks. I've written something up on each person, but I'm still working on the elusive Peter Bigsby. I can't find anything about him online. I mean nothing. He looks a little familiar to me, but I can't put my finger on why. I put in a call to Izzy, and she felt he looked familiar, too."

Jack looked at me sharply. "You don't think he's

connected to the Philly shooting, do you?"

"I really don't. If so, I would definitely know who he is. Besides, he's more like a boardroom executive, not a gun-toting thug."

His face relaxed. "Maybe he was at one of your political events."

"That's possible. I also talked to Michael about it. He said you probably couldn't bring him in and take his prints without cause. Is that true?"

"He's right. If nothing comes to light, I'll bring him in and see if he'll offer an explanation for using an alias. So how is Michael?" Jack asked. He and Michael had gotten along well during our marriage and were still friends.

"He seems to be doing fine. Reveling in his role as top-dog attorney."

"Maybe he'll come here for a short visit and hang out and watch a ballgame."

I picked up my stuff again and started toward the door. "He might enjoy that. And I'll let you know if I find anything else. I'm also checking more into Paula's past, and I have a couple of questions for Laura and Charles."

"Wait a minute. What do you mean, *questions*? That's my job. You're only supposed to be doing background."

"I'm just going to talk to them casually at lunch today. I think I can do it as part of a general conversation. I found some photos online of Laura and Niko that indicate more of a history than she's admitted to. If anything crops up, I'll tell you about it."

Jack massaged his temples, which I knew meant he was tamping down some frustration. "Now, that's vital information I could have used as soon as you found it, and, if I hadn't asked, you would have gone off half-cocked asking people questions. Remember, this is a murder investigation. Emphasis on *murder*!"

He had a point. "I'm sorry, you're right. But if the moment presents itself, I might be able to get them talking about how they knew Niko. It would be a general discussion with other people around. And I promise, I won't be all in-their-face about it."

He stared at me with his hands on his hips while he thought about it. "Okay. I'll need to question the two of them further, so take some screenshots of the photos you found online and email them to me. And don't push it. If you don't get anywhere with casual questions, back off and let me handle it."

"Absolutely, and okay." I gave him the Scouts' honor hand sign, hefted my bag back onto my shoulder, and left before he could say anything else. Of course, not being one to conform to a group standard, I never made it out of the Brownies, so that Scout sign meant I'd reverted to being a smart ass.

****

I arrived back at the Workshop and heard faint music coming from outside. Everyone had gathered in the courtyard, and as I pushed through the patio doors, I was enveloped in the sounds of the accordion and a resonant singing voice. JJ was seated, with her hands adeptly pulling sound from the awkward, yet beautiful instrument. Next to her stood Edgar. He was singing a Scottish folk song I recognized, and his voice was like velvet. Everyone was clearly enthralled with the performance.

I tiptoed over to Bitsy, and whispered, "What on

earth? How'd this come about?"

She leaned over and whispered close to my ear, "We were chatting in class about how JJ plays the accordion. She had it here in our art studio, so the others persuaded her to pull it out for a little pre-lunch entertainment. When Edgar started singing along with one of the songs, we prompted him to get up and join her. Aren't they fabulous?"

"They are. Edgar has a beautiful voice."

When the song ended, there was a healthy round of applause, then JJ suggested it was time to eat lunch.

I went up to Edgar and said, "Wow, that was beautiful."

He looked bashful as he lowered his head slightly; his silver hair shining in the sunlight. "Oh, not really, but thank you anyway."

"You're too modest. Do you sing regularly?"

"My wife and I both sang in the community choir and way back in college I was in a barbershop quartet." He paused, then said, "This was nice. I haven't really sung since my wife passed away. Maybe I'll rejoin the choir. You know, even with the obvious strain of Niko's death, some of the folks in this class have been really good for me beyond just learning more about painting, and in ways I hadn't realized I needed."

"I'm glad," I said, reaching out to touch his arm.

JJ had packed up her accordion and lugged it over to join us. "Hey, Alex, glad you caught the end of our little show. You were great, Edgar! Shall we go get some lunch?"

"A brilliant idea, my dear!" Edgar declared in full voice. A smile filled his face, and his avuncular charm radiated like the beacon of a lighthouse drawing us all to its shores.

After everyone had grabbed a boxed lunch, they drifted off into smaller groups. This was my opportunity to ask some questions. I really wanted to target Charles and Laura but knew I would be more inconspicuous if I made the rounds to everyone, so I joined the group inside first.

Annie and Monica were talking about art schools, and Spencer was regaling Bitsy and Peter with an anecdote from his early days. I was relieved to see Spencer's sense of humor returning. It meant he would make it through this.

He gave me a playful look and then addressed the others, "Sometimes, when we're getting punchy from too many hours working, we'll take a break and get wacky. Remember the dollar store challenge, Alex?"

"Uh-oh," I said, "don't you dare."

Annie chortled with glee. "Ha! That was good!"

Peter prompted him. "What was it?"

"Annie, Alex, and I ran down to The Buck Shops Here dollar store, with the challenge of buying non-traditional items for ten dollars or less, and then we had to create a masterpiece with those items in thirty minutes."

I shook my head in mock shame. "You guys were quite clever with yours. I was not."

Laughing, Spencer said, "She grabbed mustard, ketchup, glue, licorice strings, and potpourri, and then attempted to make a landscape. Not only was it fairly hideous, it also stank to high heaven."

Maybe it was stress hysteria, but we all couldn't stop laughing as I defended my choices. "I figured I could use the mustard and ketchup to create a brooding evening sky, the licorice for tree trunks, and the potpourri for tree leaves and grass. But you're right, it smelled horrible!"

Annie couldn't help adding, "In the end, we had to bag it and put it in the dumpster."

Peter said, "You guys are so lucky to have such camaraderie. You've even managed to make a difficult time more pleasant for us with your bonhomie."

This snapped me back to the here and now. I needed to try and get something out of him. I kept things light, but said in return, "We're doing our best. But you know, Peter, it's driving me crazy that I still feel like I've seen you somewhere. You're sure we haven't met before? Have you ever spent time in Philadelphia?"

His smile remained, but now it didn't quite reach his eyes. "I have been there a few times on business, but unless you were part of a company I was doing business with, which you weren't, I'm certain we haven't met. I don't have time to do much else when I'm working."

"Mmm, I guess so. Maybe you remind me of someone else."

"I'm sure that's the case," he said, and then turned to Spencer with a question about the afternoon class.

Well, that went nowhere, I thought to myself. It was time to move on. I excused myself and went outside to JJ's table.

"We could not have asked for a better day to eat al fresco! May I join you?" I asked.

"Of course!" said Marie.

As they scooted their chairs to make room for me, I asked, "How are you guys doing?"

"Quite good," Paula said. "Considering the stress of Niko's death, Annie and Spencer have carried the class forward without a hitch. We're all learning a lot. And as you saw from the impromptu courtyard concert, we're trying to make the most of our time here, and doing a fairly good job of it." She looked at me with her sharp eyes. "What about you, Alex? This can't be easy for you."

"No, it's not. But with everyone pitching in, we're doing all right. I'm more concerned with making sure you all have the best experience possible under these difficult circumstances."

Marie asked, with an anxious voice, "Is there any word about what happened to Niko? When we're with the class I can avoid thinking about this horrible event, but the rest of the time it's quite upsetting. Are there any suspects? Are we safe at the B&B? Poor Mrs. Danby is all a-twitter over this."

"The police are making inquiries, and I'm sure they will quickly figure out what happened," I said. "I'm confident you are in good hands at the B&B. However, if you'd be more comfortable, I am happy to look into moving you to the Thunderbird Lodge."

"My dear Marie," said Edgar, as he patted her hand, "I see no reason to be concerned. Of course it's unsettling to be told we must remain in town, but we're fortunate the classes have been able to continue. It provides a good distraction for most of the day. And I feel we are safe and sound with the Danbys. Paula, don't you agree?"

Paula spoke quietly, but with authority. "I do. I absolutely see no need to move. We are comfortable at the B&B, Marie, so let's not overreact. Alex, we are perfectly fine. You don't need to add us to your plate of things to worry about."

"Okay, but just know the offer stands. On a brighter note, please tell me about what you're working on today?"

Our conversation turned to pleasantries about the class, and after an appropriate amount of time, I excused myself and walked over to Charles and Laura.

"Beautiful afternoon, isn't it? Mind if I sit down?"

"Uh, sure," Charles said reluctantly, as I had lowered myself into a chair without waiting for approval.

Laura was engrossed in something on her phone and barely looked up. "Please, by all means, make yourself comfortable," she said, with just a hint of sarcasm, which I ignored.

"So how's the class going today? I know it's hard right now, but are you both doing okay?" I asked.

Charles stroked the stubble on his chin while pondering the question. "Yes, I think so. If we're stuck here, we might as well get work done. Spencer and Annie are very knowledgeable, and I've actually learned a few things today."

Laura put her phone down and looked a little bored, as if I was not worthy of her time. "I'd prefer to work independently. The group thing, with schedules and group meals, is fine for amateurs, but I like to work one-on-one or on my own. For me, this has become even more aggravating because we can't leave."

"I'm very sorry to hear that. I know it's inconvenient having to wait out the investigation, but forgive me for asking, if you don't like group work, why did you decide at the last minute to attend the retreat?" I asked, with as much sincerity as I could muster.

"Well, at the time I thought I was going to be working with Niko, and that made putting up with the class approach more tolerable."

"Oh, come off it, Laura," Charles snapped. "Get off your high horse."

I jumped in. "It's okay, Charles, no offense taken. This has been an unsettling time for all of us. And if I recall correctly, you both mentioned having crossed paths with Niko previously, so I'm sure you're feeling this loss more than most of us. Did you know him well, Laura?"

"As I said before, we ran in the same circles."

Charles looked at Laura and muttered under his breath, "That's one way to put it."

"What did you say?" Laura asked pointedly.

Charles sat up straight, his eyes flashing with anger, revealing a different, stronger personality. "I said, *That's one way to put it*. I am really getting tired of your attitude, Laura. You didn't run in the same circles as Niko. You were just one of his many flings. That does not mean you've ever been on the same level as an artist. Not even close. You were nothing more than a groupie."

"You have a hell of a nerve—"

Their voices had risen enough that Paula shifted her attention from the chatter at her own table to ours, and I saw her closely watching the exchange.

"I must apologize, Alex," Charles said, cutting Laura off. "We are behaving badly. Laura and I have always been competitive and ambitious, and we sometimes butt heads because of it. But Niko's death is prompting me to look at myself, at my life, and what I want from it—"

"What a crock," Laura interjected.

He looked at her with pity. "I'm afraid Laura and I are on different paths now. I'm learning that everyone I come across is not my competition. If I don't measure up, it's my own responsibility to improve. I shouldn't need to belittle others in order to boost myself, whereas you, Laura, seem to take great pleasure in picking everyone else apart. You were even snotty with Niko during class. And I saw you arguing with him at the Lodge Monday when we all went for drinks. What's the point? Why create drama for no reason?"

Her jaw dropped and her eyes widened. "You sanctimonious piece of—"

He held up a hand and interrupted her. "Look at Spencer. He's incredibly talented and successful, yet he's humble, kind, and willing to help everyone else succeed in their own way. Annie too. Now look at Niko. He was a pompous jerk. Yes, he was incredibly talented and successful, but a jerk. He used people, mistreated people. And for what? Where is he now? He's dead."

Throughout this speech, Charles became more and more animated. There was a bead of sweat rolling down from his sideburn, and his chest heaved from the exertion. Laura just stared at him in stunned silence.

Charles suddenly got up and said, "If you'll please excuse me, I feel the need to seek alternate company." He picked up his lunch and walked away.

"Wow. I did *not* see that coming," I said. "I'm sorry if I hit a nerve." I really wanted to find out what she was arguing about with Niko, so I needed to keep her talking.

Laura stared after him but quickly regained her composure and said, "Charles is a prima donna. I admit we will butt heads now and then because we're competing in the same market, but this 'life change' bit is just another of his stunts. He'll be back to the same ol' Charles in no time."

"Mmm, I don't know. Death can impact people in ways we can't always explain." After a pause, I asked, "So, were you in a relationship with Niko? If so, I guess that could have made this week a little awkward. Was that the cause for your argument with him on Monday night, or I should say, what Charles thought was an argument?"

I could see the muscles in her jaw clench, but she really had no choice but to answer me. "We weren't arguing. I don't know what Charles was talking about. We dated for a few months a couple of years ago. It was no big deal. It ran its course, and we both moved on. Contrary to what Charles said, I was neither a fling nor a groupie," she sneered, as she picked up her phone and started flipping through emails with impatience. "Whatever, I don't care what he thinks."

Clearly the comments from Charles did not sit well. I felt I had taken my questioning as far as I could, so I got up and said, "Well, I'll leave you to your emails. I'm sure I'll see you later."

I got no response, so I walked back toward the lounge. I could feel Paula watching me. As I opened the door, I looked back, and she held my gaze briefly before turning back to her tablemates. Her expression gave nothing away.

Back inside, Bitsy pulled me aside. "I just came

from the restroom and saw Peter looking in some of the studios down the hall. Do you want me to go see what he's up to?"

"I'll do it. I have more questions to ask him."

"Okay. Come back here when you're done."

"Will do."

As I made my way to the front desk, I texted Jack about Laura and Niko arguing at the Lodge Monday night. I then pretended to be doing busy work while looking around for Peter. When I saw him emerge from the photo lab, I walked over to him.

"Is there something I can help you with, Peter?"

"No, no. The door was open, and I'm just curious about what all goes on here. I hope that's okay. I admit I couldn't resist taking a look at the photo lab. It's great to have such a comprehensive lab for both digital and traditional film work. Your artists are quite fortunate."

"Thank you. And as long as you didn't touch anything in there, you're fine. Although I would prefer you ask someone from the Workshop to escort you if going into the studios."

"Please forgive me. My curiosity got the better of me," he said, with a look of chagrin.

"Are you interested in studying photography?"

"No, not really. It's more that I appreciate good photography. There's such a difference between someone with a good eye and a mere enthusiast. And no, don't worry, I didn't touch, I only looked," he said, with a confident grin. "So tell me, Alex, have you adjusted to the small-town pace here in Flat Rock Falls? Do you feel this is a place you will put down roots?"

"I have, and I do. I have family here and good friends. And I'm more than happy to be out of the rat race of city life. But enough about me—I still don't know very much about you. You mentioned working with companies, at lunch, but what exactly do you do in your profession?"

"In a nutshell, I buy and sell things. Or I help companies buy and sell things."

"What kinds of *things* do you buy and sell?"

"Pretty much anything that catches my interest."

Boy, he was good at evading questions. "Where are you from?" I asked.

He turned and started walking toward the lobby, which forced me to quick-step to keep up. "Originally I'm from northern California, but I consider myself an East Coaster since I've lived on this side of the country for most of my life." Reaching the front desk, he turned to me, and with a slight bow, said, "It's been nice chatting again, but I think I'll go and get a little extra work done on my painting before the next class starts."

Before I could reply, he walked away.

Chapter 11

I texted Maggie to meet me, and then I went back to the lab. A few minutes later, she walked in as I slowly looked around the room.

"What's up?" she asked.

"I caught Peter coming out of the lab. I want to try and figure out if he was looking at anything in particular in here."

"Oh, wow, okay. Let's see…" she said, and we started making our way around the room. She pointed to a scattering of prints and graphics on one of the tables, and said, "This is for the freelance job I've been working on. There's nothing noteworthy about it."

Next, we moved to her large landscape prints, some in the process of being framed, then on to some rolls of film waiting to be developed. Nothing looked disturbed. Our last stop was the computer where she had been working on the slideshow for the retreat. She pressed the space bar to wake up the computer, and the file was open with the candid pics from the classes.

"Is this how you left it?" I asked.

"Let me see," she said, bending over to click on a few images. "I was working on these portrait class photos when I went down to the lounge for lunch. I can't remember if I closed the folder."

"Maybe he was indeed just looking and not touching. Something is fishy, though, so for now don't leave anything out that you don't want people messing with, and if you'd feel more comfortable, lock the studio when you aren't in it."

"That's a good idea," she said.

"I also wanted to let you know Ryan is going to stay here in the guest suite until this is resolved."

Maggie looked relieved. She crossed her arms and leaned her hip against the worktable. "I'm so glad. I feel much better knowing someone else is in the building with you at night. There may be nothing to worry about, but it's comforting to know he'll be here."

"Yeah, I have to say I agree. I'm heading back to the lounge. Are you coming?"

"I think I'll just get back to work. I'll catch ya later."

I found Bitsy, JJ, and Annie lingering over coffee. Everyone else had congregated outside.

"Hey, guys," I said, pulling up a chair.

"So what was Peter up to?" Bitsy asked, in a hushed voice.

"He said he was just curious about the photo lab and all the equipment we have here for artists."

"Did you buy his story?" Annie asked.

"I'm not sure. What do you guys make of him?"

JJ put her mug on the table and scrunched her brow in thought. "He doesn't talk about himself very much, but he does ask a lot of questions. He's asked about you, the community, and about the Workshop."

"Ah, I wondered a little bit when he just asked me about 'planting roots' and if I had adjusted to small town life. He's certainly inquisitive."

"He's nice enough, and he has a good sense of humor. It's not that I don't trust him, but there is definitely more to him than meets the eye."

"I agree," said Bitsy. "He's not an open book like Edgar."

"What's he like in class, Annie?" I asked.

"I've found him to be eager to learn and fully engaged during class time. But I wonder why he's asking about you, Alex? That's kind of creepy. Is it just his nature to be curious, or does he have some special interest in you, specifically?"

"I don't have a handle on him, yet."

"Until you know, be careful around him."

I nodded. "Agreed." I had positioned myself where I could see if anyone entered the room from the hallway or the courtyard. Seeing no one, I lowered my voice, and asked, "What else have you noticed?"

"I've been observing Marie and Paula," said Annie. "Marie has relaxed a bit and doesn't have as much of that manic energy, thank goodness. Paula is the interesting one. It came to me this morning that she reminds me of Miss Marple. You know what I mean? She doesn't give anything away with her expression, but she's always observing, and I wonder what she's observed."

"That's a great analogy, Annie. I totally agree," Bitsy whispered.

"What about Charles and Laura? I think there might be some friction between those two after the conversation I just had with them during lunch," I said and replayed my interaction with the turbulent duo.

"Well, that explains why Charles came back inside looking worked up," said JJ.

"I hate to sound judgmental," Bitsy said, "but I find the both of them a little exhausting. They seem to bring a bit of drama to an already challenging situation."

Annie checked the time on her cell phone, then drained the last of her soda. "Sometimes artists take themselves too seriously. Their competitive nature takes over, and they stir the pot to make themselves feel superior. But you're right, it's exhausting to be around."

I got up from the table. "Hopefully this afternoon's class will be smooth and easy. Annie, when class is over, grab Spencer and stop by the office. Jack wants the two of you to look at some of the things from Niko's room."

"Okay, will do," Annie said, walking toward the courtyard to call everyone in for class.

I needed a change of scenery, so I went up to my apartment to get Baxter and leashed him up for a quick outing. While he stopped every five feet to sniff, I mentally organized everything from the last twenty-four hours.

1) Monica, Edgar, and Marie: From what I had learned about them, these folks were in the clear.

2) I still had a couple of questions about Paula. My gut said she was not involved, but there was something there behind her quiet facade.

3) Peter was a big question mark. I was trying to tamp down any anxiety, but could he be related to what happened in Philly? Maybe Jack should talk to him sooner rather than later.

4) Charles and Laura: Volatile temperaments and a history with Niko, but could either have committed murder? Charles was easily provoked, and Laura had a history with Niko and was witnessed having a confrontation with him, so for me, it was a toss-up.

I felt like I was getting nowhere. I just knew we were missing something important. An idea came to me, and I looked down at Baxter and asked, "How'd you like to go for a ride?"

****

I started second guessing myself as soon as we pulled into the parking lot for Flat Rock Falls. Baxter was becoming impatient, but I hesitated, thinking to myself, *What am I doing? Jack and his team would have been over the crime scene with a fine-tooth comb.* Oh well, I was here, so I might as well check it out.

With Baxter on his leash, we started the trek to the falls. The fall colors glowed in the afternoon light, and the air was filled with the heady scent of the season. Normally, I would linger, but I was eager to get to the top, so we kept a quick and steady pace and only stopped when we reached the spot where I had waited after finding Niko. I instantly relived the shock I felt in that moment, and my pulse quickened, but I forced myself to carry on. I wiped at the sheen of sweat at my temple from the exertion of our rapid climb, then shortened Baxter's leash and walked the path toward the clearing.

I scanned the ground, which was now trampled from the investigation, and saw nothing. I went over to the vegetation that bordered the area and scuffed at it with the toe of my boot. What was I looking for? This was really quite absurd, and I was resigned that this was just a big old waste of time.

Before leaving, I steeled myself and walked to the edge of the cliff to look down at the water. My mind's eye still saw Niko—his dark hair fanned out on the surface of the water—but in reality, there was nothing.

It looked like nothing had ever happened.

I tried to imagine the scene that day. Farther up toward the falls, I could envision the people in the class set up in each of the clearings—laughing, talking, painting. Over the sound of the falls, I imagined you couldn't hear other conversations, only snippets of voices or laughter drifting in the wind. And I could visualize Spencer wandering from person to person.

I realized from this vantage point you couldn't really see much of the other clearings. There were too many trees in between. I wanted to see what was visible from farther up, so Baxter and I went back to the trail.

Closer to the top, we stepped into one of the clearings. From here, you would have to be close to the edge and intentionally looking to see anyone back where Niko had been shoved off the cliff. If it had happened when the class was here, it was no wonder no one saw or heard anything.

I needed a visual landmark, so I took a branch and laid it on the ground half off the edge. I wanted to go back and see if I could see it from below. But before doing that, I needed to do the same thing from one of the paths below where it happened.

Baxter was a little confused by what I was doing but eagerly bounded alongside me while I repeated the process on a lower arm before ending up right back where we started. I scanned both directions. If I stood near the edge, I couldn't see the lower branch, but I could see the one above. So his fall would have been witnessed only if someone above here was standing close to the edge, looking this direction at just the moment he went over. What did I learn from this? I learned it was possible to get away with murder, right under everyone's noses.

I was deep in thought when I heard a branch crack. I spun around, and Baxter let out a low growl. "Hello, who's there?" I called out.

There was no response. I stood still, listening on high alert. A moment later I heard the sound of crunching leaves. "Hello?"

Now all I could hear was the light breeze rustling the leaves on the trees, and I said to Baxter, "Well, aren't I being ridiculous. It's probably just a deer."

But when I looked down at him, his hackles were raised. He didn't act like this around wildlife, and my first thought was that we needed to move away from the edge of the cliff. I tentatively walked toward the path, scanning the woods for any sign of a human form, when a sudden cacophony of noise came from my right. Someone was running through the woods. I quickly moved from the path to the main trail and saw a flash of gray between the trees on the opposite side.

Voices from farther up the trail distracted me, and when I looked back toward the woods, I saw nothing. Whoever it was, was gone.

I was somewhat relieved as a couple of day hikers approached, looking like they were having a great time. "Excuse me," I said, "you didn't happen to see anyone up there, did you?"

The young man smiled and said, "Nope, just us. Have you lost somebody?"

"Oh, no. I just thought I heard someone." I moved aside to let them pass.

"What a beautiful dog," the young woman said, "Can I pet him?"

I looked at Baxter and, once I saw he was back to

his normal self, wagging his tail, I said, "Sure. This is Baxter."

She reached down to pet him, then said, "Well, you and Baxter enjoy your walk. It's a gorgeous day!"

I watched them as they continued on their way and wondered how long it would be before I could truly enjoy these trails again.

Chapter 12

I followed the hikers at a discreet distance, within shouting distance if I needed help, and when I reached my car, I sat for a moment, chewing on my nail. Once I was composed, I pulled out my phone to call Jack.

After I told the story of what happened, he said, with some exasperation, "Okay, first of all, what were you thinking, going up there by yourself?"

"I wasn't by myself. I had Baxter," I replied, with more bravado than I felt.

"Right, that makes all the difference," he said, somewhat sarcastically. "Could you tell if the person was male or female?"

"No. I only saw a flash of gray, like a sweatshirt."

"Chances are, it was just some teenager out doing something they shouldn't have been doing, like skipping school, and they were more afraid of you than you were of them."

"Maybe. But what if it was the killer? Could they have been looking for something at the crime scene?"

"If it was the killer, then you were very lucky. There wasn't any evidence of significance, so I don't know what they would be looking for. Unless they were looking for Niko's phone, which we haven't found, either."

I told him about my theory that the murder could have taken place with everyone there, and he said,

"Yes. Once we got the ME report, I already had Matt and Travis check out that possibility in the hopes of narrowing the timeline."

"So I just wasted time. Oh well, I should at least sit here for a few minutes and see if anyone comes down off the trails."

"No, you should leave. I'll call the park ranger, but there are so many ways off the trails, I'm not sure it will make a difference." My silence told him I might be stubborn, so he said, "I'm waiting to hear your car start."

"Oh, okay," I said, starting the engine. In all honesty, I'd had enough of a scare and was relieved to be on my way.

****

Back in my office, I sat heavily in my chair. It felt like this day was never going to end. I was a bit frazzled and had just laid my head on the desk when my phone rang.

"Thank goodness, Izzy! What have you found out?"

"Okay, okay, keep your pants on," she bantered.

"Sorry, I'm a bit anxious today."

"Under the circumstances, that's understandable. Anyway, I'm afraid I don't have much for you."

"Oh shoot," I said, with disappointment.

"I showed the photo around, and a couple of staffers vaguely recognized him but don't know who he is. The feeling is he's from higher echelons than we would rub shoulders with. That at least tells you he *is* from this world. In what capacity, I don't know, but he's got some link to your past. I'll keep trying, but that's all I got so far."

"Thanks, Izz, I really appreciate it."

"No problem. Just watch your back. You don't know why he's there or what he wants, so be careful. And I'm not being a conspiracy theorist; I'm being practical, and a good friend."

"I know you are, and I appreciate it. This is definitely a little unsettling. Although, I don't see how it could connect to Niko's murder."

"Just keep Jack in the loop. Is Baxter still there?"

"Yup."

"Sheesh, well, say hi to Baxter for me then. Wish it was a handsome guy—you really need to get back in that saddle. But I guess a dog is at least a step in the right direction. Guys like a girl who likes dogs. Gotta run, bye-bye."

I laughed out loud to the disconnected phone call, and just as I put it down on the counter, a group text came in from Jack to Annie, me, and Spencer. —*Let's meet at Annie's and my house for dinner.*— All three of us dinged back in succession, confirming.

I needed a break from thinking about murder, so I left the office and wandered the halls. I started on the right side and stopped in the craft room where the scrapbook and card-making group was meeting. The large work tables were covered with colorful papers, card stock, stickers, ink stamps, little swirls of metal, photographs, an assortment of colored pens and pencils, and scissors. Each person had brought clear plastic bins with their own bits of ribbon and personal items for their scrapbook pages. I'm not a scrapbooker, but I like watching other people do it. Some of the card-making skills were impressive, too.

I leaned my elbows on the table and watched one

member of the group, Francis, carefully cutting out and layering card stock to create a unique and professional-looking card front. I wished I had the patience and precision to do such work. After taking a spin around the tables to look at everyone's projects, I reluctantly left the room and continued on my jaunt.

Mason was working in his studio, but the door was closed, so I watched through the window as he washed paint over a large canvas lying on the tarp-covered floor. He was working on a series of pieces with multiple mediums such as paint, paper, and metal. He looked up from his work and saw me, so I waved, gave him a thumbs-up, and moved on.

I headed down the opposite hall and passed Ryan's studio. I was happy to see he had regained his inspiration and was singing along with a song playing through his earbuds while wielding the chisel on his sculpture. I continued on until I reached the pottery studio, another of my other favorites at the Workshop. The door was open, so I walked in and inhaled deeply, taking in the earthy smell of wet clay.

Hannah was at the wheel forming a tall pitcher; her foot on the pedal of the wheel worked in perfect harmony with her hands as she shaped the graceful vessel out of the wet, pliable clay. Ethan was glazing a bowl, and I saw a batch was ready for the kiln. I was not even in the same ballpark as these two, but I loved working with clay and knew the glazes well enough to know he was using a deep blue and a dark brown. It was going to be beautiful.

"Hey, you guys!" I said.

"Hi, Alex, how are you holding up? Ryan's been keeping us up to date on things. What a bizarre turn of events," Hannah said evenly, quickly shifting her eyes back to the pottery wheel.

Thus far, Hannah and Ethan had left me alone and had not become embroiled in the drama unfolding at the Workshop. This didn't surprise me. They were both mild-mannered, kept to their own business, and showed very little range of emotion. It could have a calming effect, but at times, like when confronted with murder, I found the lack of emotion unsettling. I think I would explode if I had to keep every emotion in check. Today, though, I appreciated their reserve.

"Yes, it's been quite a shock. Everyone is hanging in there, though, and Jack is working hard to find out what happened."

"Do you need something, or are you here to get away from it all and throw a pot?" Ethan asked.

"I wish. I'm only popping in to see what you guys are up to."

"All is well here," said Hannah. "We have a lot to do to get our inventory up for the winter art festival along with our usual seasonal and holiday pieces, but we're getting there."

"Well, don't let me disturb you. I'll just linger a bit for my fix of clay."

I wandered around looking at all the tools—the hook, ribbon, and rake tools, the mud wire cutoffs, the various bats, carving tools, and calipers. I opened the heavy plastic bag encasing a block of clay and felt the coolness of it under my hand. I wished I could pull off a piece and sit down at a wheel, but it would have to wait for another day. I resealed the block and said my goodbyes.

Taking a couple of hours to visit with some of our

studio artists and people coming and going for our community classes was just the break I needed. There were a few questions here and there about Niko and the investigation, but mostly, these were people going about their daily lives without being encumbered with a murder hanging over their heads.

It was a little after five p.m. when Ryan stopped by the desk. "Hey, the fence is done, and I'm going to pop home and pack a bag. I'll be back in a little bit."

"Thanks, Ryan. Hold on, let me get you a check for your work. Do you have a receipt for the materials?"

He dug into his pocket and pulled out a wrinkled hardware store receipt. "Here you go."

While I got the checkbook out of my purse, I said, "I'm going over to Annie and Jack's this evening, but I shouldn't be gone too long."

"Okay. I'll probably still be in my studio, so stop in and let me know when you're back."

"I will."

A few minutes later, we heard the chorus of voices coming from the retreat group. As they rounded the corner into the lobby, we heard Edgar asking, "Who's up for drinks and dinner at the Lodge?"

Ryan moseyed over to them and said, "I have to run an errand first, but I'll swing by and join you guys for a bit before I come back here to get some work done."

"What a wonderful idea, Edgar," said Marie, as she took his arm and looked up at him, batting her eyelashes.

Uh-oh, I thought to myself, *methinks Marie might have a wee bit of a crush on Edgar.*

As the group congregated in the lobby, Charles was

deep in conversation with Monica. Her unpretentious manner seemed to put him at ease. In contrast, Laura was talking *at* Peter, who was listening to her with a controlled politeness. Fortunately, JJ and Bitsy rescued him and joined the conversation.

Paula held back from the group and lingered at the desk. I hoped it might be an opportunity to learn more about her.

"How was your afternoon, Paula?"

Her eyes brightened as she said. "I found it inspiring. Annie and Spencer are quite brilliant at bringing out the best in everyone."

"I'm so glad to hear that. Have you been painting all your life?"

"I dabbled, but really only started working on it after retirement. My mother and aunt were very talented with watercolors and drawing, so I hoped the gene would be passed down to me. I'm not sure it was, although I do feel someone else must be guiding my hand as I draw, because I'm not really sure how the image goes from my brain to the paper," she said, with a small smile.

"That's such an interesting way to look at it, but I'm sure you have significant talent in your own right. Both you and Marie do."

"Well, that's very kind of you to say."

"What did you do before you retired?"

"I was an analyst. Marie retired the year before me, and we spent that time figuring out where we wanted to go and how we wanted to spend our time."

Before I could ask any more questions, Marie called over to us, "Paula, come on, let's go. Alex, we're all walking over to the Lodge. Would you like to join us?"

"Thanks, but I still have some work to do, and then I think I'm going to make it an early night."

After they exited the building, the silence that followed made me feel like I was in a vacuum, so I quickly tidied up the front desk and went down the hall to find Annie and Spencer, who were finishing the cleanup in the work room.

"I'll see you guys at your place, Annie. I'm going to go change."

Spencer said, "I should be right behind you. I just need to do a little more prep for tomorrow. Can I bring anything, Annie?"

"Nah, I'm going to run into the market and pick up something for the grill. Bring Baxter, Alex. He can run around and explore the yard."

"Okee-doke. See ya in a bit."

I ran up to my apartment to change into a thermal shirt with a flannel shirt over it, then threw on a wool beanie hat with a silly puff ball on top. Perfect for being outside around the grill on a crisp fall evening.

****

Annie and Jack lived close to the Workshop, in a neighborhood with mature trees and acre-sized lots. I parked on the street, and Baxter and I took the walkway up to the inviting contemporary ranch. They did a significant renovation years ago, and the result was beautiful, with a vaulted tongue-and-groove wood ceiling, tall windows on both front and back, a large open kitchen, and a cozy den with a fireplace. Big sliding doors led out to the back covered patio and fenced yard.

I knocked while opening the front door and was

greeted with the smell of a wood fire and the heady aroma of apples and cinnamon.

"Come on in," Jack said from the kitchen.

"What smells so good?" I asked.

"I whipped up an apple pie when I got home. Should be out in about twenty."

"Ooooo, yum," I cooed, as I opened the back door to let Baxter out.

"Annie called from the market. She should be here any minute. She got some steaks, and we'll just throw some potatoes on the grill and do sliced tomatoes with a balsamic drizzle."

"Oh boy, I feel like I haven't eaten this good in days!" I said, salivating.

"That doesn't surprise me, but frankly, we haven't either, and I figured since we're going to be working tonight, we might as well eat well."

"While we're waiting for Annie and Spencer, did you hear anything from the park ranger?" I asked.

"No luck. It's a big park to zero in on one person, and it's a big errand to send them on, particularly when all we've got to go on is a glimpse of gray sweatshirt."

"I know, I'm sorry, I should have moved faster to see who it was."

"No, that would have been a bonehead move. I may think it's a longshot, but if that person was somehow connected to the case, and you just happened to be there at the same time, you potentially put yourself in a lot of danger. Can you imagine how I—how we all—would feel if we had to search for you and found your dead body up there?"

I suddenly felt a wave of nausea and put my hands up in surrender. "Yeah, okay, you're right. Point made."

"I hope so," he said, with finality. "Okay, lecture over. Catch me up on anything else from today."

"Izzy got back to me, and it looks like Peter definitely has a connection to my old life…in some way. We just don't know how. But I honestly don't think it was from the shooting. I'm confident I would know if he had been involved in that."

"Doesn't matter. I'm going to pull him out for a chat tomorrow. I don't like this hanging in the air and want it settled."

"Okay. Thanks. That would make me feel better. So, what did you find out today?"

"Well, the park rangers reported that nobody fit the description Monica gave, and no one they interviewed saw anything unusual. Of course, there was a time gap between when Niko died and the park staff started stopping people, so someone may have slipped through."

"That's too bad. Did you talk to the gallery in Chicago?

"Yes. They would like us to ship the two paintings Niko brought with him for their gallery show, and then they'll contact me afterward about where to send any money from sales. They're actually covering the shipping expenses, which kind of surprised me."

"I'm not surprised. They are having a show with pieces from an artist who has just died. The prices are going to skyrocket for Niko's paintings."

"I hadn't thought about that. But I hit a dead end with the empty shipping case. They were not expecting him to take anything back other than what they already have shipping cases for and didn't know where he was going after Chicago."

"What about phone records and bank accounts?

"Travis should hopefully get the phone dump sometime tomorrow. The big question is why he had that hidden burner phone."

"What about his financials? Anything unusual?"

"He has quite a bit of money in the bank. One account has roughly $580,000 in it, another has $80,000, and a third has about $4,000. We'll need a forensic accountant to comb through everything to see if his income matches the deposits."

I gasped. "He's pretty well-known, but that's a lot of money."

"Yeah, that's one of the things we'll be talking about tonight with Annie and Spencer. Ah, she's pulling in now." Jack said, hearing the garage door open.

"Hi! Wow, it smells good in here!" Annie said, bustling in with a shopping bag. She gave Jack a quick kiss and unloaded the groceries for dinner. "Spencer drove up just as I pulled in the garage."

"I'll let him in," I volunteered and opened the front door just as Spencer raised his fist to knock. "Hey, come on in. We're just getting prepped for grilling."

"Awesome," he said, rubbing his hands together.

In short order, we had the potatoes cut, seasoned, drizzled with olive oil, wrapped in a cocoon of foil, and on the grill. The steaks were waiting their turn, and meanwhile, Jack passed around drinks.

Getting down to business, Annie asked, "Should we look at the portfolio before we put the steaks on?"

She and Spencer took the portfolio to the couch in front of the fireplace. They examined each page, commenting more to each other than to us. They clearly had an appreciation for Niko's talent. Once done, they put it aside, and we all went outside and breathed in the delicious aroma of the grilling steaks while Baxter romped around the yard.

"We've got a lot to go over tonight. Are you up for it, Spencer?" Jack asked.

"As up as I can be," he said. "I'd certainly feel better if we can figure out what happened. And hopefully we'll be able to prove it didn't have anything to do with us or the retreat."

Over dinner, we hashed over everything—the shipping case, the hidden burner phone, the paper map, the asterisk in his calendar, the book with initials and dates, the money in his account, and the cash in the air vent.

"When I was a kid, I stashed my diary, allowance, and other important stuff in my bedroom air vent," Annie said matter-of-factly, popping a forkful of potato into her mouth.

"Amazing," Spencer said, shaking his head.

She laughed. "Hey, he's lovable now, but my brother was a menace when we were kids."

I added, "No, I get it. Even though I wasn't into girly stuff for very long, I seem to recall Jack cutting all the hair off my doll when we were kids. And Mom had to try and turn poor Bonnie's hair into an intentional pixie cut."

Jack put his hands up and said, "All right! Guilty as charged. But then you ended up putting her in fatigues with a headband around her forehead and made her into a desert commando. She became 'Badass Bonnie.' "

After a good laugh, which we all needed, I sobered.

"We're getting a bit off topic here. So, how much do Niko's paintings typically go for?"

Spencer thought about it before answering. "His prices have gone up in the last four to five years. I would say $15,000-$30,000 each, depending on the size. Not bad for someone his age, or really, any age."

"Could he legitimately have that much money in the bank?" Jack refrained from outing Ari's connection to Niko, but added, "We already know from one line of inquiry that he was broke when he was younger, so it's not like he had any family money."

"Well, I don't have that much money in the bank and my paintings sell in a similar or higher price bracket," Spencer said. "I mean really, how many people have that much money to drop on a piece of art? You have to find the right buyer, and that buyer has to want the painting badly enough to pay that much money. Then you have to remember the gallery takes their cut. So, frankly, it's hard for me to fathom."

"Me too," said Annie. "Dang, makes me feel like a slacker. And that's a lot of walking around money to have in cash. Why would he have that much with him?"

The next hour passed with our think tank trying to make rhyme or reason out of what happened. Dinner was long finished, but we were still sitting at the table talking through each part of the investigation again, when Annie checked out, lost in thought.

"Something bothering you, Annie?" I asked.

"Yes, but I can't pinpoint it. I feel like it has something to do with that portfolio."

Spencer got up and brought the portfolio to the table where he opened it between them. While they pored through dozens of images, Jack and I listened to their musings while we cleaned up the kitchen.

Annie said, "See, look at this one. It's not overt, but when you really look at it, it's not in his usual style."

"I see what you mean," he said, flipping to another page. "Hold on, what's this?" Spencer asked, feeling along the edge of the slipcover. He carefully pulled something out of the plastic sleeve. "There's another photo between two pieces of backing." He held it up, and it showed a beautiful landscape.

"Why would that be tucked away, and not front and center in the portfolio?" I asked.

Spencer said, "Because that is definitely not Niko's style. He doesn't do English countryside landscapes. More importantly, this looks like a Turner."

The table was cleared and the dishwasher was quietly rumbling, so Jack sat back down, and asked, "Can you explain in layman's terms what you guys have been talking about?"

Annie answered, "A couple of the paintings in here are unusual for Niko. He's using some color palettes and techniques that mimic some of the old masters. Maybe if he were experimenting, okay, I'd get it, but he wouldn't put those works in his professional portfolio."

"But this one," Spencer said, pointing to the once-hidden photograph, "this is a whole different ballgame. This is a direct reference to one of the greatest landscape artists, Turner. Why would he have this? And why was it hidden? Did he paint it?"

I sat for a moment trying to grab hold of something in my memory. I had seen something recently. What was it, and where did I see it? *Aha!* I got out my laptop.

"What is it?" Annie asked.

"Just a sec. Let me pull something up." I opened my browser and sifted through one of the art magazines I had been reading. "Here it is."

I scanned the article, then sat back and said, "Look, I know this might sound farfetched, but I think Niko was forging paintings."

Chapter 13

When everyone looked at me blankly, I pointed to the article, "This is a small blurb in *Art World* about a painting from the Gallawik Museum that had been sent out for restoration. It was found to be a forgery. So that got me thinking."

Annie tilted her head. "And you leapt to the conclusion that Niko was forging paintings?"

"Think about it—the burner phone, the notebook, the money, and now this." I pointed to the photo. "Is it possible?"

Spencer said, "Frankly, if Niko hadn't been murdered it wouldn't even be on my radar, but I don't know now."

Jack turned toward Spencer. "You and I talked during the official interview about your knowledge of Niko from when you lived in New York. Looking at it from this angle, do you recall anything that would trigger an alarm bell?"

"I really don't. I mean, yeah, Niko was always cocky, and he liked to game the system, so to speak. But I only really saw that when it came to angling for exposure or networking to hobnob with the wealthy art patrons. Overly ambitious, yes, but I honestly never saw anything that would be considered illegal or even a gray area. Annie, what do you think?"

"It's hard for me to fathom he would do this, and

we shouldn't jump to conclusions. If he was doing something underhanded, I can't figure out why he would hint at some of these artists in any of his paintings."

"Maybe he became careless," I suggested.

Annie continued her train of thought. "And if there's another explanation for this photo, why hide it in here? This is his professional portfolio. It's not like sticking it in with a stack of miscellaneous stuff."

Spencer shook his head, perplexed. "It doesn't make sense. Let's see if there are any more hidden photos in here." He carefully felt each page of the portfolio.

Jack asked, "How do you determine a painting is a forgery?"

Annie answered, "Aside from provenance, the paints used by the old masters have a different chemical makeup. Forgers will often deceive by carefully aging boards, papers, or canvases, but you can't recreate older paints because of modern day chemicals found in the ingredients of the pigments. And, some older pigments, such as purple, turn more blue with age. There's also radio carbon dating, or infrared reflectography, which looks at what's under the painting."

Spencer added, "It's expensive to scientifically test paintings, and very few museums have ready access to such testing. Plus, the forgers are getting better and better. Even experienced, trained eyes are fooled. So, forgeries continue to flood the market." He pulled out one more photo that had been hidden. It was of a sketch, not a painting. "Aha! What do you think Annie, French?"

She studied it. "Mmm, yes…if I didn't know

better, I'd think that could be a Corot."

I leaned over her shoulder to look. "I agree. I remember studying him in school."

"Wow. I'm not sure what to think," she said.

"I want to check something." I got up to get the notebook we found with the initials and dates, then I thumbed through a few of the pages and recited two sets of the initials. "JC, WT...could these be Corot and Turner?"

Spencer looked incredulous, saying, "Would he really be so brazen?" He took the notebook from me and scanned the pages. "Geez, you could probably pick any two initials and match them to an artist, so it could be a coincidence."

"You're right," I said, "but add everything together and it seems to me forgery is a plausible theory. And Niko could have either been the forger or the broker for another forger. Either way, not good."

"I hate to say it, but you're right," he said. "What happens now?"

Jack said, "I want to check his credit cards and see if he made any stops on his way here. I'll also call the art fraud guys, give them what we've got, and see if they have a line on anything that might link to what we have here. Then we'll have to see how this changes the lines of inquiry for Niko's murder, and who, if anyone, from the retreat class could fit this scenario."

"Well, I can think of three that could fit this theoretical scenario," I said. "Charles and Laura, because of their erratic personalities and their history with Niko. And Peter, who's been evasive when I've asked about his business. He told me he buys and sells anything that catches his interest. Maybe that includes forgeries."

****

Friday

After tossing and turning all night, I woke up at an insanely early hour. I knew trying to go back to sleep would be futile, so I got out of bed, threw on some sweats, and made some coffee. Looking out at the dark sky of predawn, my mind was twirling through everything that had happened since Tuesday.

When I had drained the last of my coffee, I realized I was no closer to figuring out which of the classmates could have killed Niko. Sitting in the dark, scowling, was not the most productive way to spend my time, so I gingerly got up, not wanting to wake Baxter, who was snoring next to me on the couch, and made a second cup to take with me down to the office. Maybe I would have more clarity there.

I stopped short midway down the stairs. There was a shaft of light coming from the office, where the door was slightly ajar. I crept down slowly and quietly, ears on high alert for any sound. A shadow crossed the path of light inside the office, stopping me in my tracks again. It couldn't be Maggie. She would have turned on the lights in the main hall, plus it was way too early. I looked toward the front door. Was it possible the mag locks weren't set last night? Damn it. I hadn't come back downstairs to check.

I tried to calm the voices in my head and stood quietly, listening. Knowing Ryan was just down the hall in the guest suite bolstered my courage, and I continued my slow pace down the stairs, although, I did look around for something to use as a defensive weapon. The only thing within reach was a big golf umbrella leaning against the bench at the bottom of the stairs. It would have to do. Step by step I made my way to the office door, pausing to silently set my coffee mug on the front desk.

I heard a soft shuffling of papers in the office. My heart was pounding so loudly I was sure it would give me away while I debated whether I should move forward or retreat back upstairs. Finally, I took a deep breath and shoved the door open with the tip of the umbrella.

"What the hell are you doing in here?" I asked, in my most authoritative voice.

A shocked Peter Bigsby dropped the paper he was holding and tried to look innocent. "I came in early to get some extra work done on my painting, but I needed a bandage for a cut on my finger. The office was open, so I thought I might find one here." He held up his hand and pointed to an invisible papercut on his second finger.

I pulled out my cell phone. "I'm afraid I don't buy that story, Peter. I'm calling the police."

Peter started walking toward me, tapping the air with his hands. "Okay, okay, no need to do that."

I absurdly struck the pose of a fencer, extending my arm with the umbrella. "Cut the crap, Peter…or whoever you are…I know you are *not* Peter Bigsby, so just sit down and don't move a muscle."

Peter complied with resignation, and I got my phone out to speed-dial Jack.

Ryan came around the corner just as I ended the call. "Hey, what's going on, Alex? Why all the racket? Peter! What are you doing here so early?" he asked, rubbing the sleep from his eyes.

"I just caught Mr. Bigsby going through my office. I've called Jack, but would you mind staying here with us while we wait for him to arrive?"

"Sure, no problem." Ryan crossed his arms and leaned against the door frame, giving Peter a look that said, *Don't even try messing with me.* "What were you doing in here, Peter?"

"Uh, I, uh, just wanted to get a little extra work done on my piece for the exhibition. I swear, the front door was not locked...come on, there's no need..."

I interrupted with, "Let's not talk any more until Jack gets here, okay?"

In the silence that followed, I paced back and forth. The only sound was the second hand ticking on the wall clock, and when Jack finally entered through the front doors, the sound echoed in the two-story lobby.

"What's going on here?" Jack asked, as he came around the front desk.

"Peter seemed to be on walkabout this morning, and I found him looking through the office. I think it's time for you to have that chat with him."

Peter heard us, and called from the office, "I told her the front door was open, and I came to do some work on my painting. I needed a bandage..." He trailed off.

Jack moved to the office doorway. "I see. Well, regardless, I do think it's time for us to have a chat, Peter. Would you voluntarily come with me, or do I need to make this more official?"

Peter looked at each of us in turn, then let out a deflated breath. "Yes, of course, I'll come voluntarily."

"I'll meet ya down there," I called out as they left the building.

I leaned the umbrella against the wall and turned to Ryan. "Did you check the mag locks before heading to the guest suite last night?"

"Oh my gosh, Alex, I didn't. I'm so sorry. I assumed Shelby locked up as usual, and she must have assumed I would do it."

"Well, we don't know that she didn't. It's possible he got hold of a key card when he was wandering around the building. And I could have come back down to check. So right now, it's no one's fault unless we find out Shelby did indeed lock up, in which case this is all on Peter. Regardless, we're going to have to be more diligent about security."

****

The single-story cinder block building that housed the Flat Rock Falls police department glowed in the early morning sun. They had attempted to warm up the 1960s industrial vibe with a taupe-yellow paint, which they must have purchased at a great discount because, otherwise, no one would intentionally buy it. Black shutters on the large plate glass windows and vintage gold leaf lettering on the front door did help with the quaint factor. However, the inside had changed little in over fifty years.

As I entered, Travis called out a hello from the desk behind the chest-high counter that ran along the front reception area. "Jack said to tell you to wait out here. He's in the interview room right now."

"Okay," I said. I walked through the swinging half door at the end of the counter and wandered over to the table with the coffee maker. The plastic tablecloth was covered with a layer of spilled sugar and powdered creamer, sticky coffee rings, and a pick-up-sticks array of used stirrers. The coffee pot looked like it hadn't had a proper cleaning in months. How badly did I really want this? Since I'd left my untouched coffee back at the Workshop, I decided it was worth a try.

Cup in hand, I went back through the swinging door to sit on the old church pew bench that lined the wall. The coffee warmed my hands through the paper cup, which was nice, but the slightly acidic smell that drifted up to my nose made me suspect what was coming before I even took the first sip.

"Ghackk," I exclaimed. "Who made this?"

Travis chuckled and said, "Jack. Need I say more?"

"Mmm, no," I said, leaning back in the pew. Jack might be a master chef at home, but he couldn't be bothered to make a decent pot of coffee here.

Within minutes I grew bored, and I impatiently crossed and recrossed my legs, tapped my fingers on the pew, and occasionally blew out a sigh like a truculent teenager, until Travis looked at me over his glasses. Finally, after reading all the public notices and adverts on the bulletin board, sorting through emails and texts on my phone, cleaning out my purse, and popping two mints to remove the coating of bitter coffee from my tongue, I heard Jack's voice coming toward the reception area.

I got up to meet him at the counter. "So?" I asked.

"We're all done here, Alex. I'm satisfied with the interview and am going to let Peter explain himself to you. Can you drive him back to the Workshop or the Lodge?"

"Yes. So he's not a danger to any of us?"

"I've been able to eliminate him from our inquiries, and after doing a little checking, I believe his story about why he's here."

"Did he say if the front door was open, or if he got his hands on a keycard?"

"He said the door was open, and he didn't have a keycard on him, so you'll have to sort that out."

Peter entered the reception area at that moment, so Jack quickly muttered, "I'll be in touch with you later when I get more information from the art fraud guys."

Peter and I walked to the car in silence. While buckling up, he asked, "Could we go somewhere and talk?"

I stared straight ahead while thinking about it, then started the car. "Sure, but I want a public place. Let's go get some breakfast."

The Café was in full swing with the morning rush. Aunt Claudia was busy bussing a table but waved as I led the way to a booth in the back corner.

"Thanks, Janice," I said, when Claudia's longtime waitress brought over the coffee pot. "I think just coffee for now. We'll order in a little bit."

I leaned back in the booth while giving Peter the look I would use with a politician who had lied to me; my eyes would go squinty and my brow would furrow. Along with folded arms, a tense jaw, and most importantly, a long awkward silence, it usually made the other person squirm.

It worked like a charm. Peter fidgeted with his coffee spoon and napkin, looking ill at ease, and I was now in control of this situation.

"Okay. Let's start from the beginning," I said matter-of-factly. "I know your name is not Peter Bigsby. You've intentionally brushed off my questions about what you do and how I might know you. I've deduced we must have crossed paths in some way when I lived in Philadelphia, which frankly, has totally creeped me out, because I don't know your motives for being here."

"Please, let me—"

I was in no mood to be polite, and cut him off. "I've caught you wandering around the building, you seem to have a heightened interest in this place, and then, I catch you looking at papers in my office in the wee hours of the morning. I don't know yet if you broke in or if the door was left open. Regardless, there's a murder investigation going on, and that makes all of this far more serious. Now it's your turn. Please fill in the blanks."

He looked me square in the eyes. "My name is Walter Sarnov."

I sat up straight and cocked my head. "Walter Sarnov?" I paused, then said, "You donated to a couple of the campaigns I was handling, right?"

Peter—*Walter*—gave me a slight smile as I worked out who he was.

My memory bank kicked in. "You wanted to be listed as anonymous on any donor lists, and you declined invitations to events, even the highbrow ones. I asked around about you, but got nothing more than an evasive, 'He's a good person to have supporting you.' "

He smiled a little more.

I propped my fist under my chin as my mind whirred a mile a minute. "What the heck are you doing here? Why with an alias? What's going on?"

"I am in business, but I have friends in certain political circles. I saw how you ran your campaigns and I liked what I saw. You won every election you handled, so I decided to put some money behind a couple of your candidates. Ones I felt were particularly important to the political landscape."

That last statement had impact, and I sensed this guy wielded some power.

"However, as you noted, I prefer to remain anonymous."

"I see." Yup, I was right. He was one of those guys you see in the movies who have a direct line to senators, governors, or even the president. Someone who has the ear of the inner circle of people in power, but in a very quiet and non-public way.

"Anyway, fast forward to your last campaign. I happened to be in town on business, and I attended bits and pieces of that trial. That's probably why you felt I looked familiar."

"Ah, that's it! I must have seen you at the courthouse."

"Yes. Once the trial was over, I kept track of you...and before you get uncomfortable, no, I wasn't stalking you. As I've mentioned, I have many acquaintances in certain circles of the political world. I was fascinated by the chutzpah you had to leave your successful career. Your name had come up a few times by those of influence as a pick for an even more powerful position in Washington, so I wanted to see where this drastic life change was going to take you."

"Wow." I was somewhat at a loss for words, which was unusual. I had, of course, done some checking on him after his donations, but only found public records in relation to his business. "So what the heck are you doing here? Why come to the retreat? Why under an assumed name? Why have you been snooping around the building, and now this morning, in my office?"

"I was intrigued when I read about the Creative Workshop, and I wanted to see what goes on here. Attending the retreat under an assumed name seemed a good way to do it. Obviously, I fumbled at that. I'm not accustomed to, and clearly not proficient at, duplicity."

I was growing frustrated. "That still doesn't explain all the skullduggery. Why were in you in my office at the crack of dawn, and what were you looking for in there? And you haven't answered why the assumed name. Why not come as yourself?"

"I told you the truth when I said I buy and sell things. I've had a great deal of success in my life buying and selling companies. I've been doing this for twenty-plus years, and frankly, the thrill is gone. In the last two years I've moved more into consulting work, both in the US and abroad."

I tapped my finger impatiently on the table.

"Anyway, to get to the point. Aside from the professional shift, I've decided I need something more in my life. So, when I read about you and the Workshop, I started thinking about a way I could invest in something that had long-term impact. I could be a part of a community, even peripherally, and do something philanthropic at the same time."

I was incredulous. "What are you saying? You want to buy the Workshop? You think you can come here and buy us out and turn it into a franchise of some kind?"

Walter remained even-keeled. "That is not what I'm saying at all. I want you to be able to keep doing what you're doing and let the artists keep doing what they're doing. I want you to be able to buy equipment if you need it, develop new programs, broaden your classes, and even add studio space. I don't want a stake in it; I want to have an impact. And I want to feel a community connection even if I don't live here."

Now he was starting to annoy me. "If that's true, then why the subterfuge? You don't need an assumed name to be a benefactor!"

"Look, in business, I typically hire someone to check things out for me. But I wanted to explore this place myself and see firsthand how you work, without you, or anyone, knowing who I was. It's the reason I came early to scope out the community, why I was looking around the building, and why I was in your office this morning."

"What were you hoping to find?" I asked tersely.

"I wanted to look at the schedule and enrollment, and I admit, I was hoping to find some financial records. That way, no one would be the wiser if I didn't like what I saw. I would leave as Peter Bigsby, and no one would see me again."

I felt a jolt go through me. "Wait, you said you came to town early. Did you happen to be on Main Street early on Friday morning?"

He said, with reluctance, "Perhaps."

"Oh my God. That was you! Do you know how much that creeped me out? Were you following me?"

"No! I like to get up early, and I was out for a walk when I saw you on Main Street. I was trying not to draw attention to myself."

"Unbelievable," I muttered to myself.

"I'm sorry, Alex. This is not how I wanted this to go, and I'm terribly sorry if I've upset you. I am very good at what I do, but this is new for me and I have totally fumbled it, particularly in light of Niko's murder. I should have come clean immediately."

I started chewing my thumbnail while thinking, then realized what I was doing and quickly put my hand under my leg. "This is a lot to take in. I'm pretty ticked off about being deceived and from having to wonder if you were sent here from Philly on some kind of vendetta."

"Really? A vendetta? How did you figure out I was even in Philly?"

"Well, when I couldn't sort out how I knew you, and you were so evasive, I sent your photo to a couple of people there. You were recognized, but no one actually knew you. That meant you had been in my old world in some way. There were some dangerous people involved in that last campaign who had a lot to lose, and then with Niko's murder, I had to wonder if you were an extension of that past."

"You thought I killed Niko? What would my motive be?"

"Well, maybe he saw or heard something he shouldn't. Or it could have been an attempt to ruin me as revenge. I don't know! But with the connection to Philly, and finding no existence of a Peter Bigsby, it's a logical progression to think you could be here for nefarious reasons, don't ya think?"

"Okay. Point taken. Obviously, I had no idea there would be a murder when I came up with my brilliant undercover idea," he said, with chagrin. Then he switched gears, and a flicker of amusement crossed his face. "The interview at the police station was a lot easier than this one. Did you know you were dubbed the 'velvet hammer' back in Philly? All professional decorum and manners until the hammer drops."

I couldn't help but laugh and put up my hands in surrender. "Yeah, all right. I will admit you had good intentions."

"Truly, I did."

I didn't want to cave so quickly, but I was curious, and asked, "I'd like to know what conclusions you've come to about the Workshop. I'm not talking about money—I would just like to know your conclusions about the community and what we are doing here."

Walter relaxed for the first time since I busted into the office wielding the umbrella. "I'm impressed, Alex. I think what you're doing here is great, and I find the community charming. I would like to sit down with you once this is over, to talk about it. Would you be willing to do that?"

"I need some time to think, but I don't see why we can't have a conversation...maybe. Let's put this on the back burner, though, until after the retreat. We have enough to deal with right now."

"Of course. Would you mind if I finished out the retreat as Peter? I really don't want to have to dance around why I came here. Everyone knows me as Peter, and I'd like to leave it that way."

"Frankly, I think that's a good idea."

I started to slide out of the booth, making motions of leaving. I wanted to go back to my apartment and think this all through.

"Great. But wait, before you go, I'd like to talk about Niko."

I sat back down on the edge the seat. "Do you know something?"

"No, not definitively. I've been trying to fly under

the radar, but I have been paying attention. Niko was a classic narcissist, but I think something more was going on. He would swing from arrogant to anxious, and he clearly had more on his mind than this retreat. Do you have any leads on his murder? And yes, I knew the minute the chief said 'suspicious death' it had to be murder."

I wasn't going to tell him anything of substance. He may have been cleared as a suspect, but I wasn't ready to trust him. "It's early days yet, but the pieces of the puzzle are falling into place."

"Good. Let's hope this gets resolved quickly. There's not a lot of time before the retreat is over."

"So you think it's someone from the class?" I asked, with interest.

He thought carefully before answering. "With the vivid personalities in this class, it sometimes feels like I'm watching a stage play. Therefore, I may be trying to look for something that's not there."

"What do you mean?" I asked.

"Well, this is a rather theatrical group of people. We have the moody, somewhat tormented artist…"

"Charles," I inserted.

"The volatile and confrontational one…"

"Laura."

"The meek, childlike one…"

"Monica."

"The quiet observer…"

"Paula."

"And so on…"

I couldn't help but add, "You forgot to include 'the spy.' "

"Duly noted," he said, with an embarrassed smile.

"But you obviously see what I mean. You must have already considered the reasons not to assume it's someone from outside. But then again, we might be looking for something that's simply not there."

I nodded. "Let's hope it's the latter."

He looked at his watch, pulled out his wallet, and put a twenty on the table. "I'm going to walk back to the Lodge and grab a shower before the class starts. Please, have breakfast on me."

He got up and clasped my arm. "Again, I'm sorry, Alex. I hope we can put this behind us. Oh, and honestly, the front door was open this morning. You should really consider stepping up your security protocols. And it goes without saying, you should tread lightly with this group. One of them just might be the killer."

Chapter 14

I stared after Peter until Aunt Claudia approached and broke the spell. "Who was that handsome man?"

"That's Peter, one of the retreat participants," I said, distractedly. The warmth from his hand lingered, and I lightly rubbed my forearm.

Aunt Claudia took a seat across from me. "Are you okay? You look like you've been dragged through a knothole backward."

I snapped my attention back to her. "Yes, I'm all right. I didn't sleep well last night, and things are just a bit stressful trying to sort out Niko's murder. But don't worry, I'm hanging in there."

"What's the word? Any developments?"

I didn't want her to worry, so I kept it short. "Things are moving along with the investigation. There have been some dead ends and some leads, but hopefully things will resolve quickly."

"Well, you just steer clear of any trouble. Let Jack handle it," she cautioned.

"Of course!" I said, feeling slightly guilty for the white lie. I looked at the menu on the table and decided a good hearty breakfast was just what I needed in order to get through this day.

****

I got back to the Workshop just before the class arrived. I would have to find time later to think on everything that had transpired with Peter.

Paula and Marie arrived first. Marie was a vision of swirling fabric, in a multi-tiered, multicolored, flowing broom skirt and matching top with an attached scarf of the same material. Her boots clopped happily on the floor as she twirled to remove her soft wool shawl, and her silver bangles clanged in harmony with her tassel belt, which had little bells on the ends.

"Good morning," she singsonged, with only the circles under her eyes betraying the strain of the week.

"Good morning, you two," I said with a smile. "Are you ready for a full day?"

"Oh yes," said Marie. "We are choosing what we want to focus on for the exhibit. I think I'll go with the portrait of Pookie. I do like to take something back to her when I travel. Usually it's a special treat or a new collar, so she'll be thrilled to see her own portrait."

I cocked my head. "I bet I'm going to do the same with Baxter when I travel."

"Oh, I know you will," she said with certainty.

"What about you, Paula?"

"I think I'll work on the still life and see if I can get that finished, and I have the one from Maggie's sitting."

"That's great."

"Paula, I'm going to go get set up. See you in there," Marie said, sashaying toward the hallway.

Paula lingered at the desk, so I put my glasses on my head and asked, "What can I do for you, Paula?"

"I just want to make sure you are managing okay," she said, gently.

"Thank you for your concern, but yes, I'm doing fine. I think everyone is feeling the strain from Niko's death, but we're all carrying on the best we can."

"Mmm, yes." She turned to leave but stopped herself and added, "Could I stop by and chat with you later?"

"Of course. I'll be around most of the day."

She simply nodded and moved on toward the hallway.

A few minutes later JJ and Bitsy bustled in. Bitsy gushed, "Oh my gosh, that will be fabulous!"

"What will be fabulous?" I asked.

"JJ has brought her cards and divining dice. The subject came up at lunch the other day, and she said she would bring some things to do a reading for anyone who wants it during lunch or after class today."

I raised my eyebrows.

JJ held up her hand, and said, "I promise, this is just for fun. I don't do full-on readings anymore, so this will only be for some light entertainment. I also brought in *The Secret Language of Birthdays* so everyone can look up their date."

Bitsy added, "Even though we've forged on in the best manner possible, everyone's been a bit stressed out, so we thought this might help lift the mood."

"You're right, a couple of hours of mindless fun would be good for all of us. Hey, I have an idea. Let's make it a game night after class. I'll pull out a few board games and put out some snacks for a little pre-dinner entertainment."

"What a great idea," Bitsy enthused.

"Agreed, and that will take the pressure off me having to be the sole entertainment!" JJ said, with relief.

"And if any of the Workshop artists want to pop in and join us, they could, couldn't they?" Bitsy asked, with an eager smile.

"I don't see why not. If you see any of them, let them know, and I'll do the same."

"Excellent!" she replied.

"So what are each of you going to work on for the exhibit?" I asked.

"I'm finishing up my piece from the falls," JJ answered.

"I'm tweaking the one from Maggie's sitting," Bitsy replied.

"I can't wait to see everything exhibited," I said.

"What's happening with the investigation? How'd it go last night at Jack and Annie's?" JJ asked.

"Things are moving quickly, but I have to be careful—too many people around. We'll talk later."

At that moment, I felt a cool whoosh of air as Edgar opened the front door and ushered Laura and Monica into the lobby.

"Good morning, how's everybody doing?" I asked, casually leaning my elbows on the front desk.

"Just fine," boomed Edgar, full of good cheer.

"It was such a beautiful walk this morning. I love fall," Monica effused. She still looked a little tired, but the brisk morning had given her cheeks a rosy glow.

Laura snorted. "It's chilly to me. I can't imagine what winters are like here."

"Aw, come now, Laura," Edgar encouraged. "It's a beautiful day. Embrace the fresh air!"

She scowled at him, preparing to retort, but any further discussion was interrupted by the muffled ringing of a phone coming from her purse. She pulled it out and quickly walked back outside to take the call.

Edgar shrugged and said, "Come on, Monica. Let's

go get an early start and figure out what we're going to exhibit!"

Charles and Peter/Walter were the last to arrive. Peter was clean-shaven and looked refreshed, which made me feel quite haggard by comparison. They were deep in conversation, so I just waved as they crossed the lobby. I wasn't prepared to pretend everything was normal with Peter and was relieved I didn't have to make small talk.

After taking care of the day-to-day business of the Workshop, I went upstairs and got Baxter so we could go for a nice long walk before lunch. I needed time to digest everything from this morning, and the fresh air would do me good.

We headed to Bennet Park, which was only a few blocks away. The park was a favorite spot for walkers, games of frisbee, and picnics. A walking path with benches surrounded the pond, with the public library perched on the hill above. The Bennet House, the original mansion to which all the park land once belonged, was now an event venue, and it resided at the far end of the pond.

The fall leaves crunched and scattered as we walked, and while Baxter crisscrossed in front of me sniffing everything with great excitement and purpose, I thought about Peter, who I now knew to be Walter. His story rang true. There were people of means and power who drifted in and out of the political world like ghosts. They had no interest in the public game of see-and-be-seen, but instead thrived on the awareness that they had the means, ability, and power to shape what happened in business and politics.

Of course, I always looked into those who made

large contributions, and donors who wished to be listed as anonymous still had to disclose certain personal information by law. But Walter had successfully kept himself at arm's length, and I had no doubt that if we had not been aligned politically, he would have been a formidable foe.

How did I feel about having an outsider involved in the Workshop? Was he sincere in his suggestion of a no-strings-attached involvement? If so, it was an intriguing thought. Even though right now everything was going smoothly, what about down the road? How could I ignore the prospect of a benefactor? I decided I was open to a discussion about this, but I chose not to acknowledge that, on a personal level, I was finding him quite intriguing.

Baxter and I reached Bennet Park, and as we made our way to the path around the pond, it was time to think about Niko. Thinking about murder seemed incongruous with the tranquil setting, with the trees reflecting red, gold, yellow, and green on the water and a gentle ripple from the ducks serenely gliding on the surface.

Forgery. I was still wrapping my head around that possibility. Okay, if indeed Niko was involved in forging paintings, who had the motive to kill him, and why? To me, the two obvious motives would be revenge or greed. Revenge didn't really work for me, though. If someone realized they had been scammed, they would simply go to the authorities. They wouldn't need to kill him. And if it was some underworld revenge, it was doubtful it would take place here, and even more randomly, up at the falls.

But what about the person who ran through the

woods when I was at the crime scene? Jack was probably right. It was likely just a kid skipping school. But what if it was the murderer coming back to look for Niko's phone or some other piece of evidence? That would mean it was someone outside of the retreat, since the class was in session back at the Workshop while I was out there.

Greed was a better fit for a motive. Did someone want in on the action? Was he being blackmailed? Did Niko want more money, and his demands or threats meant he had to be eliminated? The latter didn't fit for the location either, because unless, as Jack suggested, someone followed him, who would know he would be up there at that time? It really boiled down to why here.

Ari was in the clear, Peter was now in the clear, and I just didn't see Monica, Edgar, Marie, or Paula having a hand in this. If the murderer was someone in the class, that left Charles and Laura.

I had whittled it down to the smallest common denominator now, so it was time to ask them some more questions and either eliminate them or provoke them into revealing something. With Baxter's leash shortened so he would walk in step with me, we made good time getting back to the Workshop.

****

There was a hum of activity in the lounge as everyone was getting their lunch. People were balancing the boxed lunches, napkin-rolled utensils, and drinks while discussing whether to eat inside or out. It was the first time since Tuesday that the good spirits didn't feel as forced. I grabbed an iced tea and one of the fried chicken boxes and made a beeline for the table with Charles, Laura, Edgar, and Paula.

As I approached, Edgar got up and said, "Please, join us. Let me pull up a chair for you."

Relieved I didn't have to horn my way in, I graciously accepted, then dove into the fried chicken.

"Mmm, this potato salad is so good," Edgar said, as Paula nodded. "Tastes homemade! And the chicken is so crispy."

"All the food has been really good. And it's rare to get more than a salad option for the vegetarians, right, Laura?" Charles asked.

Laura was moving her spoon around her bowl, scrutinizing the vegetarian chili. "Yeah, the food has been adequate, which is surprising."

"I'll pass that along to my aunt," I said, choosing to ignore her backhanded compliment. "She'll appreciate hearing it. She prides herself on putting out food she would serve at home. Big city or small town, quality is quality."

"Absolutely," said Edgar. "So, Alex, is there any word on the investigation? Even though we're avoiding talking about it, I know we're all curious."

"The police are doing everything they can to unravel what happened. There's not a lot to go on, but they're making headway."

"That's good to hear."

I decided it was time to ask Charles and Laura some questions. "You guys knew Niko. Did you ever know him to be involved in anything, professionally or personally, um…let's say unsavory or unscrupulous?"

Laura asked, "What do you mean?"

I tried to look casual. "Did he have any run-ins with any art dealers or gallery owners? Did he handle his business and personal life on the up and up?"

Charles squirmed in his chair. "What exactly are you suggesting?"

"Nothing, I'm not suggesting anything," I said quickly. "I'm just trying to get a feel for Niko outside of what we saw here. It's no secret he was quite ambitious. I'm just wondering if he stepped on any toes in the process, or what lengths he would go to for success."

Paula had stopped eating and closely watched this exchange.

Edgar swallowed a bite of food and said, "I know what you're getting at, Alex. One has to look at the way a person lives their life to get a clue about them. I could see he was a highly driven individual. I can't speak for how he handled the rest of his life, but based on what I've seen here, he could easily have rubbed the wrong person the wrong way."

"I already told the police Niko had rubbed *many* people the *wrong way*," Laura said, mimicking how Edgar had put it. "He played the field a lot and left a string of girlfriends, some of whom were married, in his wake. He spent money like it was water but didn't always pay his bills. Frankly, to me, he was the typical *artiste*—highly creative, but also highly volatile. No crime in that. I still think he was just in the wrong place at the wrong time."

I didn't want to push too hard, so I just said, "Could be…"

Charles cocked his head. "You know, I do remember a time when Niko sold a painting twice. It caused a bit of a stir."

"What do you mean?" I asked.

"He had sold a painting through a gallery, and then

he was approached by an individual buyer who wanted it. He ended up taking it out of the gallery, telling them he decided not to sell it, and then turned around and sold it to the individual so he wouldn't have to pay the commission."

"Can you do that?" Paula asked.

"It's nearly impossible to get away with it, and he got in some hot water, but then things died down. He talked himself out of being blacklisted. I remember him joking that he should have just painted the same painting again, and then he would have gotten both sales."

"I didn't think high-end artists duplicated their work," Edgar said.

Charles seemed to relax now and was happy to respond. "There's no hard and fast rule about it, but, no, painters don't create exact copies of their works. They may do more than one painting of a specific subject matter, but elements would be different. For example, in a landscape, a painter may use the same subject, say a cathedral on a hilltop, but paint it in the morning light instead of afternoon or evening. The sky would be different, the light and shadow would be different."

"Like Monet's Haystack series," I added. "Each one is unique even if the subject is the same."

"Exactly," Charles said, pleased with my reference. "Buyers don't want to pay thousands of dollars for a work that's been duplicated."

"I guess that's what giclées are for, right?" I asked.

Laura answered this time. "Yes and no. Some artists will produce giclées to sell, and the high-end ones will be numbered, with a limited run. But some artists refuse to do giclées because they feel it lessens the uniqueness and value of the original piece."

Edgar was enthralled and rubbed his hands together. "This is so marvelous to be able to talk to real artists about a side of the business we don't know anything about. How do you both feel about giclées?"

"Personally," Charles said, "I don't do them. I don't want to risk my originals losing value."

"How about you, Laura?" I asked.

She sat back in her chair and said, a little defensively, "Well, that's a luxury only someone with money has. I've sold giclées of some of my works. If people want them and can't afford the original, why not make money multiple times on one piece of work? And between you and me, if someone is stupid enough to spend upward of eight hundred dollars on a giclée, then they get what they deserve. If I do that enough, I don't care if the original loses value."

"Boy, that's a jaded view of the people who buy art," Charles laughed uncomfortably. "I may not do them, but I can appreciate that giclées are a way for people to buy art who can't afford thousands of dollars for the original. Let's face it, the high-end art world is an elitist society. Allowing more people to purchase a piece of art they love doesn't make them stupid. The buyer gets something more special than a mass-produced print, and the artist earns a respectable amount for the work they do, as they should. I think your attitude is a bit skewed."

"Take it or leave it. You have to admit, the whole art scene is somewhat fabricated. People don't rise to the top because they are that much better than everyone else. They rise to the top because some dealer, collector, or gallery, decides what's a hot ticket. It's all a sham."

"Oh Laura, you don't really believe that, do you?" Edgar asked in dismay.

"Maybe I do," she said, defiantly.

Charles gave Laura a look that screamed *Stop it!* but tried to lighten the mood by saying, "Laura, I know you don't feel so negatively toward the art world." He looked at everyone else at the table and continued, "Look, our profession is like any other. It's competitive, and it's not always fair. But we get to do what we want, when we want, and we get to live a creative life. No offense intended, but compared to working a nine-to-five, we're extremely fortunate."

Laura's phone dinged with a text. "Excuse me, I need to tend to this." She shoved back her chair and left the table in a full-on snit.

Wow! That girl has some anger issues.

We sat in an awkward silence until Charles said, "Don't judge her too harshly. Laura's okay, she's just had a rough few years because she hasn't climbed the ladder as quickly as she expected to. It's made her a little bitter, but underneath that hard exterior, she's not a bad person."

Paula said, "Yes, insecurities and unfulfilled ambitions can lead one to act out. It's a shame though, because she's talented. Maybe with age she'll mature."

"Yes, hopefully she'll figure it out one day," Edgar said. "When you've lived long enough, you see life's ups and downs in a different way. Right, Paula?" he added with a wink.

She favored him with a gentle smile. "Right you are."

"So," Edgar said, "let's get back to talking about

what fun we'll have in class this afternoon. Oh, and Alex, did you hear JJ is going to do some fortune telling for any willing participants after class today?"

"I did! And you all deserve a break, so we've decided to make a party out of it. We're going to pull out some board games and have some nibbles before you all head out for dinner."

"I play board games with my granddaughters, but I haven't played with adults in a long time. Maybe we'll even have a friendly wager," he said, waggling his eyebrows at Marie.

"I'm in," she said enthusiastically.

I looked at my watch, and said, "Oops, if I'm going to join in on the fun with you guys, I better get back to the office. Thanks for inviting me to your table. It was nice to sit and chat for a bit."

I piled Laura's abandoned lunch trash on top of my own and made my way toward the door, stopping to talk briefly with JJ, Bitsy, Annie, and Spencer, to let them know everything would be set up and ready after class.

On my way back to the office, I noticed Laura's leather bag sitting on the bench in the lobby. I walked over and idled by it. Maybe I could take a look at her phone to see if she had texts or messages to or from Niko. *Should I?* I looked over my shoulder and listened carefully for footsteps in the hallway. I fingered the soft brown leather, then dropped my hand inside.

"Excuse me, what are you doing?" Laura barked, having entered the lobby.

Chapter 15

I jolted and yanked my hand out her purse as if it had been bitten by a snake. "Oh, you startled me! I was just checking to see who this belongs to. As safe as this building is, it's never a good idea to leave an unattended bag in the public spaces."

"Clearly, it's not," she shot back, as she grabbed the bag and stomped off.

My pulse was racing a mile a minute. Man, that was close. *I'm such an idiot!* What had I been thinking? I tried to appear casual as I walked to my office, then I closed the door and plunked down in the chair, taking some deep breaths to pull myself together.

I was back at work when I heard a light knock on the door. "Hi, Paula, come on in!"

"Thank you," she said, taking a seat. She carefully smoothed out her navy slacks before she crossed her legs and lightly clasped her hands in her lap.

Her hands were delicate, soft, and just beginning to show the signs of age, with a few veins showing through the thinning skin. Her nails were perfectly manicured with a pale pink polish, and the subtle scent of French perfume gently drifted toward me. I admired Paula's demeanor. She made no excess movements. No wasted energy, either in words or motion, and I imagined she was always put together, finished, and refined.

I couldn't imagine her ever sticking her foot in her mouth with a stupid comment or making rash decisions that could bite her on the rear end…like I had just done with Laura's purse. Granted, while part of me wished I could be so punctilious, I knew I never would be, and I'd accepted that. Besides, I'm sure Paula never had a bag of cookies for lunch, and who would want to give that up?

"What can I do for you, Paula?"

"I'm assuming you're looking into Niko's death, yes?"

"Well…"

She held up her hand to stop me. "Wait, that was more of a rhetorical question. If I were to guess, I'd say you've been looking into the class participants and have been asking some seemingly innocent questions to flush out a motive, a suspect, or possibly clear a suspect. Is that accurate?"

I waited.

"Okay, now *that* was a question," she said, with her smile reaching her eyes.

I grinned back at her. "I've noticed how observant you are, Paula, but as I said at lunch, the police are handling this, and they're making inquiries into Niko's death."

"Yes, you did, but I've learned a little about you since we've been here and I would imagine there's more to it than that. I would also surmise your reluctance to talk has something to do with not finding much about me or my history when you've been digging around. I've actually been waiting for you to approach me about it."

Boy, Paula was astute. "Well, now that you

mention it, I have been curious about a couple of things."

"Why don't I fill in some gaps for you." She looked at her hands and then raised her eyes to meet mine. "When I was studying statistics at William and Mary, I was approached by a government agency."

Whoa, I was not expecting that. "What government agency?"

She dismissed this with her hand. "It's of no importance. I was at the top of my class, and at that time it was not unusual for the top percentile of students at the ivy league universities to be approached."

"I did find out you went to William and Mary."

"Yes. And then, via the agency, I worked for GMRA, Inc., an acronym for Global Market and Research Analysis. There were two divisions. One was legit market research, and the other was doing analysis for the government. It suited me to work on more clandestine matters. So, my friends and family knew where I worked and thought I did market research. Since I've retired, what I did is not a state secret, but it's not something I talk about, and I must rely on your discretion."

"Of course. But boy, this is fascinating. What a life you've lived."

"It was often mundane work. But occasionally, yes, it could be quite exciting. Anyway, GMRA was closed down years ago, and the building was torn down to build some condos or something. Due to the nature of my work, no trace of my work history would be public record."

"If I may ask, what did you do there?"

"In a nutshell, I read a variety of materials, looking

for keywords, phrases, or patterns that might indicate covert communication, and then I created reports based on compiled data. Keep in mind, a good bit of my service was before the internet and all that came with that. I also analyzed and reported on data provided by other divisions. I'm good at languages, which, paired with my degree, made me a desirable hire. That's my backstory."

"Wow." I was gobsmacked. "I knew there was something more to you. I could see the way you observe everything around you, and I've found that intriguing."

"And I, in turn, could see you doing the same. I can't help but wonder if we've come to the same conclusions about Niko's murder," she said, closing the topic of her past. "Of course, we're all hoping it was an outside person that did it. But it's impossible not to look at the people around us since he was here specifically for this retreat."

My gut told me Paula was the real deal, but I knew I should proceed with caution, so I asked questions instead of giving her my thoughts. "What's your take? You've been with these people all day, every day."

Paula shifted in her chair and became all business. Gone was the genteel older woman. Her eyes brightened and she spoke as if she had been cataloguing information in her head and was ready to give a report. I hoped she might have some valuable insights or new information for me.

"I took JJ and Bitsy off the table immediately. They have no connection to Niko. Spencer knew Niko back in New York, but after piecing together the timeline up at the falls, it doesn't appear he had

189

opportunity. Since he was leading the session, he was sort of everywhere and always visible."

I nodded in agreement. "Yes. Plus, Spencer has it good here, and there's no reason to think he would jeopardize that."

"Next, I crossed off Edgar. Since we are closer to the same vintage and share a generational history, I've chatted with him quite a bit. He's a happy soul and fills his life with things that bring him joy. He's uncomplicated. He has no connection to Niko, nor a motive."

"True. He's such a lovely man. Granted, that doesn't give him a free pass, but I agree with you. He doesn't appear to have a motive."

She took a breath and continued, "I really don't consider Monica as a suspect either. She's the type who lives her life like someone who doesn't color outside the lines. I doubt she would get a speeding ticket, let alone take a life."

I thought back to when I met her at the reception. "Yes, she said she went into the profession her parents wanted instead of doing what she wanted with her life. She doesn't want to disappoint people."

"I don't see Monica as a person who is simmering and ready to blow, either. Granted, if someone is pushed far enough, they can act out of character, but to me, she's a rule follower."

"What about Peter?" I was curious to hear her take on him.

"Peter's an interesting person. I believe he's more affluent than he lets on. He engages with everyone, but he doesn't reveal much about himself. We've learned a lot about both Bitsy and JJ, Marie talks about her friends at the community center, Monica has relayed funny family stories, like when she was in school and she and her sister would switch places to prank people. Edgar talks about his travels…by the way, he has fascinating stories. Even Charles talks about his younger years as a painter. But nothing personal from Peter. I like him, but I don't know why since I don't know much about him or his life."

"Is it that you feel he's trustworthy?"

"I think it's that his confidence is comforting. Not at all cocky…there's a difference between confident and cocky. It's that you instinctively feel you're in good hands. That he could handle any crisis and make you feel safe."

Her take was interesting. "Mmm, that makes sense."

"All right. The last of this group are the two I have the most reservations about. I'll start with Laura. She's chock full of insecurities. I know artists can be sensitive, but I have rarely heard anyone whine as much as she does. I generally try to be magnanimous, but she's quite tiresome to be around."

I nodded in agreement. "I've noticed some attitude when I've dropped in on the class and at lunch. She seems a bit defensive and frequently picks fights. She was a last-minute addition to the class, and I'm not sure why she was keen to come since she doesn't want to learn or have anyone give her constructive criticism."

"That makes me wonder *why she's here* if you get my meaning. Did she have a reason aside from the retreat? Did she have a motive? I'm not sure. Do I think she could kill someone in a fit of anger or passion? I think so."

"You may be right."

"But I could also be passing judgment purely because I find her a distasteful person, which does not make her a murderer."

"True," I agreed, realizing I was guilty of the same judgment.

"And lastly, Charles. He's one tick above Laura in the personality department. Initially, he was particularly condescending toward Marie. Granted, Marie isn't everyone's cup of tea, but she's a kind person and she does not deserve to be treated poorly."

"Absolutely not. There is no excuse for that kind of behavior," I said, firmly.

"He was fairly dismissive of the rest of us nonprofessionals too, as if engaging with us would somehow diminish his own reputation. And he's mildly misogynistic. But he's mellowed since Niko's death. Spencer and Annie have been a good influence on him because they don't take themselves too seriously."

"I've seen a change in him, too. But is it possible to have an epiphany and change that quickly, or is there more to it?"

"Did he have a motive to kill Niko? Does he have the will to kill? It's possible. Both he and Laura knew Niko outside of this retreat, but I don't know their full history." Paula uncrossed her legs and leaned forward. "So, there you have it. Tell me how it lines up with your perceptions. And if you are so inclined, we can hash over some details."

"Whew," I breathed out, "I would imagine you were very good at your job. Okay. I'm sure you understand I'm not at liberty to go into any details about the investigation, but my own take on this group is similar to yours. Charles and Laura are the wild cards. I have one question for you. Did you notice Charles drinking while up at the falls? I saw him pull out a flask while the group was waiting to talk to Chief Maddox. If Niko's death was from a flash of anger, alcohol could be a contributing factor if coupled with his somewhat volatile personality."

Paula considered this. "I've seen him drink from that flask throughout the week, but at the falls? I don't think so. At least not that I saw. It could be more like the anxious smoking he does, which is just a stress reliever. However, I've been thinking a lot about after we came back from the falls and how people were acting *before* we knew Niko was missing. Charles seemed invigorated, like the morning had been a good experience."

I leaned forward. "I do remember thinking he had some color in his cheeks, and it looked like the fresh air had done him some good. But was that the rush of fresh air, or the rush of killing Niko? I tend to think the former."

"I agree. Charles's type would be twitchy and nervous. I don't think he could fake nonchalance if he had just killed someone, and he seemed genuinely unsettled when what we thought was an accident became a suspicious death. I just don't think he could have pulled it off."

I mulled this over. "I don't think we can rule him out, though. He's blossomed since Niko's death. Maybe it's because Niko's gone, and he thinks he got away with it. Maybe there was a professional situation where Niko was undermining him, or something happened involving a personal relationship."

"It's possible. But then that could just as easily be relief as opposed to revenge."

It felt like we were going around in circles. "There are still too many questions. But speaking of personal, did you know Laura and Niko were previously in a relationship?" This had been outed at the lunch table, so I saw no harm in mentioning it.

She raised her eyebrows. "No, I didn't. But it does explain some of her contempt toward him. During the short time we were with Niko she waffled between trying to attract his attention and being aloof and snippy. That smacks of a woman scorned," Paula said.

"Yes. And from what I've seen, she has the temper to kill him if pushed too far. But perhaps she's simply immature." I blew out a sigh of exasperation. "We're faced with the same waffling as with Charles. We need the smoking gun, so to speak."

"Well, you just keep pulling at threads until one lets go and everything unravels. I do have one nagging question about Laura. Why does she have two phones?"

"What?" I asked.

"She has two cell phones. On the first day I noticed her cell phone because I liked the case. It was a color palette. Little paint pots with smudges of paint. Every time she pulls it out, I mean to ask where she got it. However…"

"However," I interjected, "this morning she pulled a phone out of her purse to take a call and it had a plain black case."

"Yes," Paula said, and gave me a conspiratorial smile. "I saw it after class on Wednesday."

"Hmmm. It might be nothing. Maybe one is personal and one is for business. Although we have to ask ourselves if it could be Niko's missing phone. I will mention this to the chief." Now I was wishing I could have gotten hold of the phone in her purse.

Paula looked at the clock. "Oh dear, I must run. Class is going to start in a couple of minutes. Thank you for chatting, Alex. I do hope we have the opportunity to talk again."

"I would like that. And if you don't mind me saying this, I hope to grow up to be just like you one day."

She laughed, but then became pensive and paused in the doorway. I could see the wheels turning behind her eyes. "Alex, I've just had a thought. Has Maggie looked at all the photographs yet?"

"She's been going through them each day to pull good ones for the slideshow at the reception."

"I would suggest you or Maggie go back and look at all the photos, including the discarded ones, paying close attention to background of each one, even the blurry bits. You might just get lucky and find a clue."

Chapter 16

After Paula walked away, I sat at the desk trying to grasp everything that had happened today. Holy cow. Peter was actually Walter, and Paula was a spy. What a group, what a day! The first order of business was to follow Paula's advice.

When I entered the photo lab, Maggie was bent over the worktable, aligning a large landscape photograph on a wooden board. I knocked lightly before entering so as not to make her jump.

"Do you have a minute?"

"Of course, what's up?" She lifted her arms above her head and did some side stretches.

I closed the door, and said, "It's been suggested that we need to look through all the candid shots to see if there's anything in the background that might reveal something pertaining to Niko's murder. You haven't permanently deleted anything yet, have you?"

"No, I always keep everything. That's a really good idea, Alex."

"I wish I could take credit for it. Paula suggested it. I just had a good chat with her."

"Well, that's interesting. You'll have to fill me in later. You know, it wouldn't hurt to widen the net, and under the guise of looking for slideshow photos, ask people in the class if they want to give us any of the pics they've taken."

"Great idea. Look at everything—body language, facial expressions, who's spending time together—and pay close attention to the time at the falls. I know that's a lot of work, but maybe something will come out of it."

"I don't mind. It's nice to be able to do something to help. There are hundreds of them to go through, so I'll get started this afternoon."

"Okay, thanks. You can do it here, but make sure the computer screen isn't visible from the door or windows, and close everything down and lock the door if you leave the room. Better safe than sorry."

"I agree. Help me with this table, and then I'll move the computer over."

We moved a square wooden table so her back would be against the wall, and then she moved the computer. Now Maggie could see anyone coming, and the monitor wasn't visible to any prying eyes.

I went up to my apartment to let Baxter out. *Note to self: get a doggy door, pronto.* I left the door open while I punched the button to brew a cup of coffee, pulled out the bag of peanut butter cups I had stashed in the cabinet, and put my phone on speaker to call Jack.

"What's the word from the fraud guys?" I asked.

"They've been tracking some movement in the forgery market. It appears over the last few years some pieces were purchased by a couple of high-end collectors that later turned out to be fakes."

"That's interesting, I was only thinking about museums, not individual collectors. This seems a more likely scenario."

"It happens more often than we might think," he said.

"Of course, I've read about the black-market stuff; you know, pieces that may have been stolen or had sketchy ownership or, even worse, a piece that was part of the looted art from World War II. Those collectors covet the possession and don't look too closely at the provenance."

"And slipping a forgery in here or there is big business."

"So what are they going to do now?"

"The local cops in New York went through Niko's condo. They have his computer and his ledger of painting sales. I also scanned and sent them the pages from the notebook with the initials and numbers."

"Have you heard anything back yet?"

"What we know so far is that his painting sales and tax records don't match his deposits. We don't know where the extra money is coming from, but it's likely from an offshore wire transfer. They'll have a forensic accountant dig deeper."

"Wow, this is major stuff."

"They'll also scour his hard drive and have a specialist come in to do a thorough search of his art studio to see if there are any materials a forger would use. Oh, and thus far, no will has been found, which means Ari is the sole heir."

I walked over to close the back door after Baxter returned. "Poor Ari. I'm guessing she'll have to go to New York to straighten out his estate, inventory his paintings, all the stuff in his studio and condo, and then wait while the forensic accountant determines what money is legit and what isn't. That could take a while."

"No kidding," he said. "I don't envy her that task. Of course, she could just hire an attorney to handle things, but it would probably be best for her to at least go and scope everything out."

"Bitsy's husband might know someone, and I could also ask Michael if he can come up with a contact in New York for her to reach out to for help."

"Good idea. So, have you got anything for me?"

As I plucked another peanut butter cup from the bag, I relayed my conversation with Peter/Walter, which Jack confirmed was the same as his interview.

"Before I released him, I made some phone calls and did a background check on him. His story lines up," he said.

"Good. I haven't had time yet to do that. I've had my hands full around here today." I then filled him in on my chat with Paula and relayed her suggestion to check the images from the photos. I also told him about the conversation from the lunch table, and the two cell phones Laura had been seen with.

"Can you ping his cell phone, to see if it's been turned on since his death?" I asked.

"First, the phone has to be on to be pinged. If we can get the danged phone dump from the carrier, we could see if any calls or texts have gone out since his death. It's taking way too long."

"Okay, can I do anything else?" I asked.

"I want to talk to Laura and Charles again, so I'll be over in a little bit to pull them from class on the premise of needing more background info. You've had a full day, and I'd rather you not draw any more attention to yourself than you already have, so lie low now, right?"

"Got it." After hanging up with Jack, I set my phone down but picked it right back up to call Izzy.

She answered with a breezy, "What's up, duck?"

"Well, you are not going to believe my day. I now know who Peter is!"

"Oooo, wait, let me tell the person on the other line I'll call them back."

"If it's not a good time, I can try you later."

"No worries. This guy's a big blowhard. I'm happy to put him off."

A moment later she was back, and I gave her the full scoop. She let me tell the whole story without interrupting, although I heard a hushed exclamation of *No kidding!*

Once I was finished, she said, "Walter Sarnov! Of course! I've heard his name over the years. I remember someone pointing him out to me once when I was at the Senate Chamber in Harrisburg. From twenty yards away, I could tell he was a man with nothing to prove, which in our business is rare. This could be amazing, Alex."

"I'm still not sure about it."

"Well, he's clearly taken with you. Imagine what you could do with the Workshop, and bonus, it might keep you from being totally cut off from civilization to rub shoulders occasionally with someone like him."

I laughed. "One thing at a time. First, we have to get Niko's murder solved and finish the retreat. Then we can worry about Walter and what that might entail."

"He's kind of cute though, isn't he? Maybe this won't just be about the Workshop," she said coyly.

"Sheesh. Cute? What are you, twelve? I haven't had time to think about what he looks like." Okay, I had actually thought about it, but I wasn't going to give Izzy any more fuel for teasing me.

"Mmm, he does tick all the boxes, though. Well, kiddo, thanks for calling to update me, and I'm super glad you aren't in any danger from him. What a relief. All joking aside, I've been worried. Time to call the blowhard back. Kiss, kiss, hug," she said.

"Back atcha," I said and hung up.

While I was at it, I thought I better give Michael a call and let him know the Peter issue had been resolved. I gave him an abbreviated version of the story, and then he asked how the investigation was going.

I gave him the full update from Ari's marriage to Niko to the forgery angle and concluded with "I think we're getting closer."

"*You* aren't getting too close to all of this, are you, Alex?"

"Nah. I've asked a few questions here or there, but mainly I am staying out of it." I refrained from relaying my excursion to the crime scene.

"Okay. Keep it that way. Someone has killed once. If they feel threatened, they might strike again. How's Annie handling it?" Michael still had fond feelings for his in-law family, regardless of their being ex-in-laws now.

"She's doing fine. I think it helps that Spencer's there with her, and we're all looking out for each other. I'll tell her you said hello. And Jack said he hopes you'll come sometime in the spring to hang out for a couple of days and watch a ballgame with him."

"That would be great. Tell him I'll make it happen."

"Will do. Oh, and can you do me a favor and send me names of anyone you know in New York who could help Ari navigate through the red tape of Niko's estate?"

"Sure. I might know of someone. And let me know what happens with all of this. Hopefully it'll be a quick resolution. Promise me you'll tread lightly."

"That's my intention, I promise."

After I hung up, I tried to remember the idiom about good intentions...oh yes, *The road to hell is paved with good intentions*. I pondered this, then dismissed it, as I ate another peanut butter cup.

****

Jack showed up an hour later, and we headed down the hall to the classroom. There was a happy hum in the air as they worked on their pieces for the exhibit. They were seeing their works come to life, and the buzz of excitement was palpable. Annie was hovering over Monica, showing her little fixes to blend the background of her painting, and Spencer was laughing as Marie bantered with Bitsy. I hated to break the spell, but it had to be done.

Jack cleared his throat. "Sorry to interrupt..."

Everyone looked at us, and their smiles either froze in place or quickly deflated.

"Don't be alarmed. I just need to speak with a couple of you in the hopes that you can assist us further with the investigation. It won't take long, and you'll be back at the easel before you know it. Charles, could I have a moment, please?"

The faces shifted from us to Charles as he slowly put his brush down and got up from his stool. The muscles in his neck became ropey with tension, but he calmly followed Jack from the room.

"Really, there's nothing to worry about. Please go back to what you were doing," I said.

I walked over to Edgar's easel and got him talking about what he was working on, and thankfully Bitsy and JJ picked up the cue, and along with Annie and Spencer, we got everyone back on the happy train.

When Charles reentered the room, everyone looked up, but quickly averted their eyes and returned to their work. I could tell their attention was divided, but they attempted to pretend they weren't interested in what was going on. Charles walked over to Laura and leaned down to whisper in her ear. She snapped her head back to look at him, visibly annoyed.

"He just wants to ask you some questions. It's nothing to get upset about. We knew Niko outside of this retreat, and they need additional assistance," he said, in an urgent hushed voice.

Laura slammed her brush down on the easel lip, then scraped the legs of her stool on the floor and elbowed past Charles before flouncing out of the room.

"Is everything all right, Charles?" Monica asked, with concern in her voice, while she nervously fussed with her charm bracelet.

"Sure, everything's fine. Chief Maddox needs to talk to those of us who knew Niko to get more background information. It's no big deal. Laura needs to just calm the hell down."

"Ah, youth," chimed Marie, in a singsong voice. "Everything is full of drama when you're young. She'll grow out of it. Maybe." She laughed.

Thank you, Marie, I thought to myself. Once again, the spell was broken, and the amicable chatter resumed. I walked around the room, impressed by the progress of everyone's work. This was definitely an odd group of people, but all of them seemed to have some talent, each with their own unique style. Under normal circumstances, this week would have been a real success story.

Eventually Laura returned, and this time everyone just ignored her as she stomped back to her easel. I couldn't help but notice the venomous look she gave me, but I pretended I hadn't seen it and continued milling around a few minutes longer to chat with everyone about their pieces. Once I was sure the drama was over, I left the room to look for Jack, but he was already gone, so I went back to the office.

I sat for a few minutes, my mind twirling around the events of the day. I was exhausted, but also fidgety, and I felt the need to move, so I grabbed my bag and headed to my car.

****

After driving around aimlessly, I pulled in and parked at the Café. Being midafternoon, only a handful of customers occupied tables, so I sat at the counter next to where Aunt Claudia was sorting the lunch tickets.

"Twice in one day! Nice to see you again, but you look even more frazzled, if ya don't mind me saying so," she said, looking at me over her reading glasses.

"I am a bit frazzled." I breathed out like a turbulent teenager.

"How can I help?"

"Thanks, but I'm afraid I just have to try and unravel all the stuff in my brain. I could use a little homey comfort."

"Well, your brain is not someplace I would like to spend any time, but I'm happy to fulfill the need for homey comfort."

I smiled at her. "Thanks. Could I get some fries?"

"Sure," she said. She popped her head through the swinging door to the kitchen and called in the order.

I swiveled on the stool to see who was here at this time of day and saw Brenda Danby having a cup of tea, flipping through a magazine. "Be right back," I told Claudia, and hopped off the stool.

"Hey," I said, sitting on the edge of the chair across the table from her. "I don't want to intrude, but just want to see how you're doing."

"Oh, I'm all right," she said, looking up from her magazine. "Thanks for asking."

"Do you feel like things are getting back to normal at the B&B?"

"It's quieted down a little. We're still getting calls from the press, and we've had some extra visitors, but, all in all, things have settled down."

"What visitors?" The initial excitement was over for her, and she seemed a little worn out by the sudden notoriety.

"Oh, you know, friends and neighbors who stop by under the guise of checking on us, but we know they just want to see where Niko was staying or get some snippet of gossip. Most are people we know, but we've had a handful of strangers come knocking on the door too. Some have even asked to see his room. Can you believe that?"

"Mmm, sadly, yes, I can believe it. That side of human nature is sometimes baffling, but it seems to be universal," I said, then realized she was saying something quite significant. "Wait, what strangers? Did you let them in? Did they give their names?"

"Oh heavens no, we didn't let them in. We can't

have strangers coming inside willy-nilly. Now we have had a couple of people from the retreat come by, but they don't really qualify as strangers."

"Which ones?"

"Let's see, Peter Bigsby stopped in to visit with Edgar, Marie, and Paula. He's actually been here a few times during the week, usually before or after they all go to dinner. And Lisa? No, Laura, she came by a couple of days ago."

"Was she there to visit with the others?"

"No. She dropped in before the others had come back. She said Niko had something of hers, and she needed to get it."

"Do you remember which day that was?"

Brenda tilted her head back and looked at the ceiling. "It's such a blur, but I think it was either Tuesday or Wednesday. I remember now, I was making pot roast for dinner, so that would have been Tuesday. I was in the middle of mashing some potatoes when she came, so I just gave her the key and told her which was his room so I could get back to the kitchen. I heard her leave shortly after that, and she left the key on the desk." She noticed my furrowed brow, and quickly added, "Did I do something wrong? I mean, she's in the class with everyone else, so it seemed perfectly innocent to me."

"No, no worries. I'm just asking questions. Do me a favor, though: if any more strangers come by, please let Jack know. He may want to bump up the patrols near your house. And if you don't mind, I think I'll mention it to him, too."

Brenda became nervous. "Oh dear…"

I patted her hand. "Don't fret. You guys are

handling things really well. It's just better to err on the side of caution, right?"

"Okay, thank you, Alex." She grew pensive, then said, "You know, our bookings have gone up since this all happened, but truth be told, I'll be relieved when this is all over and we can get back to normal."

"You and me both, Brenda. Oops, my fries are up." I stood up. "Don't hesitate to call me if you need anything."

Back at the counter, I dove into the basket of hot crispy fries while mulling over what Brenda had told me. I wiped my fingers on a napkin and pulled out my phone to text Jack about Laura's visit to Niko's room, which happened before he had examined its contents. Did she take something? We needed to find out. I also relayed about the strangers, and he agreed it would be a good idea to bump up patrols.

I felt that, for now, my extracurricular job was done, and it was time to focus on the Workshop. I left the Café and made a quick twirl around the Bushel Basket Market and filled my cart with food for the game night. The B-B, as we called it, played an eclectic mix of music for their shoppers, and I even found myself doing a little step-tap dance to a James Brown tune.

Chapter 17

Soon after the Workshop opened, I started accumulating an array of board games and puzzles for the lounge. Playing a game was a great way to break the ice when we were all getting to know each other, and during the winter, I liked to put out a jigsaw puzzle for everyone to work on. The larger part of the room had the tables and chairs we'd been using for lunch, plus an area with a couple of sofas and plush comfy chairs scattered around.

A functional kitchen was in the back of the room, separated by a partial wall. When renovating the original school lunch room, I opted to keep the vintage black-and-white checkered linoleum floor tiles. They conjured up nostalgic memories, and I loved the way shoes sounded click-clacking on it.

After rummaging around in the cupboard under the bank of windows, I decided on Scrabble, Masterpiece, and backgammon for tonight. Maggie and I set up one of the long tables with trays filled with hummus and veggies, cheese and crackers, fruit, and artichoke dip with a sliced baguette. I had just put out the cups and drinks when we heard voices approaching the lounge.

Once everyone was in the room milling about, I held up my hand and made an announcement. "Hello everyone! Please help yourself and have a bite to eat. In a few minutes, I'll go over your options for game night!"

While the gang filled their plates, I pulled JJ aside. "Where do you want to set up, and do you want me to give an intro about your part of this?"

JJ walked to one of the smaller round tables. "Why don't I set up here, and then the board games will be closer to the food and drinks. And sure, why don't you give the intro about what I'll do, and I can explain in more detail only to those who are interested."

"Sounds good," I said, watching JJ put a pretty yellow, gray, and white damask cloth over the table, with a smaller round gray felt cloth on top of that. She untied a leather bag and shook out three dice, then set a deck of playing cards near the edge of the table.

Maggie pulled me aside to tell me she was heading back to the lab to continue scrutinizing the photos. "I'm about halfway through, so I want to get back to it before it's time to call it a night," she said. "Oh, and I also got a good batch of pics from people in the class. I had them forward them to my email."

"Thanks for the hard work on this. I know it's tedious, so why don't you grab some food to take with you," I suggested.

Paula, Peter, and Edgar were already laying claim to the Scrabble game. Marie, Annie, Bitsy, and Monica were looking with interest at Masterpiece, and Charles was trying to coax Laura into a game of backgammon. Ryan and Spencer arrived at the same time and joined in.

We were ready to start. "Okay, everybody, here's how we'll do this. JJ will start the evening with anyone interested in some parlor-game fortune telling, and she wants me to remind you this is purely for entertainment purposes, sort of like reading your horoscope in the newspaper. She'll explain all the details. So, anyone who wants to do that, go to her table. When you're done, you can shift to the board games. If you don't see something here you like, let me know, and we can rifle through the game cupboard. And of course, help yourself to food and drinks. Let the games begin!"

Various whoops and cheers followed as the group dispersed. A few wandered over to JJ's table, and I followed, curious to see how she was going to do this.

"I have two options for you to choose from," said JJ. "Divining dice or playing card readings. Both are quick. Why don't I start with Alex so you can see how it works," she said, looking at me with a *gotcha* glint in her eyes, knowing I didn't like attention focused on me.

"Ahhh, I don't know, one of you guys should go first…"

"Come on, Alex, go for it," cheered Marie. "This will be fun!"

Realizing there was no way out of it, I took a seat across from JJ. "Okay, here goes nothing!" I laughed, putting on a good face.

"Which would you prefer, the dice or the cards?" JJ asked.

"Let's do the dice."

JJ shook the three dice in her hand. "All right, here we go." She let them roll onto the gray felt circle. "So, we have a one, one, and three. Interesting," she said, pausing for effect. "Your total is five. The number five signifies that a stranger brings you happiness. It could also mean a pleasant surprise. And you will meet someone who impresses you in some way."

I found myself thinking about Peter/Walter, and

that this was a bit uncanny, but I quickly came up with a simple response to my reading. "Well, I would say that's accurate since each of you have impressed me with your artistry this week, and while you came here as strangers, you leave as friends." I was relieved. JJ was indeed doing this like reading your horoscope from the newspaper.

Marie clapped her hands and said, "Me next! I want to take a spin at this."

I got up and waved my hand at the chair. "It's all yours, Marie." I shot JJ a look, and she winked back at me, clearly enjoying the moment.

Marie also chose the dice, and JJ went through the same routine as she had with me, although Marie's number included the prospect of a potential admirer.

"Doubtful," Marie countered with a laugh. She then shifted her attention to the book JJ had brought, *The Secret Language of Birthdays.* "Can I look up my birthday in here?"

"Sure! It lays out a variety of characteristics for each date. Not the year, but the month and day. Sometimes it's pinpoint accurate, although, on occasion I've found it misses the mark, so don't take it too seriously. Now, who's next over here?" JJ asked. "How about you, Monica?"

Monica was reluctant, but the others persuaded her, and she shyly slid into the chair. "Oh okay, I'll play," she said. "Could I do the cards?"

"Sure." JJ handed the deck of cards to Monica. "Please cut the deck." She then spoke to the small circle watching. "Similar to astrology, the suits of the cards represent the elements of water, fire, earth, and air. I'll explain more as we go. So, Monica, pick three cards.

The first will represent the past, the second for the present, and the third for the future."

Monica cut the deck, drew three cards, and put them face down on the table. JJ turned the cards over from left to right, then sat for a moment, pondering them. As everyone watched her expectantly, she laughed a little and said, "Huh, you know what? I should have had you shuffle them first. Shuffle those cards really well, Monica, and let's try this again."

Monica repeated the process and laid down three more cards. This time when JJ turned them over, she quickly got down to business.

"So, the suit of hearts corresponds to the element of water, and represents love and friendship. Generally, these are happy cards. The other suit you have drawn is spades. The suit of spades corresponds to the element of air, and generally signifies the changes or challenges in your life. The ace of hearts as your first card represents love and happiness, a content feeling of home in your past. The nine of hearts is the card of wishes. For the present, it represents a dream or wish fulfilled. And for your future, the seven of spades is more of a cautionary card. It shows an obstacle to success, and that obstacle may actually come from you, yourself."

"Wow, that's deep," Ryan said, through a mouthful of cheese and cracker.

"Oh, it could really apply to any of us," Monica said shyly.

Annie said, "True, but it definitely applies to you. You've talked about your happy childhood with your close-knit family and friends. And do y'all remember? She told us about her desire to go back to school to get her degree in art. It looks like you need to be careful not to allow anyone, including yourself, to stop you from fulfilling that dream! This is so much fun. I think I want to give it a try."

It looked like JJ was rolling along just fine, and everyone was having fun, so I was free to move on. Hannah and Ethan had come in, as had Shelby and her assistant Claire. I wandered over to where Paula and Peter were in the middle of a game of Scrabble. Both were deeply focused on their letter tiles, alternating between scrutinizing the words on the board and rearranging their tiles. Sheesh, I was pretty good at Scrabble, but these guys were way out of my league. They'd come up with complicated, high-scoring words: *zymurgy* and *sjambok*.

I found the soft clicking sound of the tiles somewhat mesmerizing as they were moved around on the wooden easel and then on the board, and I couldn't pull myself away. I sat down to watch them finish the game and was instantly lulled into a pleasant suspension of time. Later, when Paula and Peter congratulated each other on a game well played, I roused myself from my Scrabble reverie.

By this time, JJ's circle had broken up, and everyone had split off into game groups. A few other studio artists had also wandered into the room and were talking amongst themselves while grabbing a snack. Marie, Annie, Bitsy, and Monica were playing Masterpiece. As Bitsy counted her money, her serious face was a contradiction to the bobbing head of the woodpecker affixed to the side of her headband, and Marie's bracelets jangled as she picked up a card depicting a Picasso painting.

At the next table over, Ryan and Charles, each with

a beer in hand, were enjoying a friendly game of backgammon, while Laura vacillated between watching them and being distracted by what was going on at the Masterpiece table. The rest were either playing cards or chatting by the food table.

I poured myself some iced tea, took a big gulp, then set the cup back down to pick up an empty tray to take to the kitchen, where I found JJ doing a little cleanup. She had pulled out a few glass containers for storing leftovers and had neatly lined up the boxes of crackers.

"Hey! It looked like everyone enjoyed doing the readings," I said, leaning my backside against the counter.

"I think so, too. We also had some fun talking about astrological signs afterward. By the way, thanks for being a good sport. I knew no one would want to go first."

"No problem. At least nothing embarrassing cropped up." I laughed.

"Well, if it had, I would have gotten you out of it. That's the difference between a true reading and just having fun. For example, you saw I had to have Monica redo her cards." She placed the extra cheese and fruit on the cutting board so she could wipe down the counter.

"Yeah, why was that?"

"Well, I *had* shuffled the cards, but the present and future cards were a little dark. Granted, dark cards don't necessarily mean something bad, but it didn't seem right for the moment, so I just had her reshuffle."

"Well, you covered well. The board games are a hit, too. Boy, Paula and Peter would wipe the floor with me in Scrabble. They both scored over four hundred!"

"Oooh," JJ said, "I might have to get in on some of that action. You know I love Scrabble, and I don't mind losing to a good player. Well, actually I do! It does bring out my competitive side, but I can be a good sport too, if I must. Game on!" she said, with mock bravura.

I laughed, and said, "You'll be in good company then!"

We returned to the lounge, and JJ plopped herself down at the Scrabble table, ready to engage in battle.

I grabbed my iced tea and wandered around to watch the games in play. I was feeling relaxed, enjoying a moment where everyone was having a good time. Ryan took a victory lap, having beaten Charles in a best of three backgammon games, and then he piled some food on a plate to take to his studio to work on his sculpture. The rest of the Workshop gang waved to me from the door as they followed him out. The room was quieter now with just the retreat class remaining, but spirits were high.

JJ was taking her spin at Scrabble with Peter, and Paula and Edgar were playing a game of gin rummy. The Masterpiece group was wrapping up their game, and Laura looked on as they discussed the various works of art they had collected. Bitsy bemoaned that one of her favorite masterpieces had been deemed a forgery, while Annie congratulated herself on getting all high-value paintings.

I picked up the card with Hopper's *Nighthawks* painting. "Even as a teenager, I always went for this one first," I said.

Bitsy said, "You had a good eye for art at an early age. It's very evocative."

215

I wanted to just sit down and relax, but I knew they'd take off soon for dinner, so I set my tea down again and cleared the buffet table. I was wrapping up leftovers for future snacking when Annie came around the corner.

"We're all going to the Lodge for dinner. Do you want to come along?" she asked.

"You know, I just might." It had been a long day, and I wasn't sure I wanted to go upstairs and stew in my own brain. "I have a few things to finish up, and then I'll be along."

"Okay, great. I'm going to run down and see if Maggie wants to join us, and then I'll start wrangling everybody."

I was wiping down the counters when I heard Annie rounding up the group. There were the usual sounds of chairs being moved around and the swoosh of jackets being donned as they prepared for the brisk walk to the Lodge. I reentered the lounge after they left, and the sudden silence in the room had a lingering aura of good cheer.

However, as I was cleaning up, I started to feel light-headed. I paused with my hand on the kitchen counter to steady myself. When did I last eat? Maybe I was hungry. I grabbed a banana from the bowl on the counter, thinking that might help. It didn't. I still felt disoriented but forged ahead and finished tidying the lounge.

My legs felt heavy, and after what felt like an arduous climb upstairs, I let myself into my apartment. Maybe some fresh air would do the trick. I opened the back door and followed Baxter down the exterior staircase. He bounded down with abandon, but I went more slowly, inhaling deep breaths as I went, hoping to clear the fuzziness in my head. When I reached the ground, the chill in the air felt good. Baxter was happily sniffing around the yard, tracking every bird and squirrel that had traversed the area during the day.

I looked out toward the tree line at the back of the property. The trees were swelling and receding, going in and out of focus. *What's going on?* I looked from Baxter to the building. It was like looking through a distorted lens; everything was ebbing and flowing.

I started to take a step forward, then felt myself falling in slow motion. I landed heavily on my knees. Even though I knew it was an absurd idea, I just wanted to lie down and rest, so I did. I could smell the pungent scent of the earth, and the damp grass felt prickly against my cheek and ear. I reached out my arm to push myself up, but the effort was too much, and I lay back down on the ground.

Baxter sniffed around my neck and hair and nudged me with his nose, as if I might be playing a game with him. He barked, but it sounded like he was getting farther and farther away. Then, there was nothing.

Chapter 18

Voices; nagging voices. *Why are they bothering me?* I was floating, drifting in the deep cool water, but from the surface of the water, voices intruded.

"Alex! Alex, wake up!" Ryan shouted.

"What's happened to her?" Maggie cried.

"Alex!" Ryan called out, with urgency.

What's he going on about? ...just want to drift.

"We need an ambulance at the Creative Workshop, 1715 Main Street, ASAP. We don't know what's happened, but we've just found Alex Montgomery. She's breathing but unresponsive. We're out back in the courtyard area."

Can't they tell I just want to be left alone?

"Jack, get over here. Something's happened to Alex. She's face down in the yard, and we can't rouse her. An ambulance is on the way."

"Alex! Can you hear me? Come on, open your eyes," Ryan pleaded.

Someone reached down into the water to pull me up toward the surface. *Noooo, let me float!*

"It's okay, Alex. Help is coming," Maggie said.

I felt a gentle stroking on my hand. It was nice, like the flutter of a fish, or maybe a feather. *Maybe I'm dreaming.* Now the fish was smoothing my hair and stroking my forehead. How nice...I liked swimming with fish. What kind of fish was it? I slowly opened my eyes, felt a topsy-turvy spinning, and closed them again. *Wait a minute. That was not a fish.* In the brief moment I had opened my eyes, Maggie's face floated above me.

"Mmm, what's happening?" I mumbled.

"Lie still, Alex. Help is on the way," Maggie said in a hushed, worried tone of voice.

"Okay, I'm gonna swim with the fish some more..." I mumbled and drifted off again.

****

The sound of beeps and hums filtered into my consciousness. I opened my eyes and slowly surveyed my surroundings. There was a door, almost closed, with a sliver of light coming through. A dry erase board was hanging on the wall with some illegible writing on it, and farther down from that, another closed door. To my right I saw tubes running from my arm to the beeping machine, and to my left, Jack was sleeping in a chair.

What the hell happened to me? I tried to sit up.

"Whoa, take it easy," Jack said, unfolding himself from the chair to came to the bedside.

I cleared my throat. "What's going on? Why am I here? How did I get here?"

"What do you remember?" Jack asked, pressing the call button for the nurse.

I lay back and tried to find my last memory. "I remember cleaning up in the lounge, and then I started feeling a little woozy. I headed upstairs to let Baxter out and went down with him, thinking some fresh air might clear my head." I shook my head in frustration. "That's the last thing I remember. What happened?"

"Ryan was working in his studio and heard Baxter barking. He went to the windows to take a look and saw you face down in the yard. You don't remember that?"

"No, it's like my memory is in a deep fog. What's all this stuff?" I asked, holding up my arm with the IV.

"They're flushing you with fluids. We're waiting on bloodwork results."

A nurse bustled into the room. She wore a colorful hospital smock with hearts and little animals on it over navy blue scrubs and equally colorful clogs. She looked young, but her demeanor was efficient and professional.

"Nice to see you awake!" She beamed, as she pushed some buttons on the beeping machine. "How are you feeling?"

"Uh, I'm okay. A little foggy, and really thirsty. How long do I need to stay hooked up here?"

She went to the sink to pour ice water into a cup from a blue plastic pitcher and brought both over to the tray next to the bed. "Hopefully not too long. We're flushing your system, and the doctor will evaluate everything once your bloodwork comes back, which should be soon," she said, checking her watch. "Your vitals are looking good, which is encouraging. Lie back and relax, and he'll be in shortly."

After she left, I sat back up and asked Jack, "What's going on here? What do you think happened? Am I sick?"

"Alex, the doctors think you were drugged. When you're ready, we need to go over everything that happened from yesterday afternoon on. I need you to try and remember what you did, what you ate and drank, and who was there."

I looked at him in disbelief, then took a deep drink of the cold water and chewed on a few soft ice chips while I processed it.

"Someone drugged me? I don't believe it. This is crazy. Are you sure about this?"

"Yeah, they're fairly certain. We're just waiting for the test results. So, think back. Walk me through the afternoon."

I pushed the button to raise the back of the bed so I was in more of a sitting position.

"I went to the Café in the afternoon and had some fries. I chatted with Brenda and then texted you. After that, I stopped at the market to get the food for the game night, then went back to the Workshop. Maggie and I set up the room, and everyone joined us after class. I started feeling funny while I was cleaning up after they left for dinner."

"What did you eat or drink?" Jack prompted

"I only had iced tea. Oh, I ate a banana once I started feeling woozy. Then I went upstairs to let Baxter out, and went down to the yard with him hoping the fresh air might help. Like I said, that's the last thing I remember."

"Was that tea always in your possession?"

I thought back. "No. A couple of times I set it down to go take care of something. Why? You don't think someone put something in my drink, do you?"

"I think it's possible. We'll know more soon. Who was there last night?"

I thought back and then rattled off the names. "Spencer, Annie, Ryan, and everyone in the class. Hannah, Ethan, Shelby, and Claire dropped by, along with a few other Workshop artists. And Maggie, but she left before we got started." I moved the covers back and swung my legs over the side of the bed.

"What are you doing?" Jack asked.

"I want to get up and dressed."

"No, you need to stay put."

"Jack...don't—"

The doctor came through the door with a clipboard in his hand. He looked to be in his early forties, with close-cropped hair, black rectangle-framed glasses, smooth mocha skin, and intense blue-green eyes. He had an air of authority, and I meekly tucked my legs back under the covers.

"Hi, Alex, I'm Doctor Gray. Hi, Jack," he said, looking from me over to Jack.

"What's the report, Dominic?" Jack asked.

He came to the side of the bed. "Alex, ketamine showed up in your bloodwork."

"Ketamine?" I asked.

"Yes. Have you heard of it? Jack, I know you're aware of it."

"Yup. Alex, you've probably heard it as Special K, or the 'date rape' drug. It's also sold on the street as a powerful pain medication," Jack said.

"Oh my God! You mean someone slipped me a date rape drug?" I felt panicky and pawed at my hospital gown.

The doctor looked at my chart while moving toward the machine I was hooked up to. "I'm going to let Jack handle the how and why. Thankfully, there's no indication of an assault. Your vitals are good, and you've had enough fluids go through you to flush this out of your system."

Sensing my anxiety, he gently laid his hand on my arm and gave it a soft squeeze. "You're going to be okay. From my standpoint, you can be released, but I will recommend you get some rest and continue to drink lots of fluids. You might not regain your memory of the moments leading up to your blackout, but you're going to be fine other than some fatigue and fogginess, which will go away soon."

"Thanks, Doc. When can I get disconnected?" I asked, holding up my arm.

"Hang tight, the nurse will be back in shortly. I'll get the paperwork started for your release, and Jack, I'll fill out the medical report for you."

While we waited, Ryan came in from the waiting room, and the three of us started to hash things over to figure out what happened. We quickly eliminated the possibility that the ketamine was intended in the club sense, as a date rape drug, which meant it had to be related to Niko's murder.

****

By the time we returned to the Workshop, it was well after midnight. We stopped in the kitchen first for me to find the cup I had used for the iced tea. Jack used a paper towel to pluck it from the recycling bin, then bagged it up so they could run tests to confirm or rule it out as the vehicle for the dosing of ketamine.

Once upstairs, I unlocked my apartment door with both Jack and Ryan still in tow. Something crinkled under my foot as I stepped through, and a Laurel and Hardy collision ensued behind me when I halted our progress to pick up the piece of paper that had been shoved under my door. We shuffled into the living room while I unfolded and smoothed the paper. Two words were scrawled in jagged black letters: "BACK OFF."

I held up the warning note for Jack to see. "Don't move," he said, going to the kitchen. "Where are the baggies?"

After banging around to find what he wanted, he came back and followed the same routine he had with the cup, then called Matt Wallace, another of his deputies, to come over and dust for prints.

While Ryan went to the kitchen to put some water on for tea, Jack got me settled on the couch and tucked a blanket around me.

Ryan brought the big steaming mug of tea over to me, and Jack said, "I really appreciate you being here to look out for her, but I need to go over some things with Alex on her own. Would you mind waiting for me downstairs?"

"Not at all. I'll be in the guest suite, and I'll update Maggie and the gang. They're anxiously awaiting news. Do you need anything else, Alex?"

"I'm fine, and again, I can't thank you and Maggie enough for your quick action tonight," I said and got up to give him a long hug.

Jack held up his hand as Ryan opened the door to leave. "Ryan, could you text me the contact info for any of the Workshop artists who were there last night?"

"Sure thing."

Once the apartment door closed, Jack said, "Let's go over the day again. You've been asking questions, right? Who could you have pushed into a corner?" Jack asked.

"Well, yes, I have been asking some questions, but I didn't think I was being that obvious. I was really careful, or at least I thought I was..." I trailed off and avoided looking at him.

"You look uncomfortable. What did you do?" he asked, with an edge to his voice.

I didn't want to tell him about looking in Laura's purse, but I had to. "Well, at the end of lunch today, I saw Laura's purse out in the lobby. No one was around, so I thought I might take a little peek, and, well, she caught me."

Jack exploded. "What? Are you crazy? Do you realize how dangerous that was?"

"I know, I know! You don't have to rub it in. I know it was stupid. But really, I think I covered well. It was out in the lobby. Anyone could have left it, like someone in Shelby's class. So I had a built-in excuse."

"Doesn't matter. If she's involved in this, she's already feeling paranoid, and if she felt you were getting too close, it could push her to warn you off."

We heard a knock at the door, and Jack let Matt in. He got him started dusting for prints on the door and then sat back down on the couch and resumed his questioning in a more normal tone of voice.

"I think it's a safe bet we're looking at Laura for this, but let's go through the day anyway. You didn't do anything else to get yourself in trouble, did you?" he asked.

I rubbed my eyes before starting. "This has been an unusually full day, but no. I promise. After Peter and I talked, Baxter and I took a walk around Bennet Park, then lunch and the unfortunate purse incident. I had the chat I told you about with Paula, then I went down to the photo lab to talk to Maggie, then upstairs to get some work done."

"And then?"

"I meandered around the class while you were interviewing Charles and Laura again. Laura shot me some daggers when she came back from her interview with you. Since she was gone a long time, I was going to ask you how it went with her, but you had already left when I came out to find you. Then I went to the Café, and that's where we started earlier with the chain of events."

"Did you notice anything during the game night? I know you're tired, but try and think."

"No, it seemed like it was a pleasant evening with everyone unwinding a little from the stress of the week. Plus, with the gang from the Workshop popping in, I just don't get when and how it could have happened," I said, perplexed. "We were having such a nice time."

Jack cocked his head. "Wait, back up. What did you mean that the interview with Laura seemed to take a long time?"

"Well, she was gone for quite a while. I assumed you were getting somewhere with her interview."

"No, actually I didn't spend any more time with her than I did with Charles."

"No wonder you were already gone when I came out to find you. Where was she?"

"I don't know, but we'll find out. Is there anything unusual about this paper, or the writing?" He handed me the now-bagged slip of paper with *Back Off* on it.

"The paper is just lined notebook paper, but it looks like an artist pencil was used. Of course, you can find one of those in almost every room in this building. Look, Jack, I'm so tired, and my brain is still really foggy. Can we pick this up in the morning?"

He patted my leg. "Of course. And I'm sorry if I was terse, but this scared me. I couldn't live with myself if something happened to you."

"No apology needed. It's my own damned fault for

going too far."

"You just get some rest. Matt will be done soon. I'm going to pass the note and cup off to him to take back for testing. I'll also talk to the Workshop people and see who saw what, and when."

"Can you get a warrant to search Laura's room?"

"Not yet. I can question her about where she went after the interview and what she wanted from Niko's room, but it's too circumstantial to get a search warrant unless her prints are on your door. For now, I'm going down to talk to Ryan, and then I'm sending him back up here to bunk down on your couch. I don't want you left alone tonight, and don't argue with me about it."

"I'm not gonna argue about that, and anyway, I'm too tired to fight."

I sat in a stupor while Matt finished up, then moved on autopilot to wipe down the fingerprint dust from the door after he left. I had just changed into my green plaid flannel PJs when I heard a light knock on the door. It was Ryan, returning with his pillow and blanket from the guest suite. I offered him the guest room, but he wanted the couch so he would hear me if I needed anything, so I got him settled, said my goodnights, and called Baxter, who bounded along with me and jumped on the bed. I lay there for a while, staring at nothing, with my arm draped over his body, until eventually, his gentle doggy snores lulled me into a deep sleep. It must have been the effects of the drug that made my sleep a dark abyss.

Chapter 19

Saturday

The next morning, I didn't recognize the person in the mirror. The dark half-moons under my eyes and the ashen quality of my skin were a visible manifestation of the strain I was feeling from the last week. Staring at my reflection, I decided it was time for this to end. I tilted my head back and closed my eyes to let the eye drops work to get the red out, then grabbed my bag and headed down to the office.

I tossed my keys on the desk and was turning back to go to the lobby when Annie, JJ, and Bitsy crowded into the office and closed the door.

"Are you okay?" Annie asked, her voice rising in concern. "Ryan and Jack filled me in, and I called Spencer, JJ, and Bitsy. Everyone is up to speed."

"This is unbelievable!" JJ exclaimed. "Such a violation!"

"Are you sure you should be up and about? How are you feeling?" Bitsy asked, looking me over from head to toe. "You don't look so good."

I felt my hair. I hadn't even brushed it before tossing it up on my head. I was just happy to see I had put on clean jeans and a shirt, and both my shoes were from the same pair. Knowing Bitsy, though, I knew she wasn't talking about my attire.

"I'm okay, you guys. Really. I'm past being scared and confused. Now I'm mad, and it's time to get to the bottom of this."

"What are you going to do?"

"I'm going to talk to the class this morning," I said. "I'm no longer interested in tiptoeing around."

After a few more minutes talking over last night, I said, "Okay, let's go."

Before leaving, JJ grabbed my hand. "This is an amethyst. Keep it with you. It has a calming, healing energy, and you need that right now." She placed the necklace in my hand.

"Thank you, I'll take any help I can get." I heard my phone ring and darted back to the desk to get it. "You guys go on, and I'll be there in a minute."

"How are you feeling?" Jack asked, when I answered.

"I'm doing okay."

"I wanted to let you know that since Matt found prints on the lower part of the door, he and Travis are coming over to take everyone's fingerprints. Travis will then remain on the premises, both for your safety and that of the class. I'll also need prints from the staff for elimination purposes."

"I'll let them know. If you end up searching Laura's room, I want to be there."

"We'll see. One thing at a time," he stated.

I took a deep breath and walked with determination down the hall to the classroom. My confidence waned when I reached the door, but I put up a good front.

"Good morning," I said in a formal tone. "I need a moment of your time, please."

Everyone turned to look at me, some with a look of

anticipation, others with apprehension. I forged on.

"Last evening, while we were enjoying game night, someone slipped a drug into my drink."

Marie put her hand to her chest. "What?"

Peter stood up quickly, his stance was tense.

"After you all left for dinner, I ended up unconscious in the yard out back. If not for the quick action of Ryan, who just happened to be working in his studio, I would be in a very different place right now."

"Are you all right?" Peter asked.

"I'm fine…I'm *going* to be fine."

"Oh dear," Edgar whispered.

"Two deputies will be here shortly to ask you some questions, and one of them will remain on site the rest of the day. I need you to please think back to last evening and let them know if you saw something out of the ordinary. Even if it seemed insignificant at the time, it might be important."

I intentionally didn't mention the note or the need for fingerprints. I didn't want to spook Laura or anyone else who might be involved. And I still wanted them to think it could have been someone from the outside, even though I knew that was no longer a possibility.

Marie's brow was furrowed in deep thought. Paula had a look of sad resignation, as if she had known things would escalate to some degree.

Monica was worrying her bracelet charms, muttering under her breath, "I'm so confused. How could this be?"

Charles darted anxious looks all around the room. Laura had crossed her arms and managed to mutter something to him while also looking defiant. Edgar sat next to Monica and his usual bright disposition was dampened by worry. And Peter met my gaze with a silent acknowledgement that I had just catapulted myself into uncharted territory.

Spencer took a step toward me, but I discreetly put up my hand to stop him and stepped back into the hallway just as Travis and Matt rounded the corner.

"Let's go to the lounge to do this, and I'll get yours first," Matt said, all business. "Travis will position himself where he can keep an eye on everyone."

When we reached the lounge, I had the strange feeling I had experienced before during a crisis. The air felt different and colors were more muted. It was as if my senses had squished everything into a tighter space. It was usually only recognizable when on the back side of it, when suddenly colors seemed more vivid, the field of vision seemed more expansive, and the air felt like it had more flow. I instinctively knew I would eventually get to the back side of this and simply acknowledged the tightening of the senses.

New technology allowed Matt to quickly take a digital image of my ten digits and my palms, and we were done. I then went back down the hall to the classroom and called Spencer to go in next. Knowing Travis and Matt had things well in hand, I went to find Maggie and Ryan.

Ryan was in his studio, so I sent him on down to the lounge to wait for his turn. As I entered the photo lab, Maggie got up and rushed at me with outstretched arms. After giving me a big bear hug that almost knocked me over, she backed up and said, "Ryan filled me in after you guys got back from the hospital. Are you okay? I was so worried!"

"I'm a little groggy, but fine. I'm just so grateful

you two were here."

"Who do you think did it?"

"Jack has to go through the process of gathering the evidence, but I have my suspicions."

"Who?" she repeated.

"Frankly, I think it was Laura. Jack will hopefully have enough probable cause to get a search warrant later this morning, and if so, I'll meet him at the Lodge. I want to look around her room."

"Wow. It would be bold of her to dope and threaten you when she's basically stuck here."

"I know. Just based on her attitude and behavior she's called attention to herself, which is kind of stupid. But until they take prints, we don't have much to go on other than suspicion. How's it going with the photos?" I asked.

"I've got two more batches to go through, plus some of the camera dumps from the class. It takes time to look at each one carefully with them magnified. I don't want to miss something, so I'm going slowly, and I'm going over the ones at the falls twice."

"That's okay. If something is there, I know you'll find it. Listen, Matt is down in the lounge. You'll have to go down there to have your prints taken. They found some prints on the lower part of my door, and we need to have staff prints for elimination purposes."

"Gee, okay. How will it eliminate us? So many of us have been to your apartment."

"Well, they're going to be looking for a match from someone who would have no reason to have been near my door, and I'm assuming any prints found on the lower part would be from someone shoving the paper under the door last night. If none of the outsiders are a match, then it's a big zero for helping us nail the person who's behind all of this."

"I'll keep my fingers crossed," Maggie said.

We walked to the lobby together, and then I split off to go back upstairs. I was on the couch with Baxter when Jack called. "Matt is still processing prints, but he texted to let me know he got a match for Laura's. Both on your door and on the note. So I moved forward with the search warrant, and I'll be heading over there soon."

"Wow, that was fast."

"I'd already given Judge Collier a heads-up and had written the warrant. So all I needed was her signature."

"I'll meet you at the Lodge."

"You don't need to do that. Why don't you stay there and rest?"

"No. I need to keep moving."

****

As I walked into the lobby of the Thunderbird Lodge, the warmth from the fireplace made me want to curl up in one of the lounge chairs by the fire, sipping a nice cup of coffee. Instead, I went straight to the front desk, told Dustin I was there to meet Jack, and asked what room he was in.

He tapped some keys on the computer and said, "Room 136. That's down the left hallway."

Dustin looked like he wanted to ask me some questions, so I said a quick thanks and bolted through the lobby. When I reached room 136, I knocked lightly, and Jack opened the door in an officious rush.

"You really should be resting," he said, but ushered me in anyway.

"I know, but I also told you I need to keep going.

So, let's drop it. Tell me what you've found so far."

His manner softened. Jack knew me too well, and he could see from my clenched jaw that if I couldn't be proactive, I'd fall apart. He handed me a pair of gloves.

"I've just arrived. So as long as you're here, let's divvy up the space." While we got ourselves organized, he said, "I've talked to the additional people from the Workshop. I wasn't expecting an 'aha' moment, but unfortunately, they didn't see anything out of the ordinary during their time in the lounge last night."

I sighed. "Oh well, can't say I'm surprised. I didn't notice anything either."

Jack clapped his gloved hands. "Let's get to work. I'll start in the bathroom, and you start over there."

I could hear him going through Laura's toiletries as I looked around the rest of the room. I first picked up a pile of books and magazines and set them on the bed. I took each one and fanned them open to make sure there was nothing tucked inside. Once done, I set them aside.

"Nothing in the bathroom," he said. "I'm moving to her suitcase and the closet."

He pulled out her roller bag suitcase and flopped it onto the bed, then turned back to the closet while I set a big black toolbox on a chair and opened it. This was where Laura kept her extra travel art supplies. As the lid raised, it pulled open accordion-style shelves holding brushes, pencils, painting tools, cleaners, and a few rags. I fingered through the contents, then closed it back up.

We worked quietly, and I could see Jack had moved from the closet to the suitcase. He was going through the clothing Laura hadn't unpacked, checking anything with pockets, and feeling around the lining of her suitcase. He was faster than me, working with the efficient speed of experience.

"Aha!" Jack exclaimed, holding up a pill bottle.

"What is it?"

"There's no label on it, but my guess is it's the ketamine since it was hidden in her suitcase lining."

"Really!"

"Yup. Right here." He showed me where the bottle had been hidden in the lining along the right edge of the suitcase.

"How long will it take to check what it is?"

"We can do basic drug tests at the station, so not long. I also want to dust for prints," he said, dropping the pill bottle into a little plastic bag. "Let's keep going."

My head was reeling now, but I carried on and started pulling the painting boxes and cases out from against the wall. Like Niko, Laura had painting cases: two cardboard ones, and one shipping case. The cardboard boxes were empty. My guess was she had brought them to transport home whatever she worked on here. I then opened the shipping case. *Oh my. What have we here?*

I got down on my knees and leaned over to scrutinize the small painting in the case. It was a portrait of a young girl sitting on a wall, and it had a sophisticated blend of both portraiture and still-life details.

"Uh, Jack, I think we have a situation here."

Jack stared at the small piece. "What's this look like to you?"

"Well, we need Annie or Spencer to confirm what I'm thinking, but to me, based on the subject matter and materials, this looks like a seventeenth- or eighteenth-century oil painting on a wood panel. Let me see if I can find a signature on this. I guarantee Laura didn't paint it." I pulled my glasses down from my head and scrutinized the lower corners of the painting. "It looks like 'B Murillo.' I know his work, but I need a magnifying glass to say for certain that's what the signature is."

"What's she doing with this?" Jack mused.

"I think you need to dust the case for prints. My gut tells me this is what she took from Niko's room when she went to the B&B. If this was the real thing it would be incredibly valuable, and not left sitting in a vacant hotel room, so I think it could be a forgery. Personally, I don't think she could pull off a painting like this, but Niko could."

Jack looked at his watch. "Matt should be done at the Workshop, so I'm going to get him here to take prints. I want this evidence as pristine as possible, so I'm not going to risk any smudging or cross contamination. Once he's done, it can be moved to the station."

While Jack called Matt, I sat on the bed looking at the painting. It saddened me to think such a beautiful piece of art could be the impetus for grief, fear, and death.

Jack's voice intruded on my thoughts. "While we wait, let's hit everything else in the room. There's enough with the pills and the painting to bring her in, but I want to cover every inch of this room first. Maybe she left that second cell phone here."

He started by lying on the floor to look under the bed, dresser, and nightstand. We then lifted the mattress to make sure nothing had been tucked into hiding. He looked behind the wood headboard and every other nook and cranny in the room while I searched every drawer.

As I restacked the books and magazines, I noticed a small spiral notebook on the TV credenza. I held it under the lamp to flip through the pages, and as I set it back down the desk lamp highlighted the imprint of writing on the soft cardboard cover. I tilted the notebook back and forth under the light. A variety of letters and numbers stood out, but then, there it was; the outline of "Back Off" imprinted on the cover of the notebook.

"Jack, take a look. Laura wrote the 'Back Off' note on here. She must have been pressing hard enough with the drawing pencil to leave an impression." I handed him the notebook and stepped back with my arms crossed in an instinctively self-protective pose.

I had a vision of Laura, full of anger, returning to the room to get the pills and draft the warning in a heavy hand before rushing back to the Workshop. This must be where she was during the lapse between Jack's interview and returning to the class.

"Does Dustin have cameras in the lobby?" I asked. "She must have come here after you interviewed her yesterday."

"I'll go check. You stay here and make sure we covered everything in this room," he said, putting the notebook in yet another plastic bag.

As Jack left, Matt entered and got to work dusting the pill bottle, the shipping case, and the notebook. I was having difficulty focusing and basically just swiveled around the room looking but not taking anything in.

Jack returned in short order. "Okay, let's go. Dustin's pulling up the video from yesterday afternoon. Matt, we'll need to get all this stuff over to the station, so if you're finished before we get back, close up and swing by the front desk."

"Sure thing, won't take me long," Matt replied, lightly twirling a brush on the surface of the shipping case latches and edges, where he had sprinkled the fingerprint powder.

****

In Dustin's office behind the reception desk, Jack and I pulled up chairs and leaned forward to watch the video monitor.

Dustin had it cued up and explained, "Okay, this is starting at about one p.m. You can increase the speed in increments so you don't have to wade through minute by minute. And here's a thumb drive in case you need to copy anything." He showed the various commands to Jack, then left, closing the door behind him.

"Let's zip down to around two p.m.," I suggested. "You came to talk to them when they had been back in class for a bit after lunch, and I left to go to the diner midafternoon."

We watched the high-speed comings and goings in the lobby as Jack fast-forwarded, then slowed to double speed as we neared two p.m. I was growing impatient, but suddenly perked up when Jack stopped the tape and we saw Laura's frozen image entering the lobby at two twenty-four p.m. Then he slowed to real time, and we watched her hurry through the lobby.

"Aha!" I said softly, grabbing Jack's arm.

"Gotcha,'" he said, continuing to scroll through

until we saw Laura leaving four minutes later.

I leaned back in the chair while I did some calculating out loud. "Let's see. It takes about ten minutes to walk leisurely from here to the Workshop, and let's say she was bookin' it to get back before she was missed. She could probably do it in seven or eight minutes. Four minutes here, same fast pace back, with a couple of minutes to pull herself together before reentering the class...so roughly twenty minutes. It took some chutzpah to risk it, but she did it. Maybe she figured if she got caught, she could cover and say she needed something from her room."

"Either way, with everything we've got, it's a slam-dunk case." He inserted the thumb drive to copy the video. "I'll pass this security footage off to Matt, and then it's time to go get her."

****

Back at the Workshop, Jack and I went down the hall to talk to Travis, who had remained on site for security reasons. Jack filled him in on the search and video evidence at the Lodge and asked how things had gone here.

"People had the typical range of attitudes—helpful, cautious, nervous and anxious, or annoyed. But we didn't have any real problems. No one saw anything suspicious, and all seemed perplexed by what happened. I've emailed you the print results."

"Okay, let's go get Laura."

The three of us walked to the classroom without speaking, our footsteps echoing in the empty hallway. When we entered the room, all eyes, once again, turned toward us.

Jack stepped forward and said, "Laura Mason, I am

arresting you on suspicion of assault, theft, and the murder of Niko Romano. Please stand up and put your hands behind your back."

With mouths hanging open, everyone turned to look at Laura.

"What are you talking about?" Laura yelled. "I did not murder Niko!"

"You have the right to remain silent..." Jack continued reading her rights as he put the handcuffs on her.

Chapter 20

Laura protested loudly as they walked her out of the room. "You're making a mistake. I didn't do anything!"

Everyone was speechless for the first few minutes after their departure. Then Charles said, to no one in particular, "I knew it. I just knew it."

That started the rounds of comments and questions.

I took a seat over by Annie and Spencer, suddenly exhausted, and put my head in my hands.

"I don't even know what to say," Annie said.

Spencer asked, "What evidence did you find?"

I got up and motioned them out into the hall. Lowering my voice, I said, "We found an unmarked pill bottle, a painting in a shipping case that looks like it could be a forgery, and a notebook with the impression of the 'Back Off' note on it. Plus, there was video footage of her coming and going from the Lodge after her interview yesterday with Jack."

Annie's eyes widened. "Wow."

Spencer remembered they were in the middle of class. "I should call a break, and then we'll try and carry on. What do you think, Annie? You think we'll be able to keep going with the final stretch of the class?"

"I do," she said. "Frankly, I think everyone will be relieved this is over, and let's face it, if someone was going to be the villain, Laura was a likely choice. I don't think anyone actually liked her. They tolerated her but didn't like her."

Spencer entered the room to address the class, all of whom were now standing in a cluster talking about Laura.

"Let's take a break and regroup in fifteen or twenty, okay?"

Everyone nodded their heads and wandered out of the room, still whispering their disbelief over what had just happened. JJ and Bitsy hesitated, but I urged them to go on with the group.

I looked at Spencer and Annie, and said, "I'm going over to the station to see if Jack will let me watch the interview. Since she doped and threatened me, I want to watch him make her squirm! I'll be back in a bit to help get the exhibits set up for tonight. What time does everyone break for the afternoon?"

Spencer looked at his watch. "We're taking lunch at twelve thirty; after that, everyone will have a few hours to finish up. Ryan and I can handle getting everything upstairs and finish hanging the exhibit, so don't worry about that."

"Thanks, but I'll still try to be here."

"I had Ryan take Niko's paintings up there on Monday. Although, I'm not sure we should even hang those. We can decide later. While we're doing that, the class has a little down time before the reception."

"Okay. Oh, Annie, I forgot to check in with Aunt Claudia about what time they're bringing the trays for the reception. Would you mind calling her?"

"No problem. Don't worry about a thing. Spencer and I have this under control. I'm just glad we can all breathe a sigh of relief knowing this has been resolved before tonight. It's devastating, but at least it's over."

****

When I arrived at the station, the small-town Mayberry vibe was gone. There was a hum of activity, and everyone was all business. I bypassed the reception counter and headed down the hallway to the precinct room, pausing outside the door to look at the work Jack and the team had done this week. There was the ubiquitous white board with Niko's photo held in place by a magnet.

On the left side, someone had listed the Workshop staff and retreat participants. The rest of the board had scribbled notes on the forgery investigation and a few bullet points on specific people from the class. Laura's name was in the center, with a list of evidence against her, and my photo was up on the board as a victim of the doping and threat. To see it in such a clinical way made my stomach queasy.

Four desks filled the rest of the space in the room, each with a computer, phone, a clutter of folders, papers, and coffee cups. A door at the back of the room led to the storage and evidence room, and along the left wall, the door to Jack's office was open and empty. I moved on down the hall to the interview room.

I took a peek through the one-way glass in the door. Jack and Travis were at the table with Laura. I didn't see anyone to give me permission to listen in, so I slipped into the observation room and flipped on the intercom. They had just started the interview.

Jack said, "You've asked for an attorney, so we aren't going to ask you any questions, but here are some things to think about while we wait. We have you on video returning to the Thunderbird Lodge after our interview at the Workshop. We have your prints on both the pill bottle and on Alex's door. Niko's prints are on that same pill bottle. We have an imprint of the threat on a notebook in your room. We have a painting in a shipping case that was found in your room that has both your prints and Niko's prints on it. You're looking at some serious charges on top of the murder charge. So think about this carefully. If you cooperate, you'll have more options."

"I did not kill Niko!" Laura barked.

"Please, Laura, don't say anything else until your attorney arrives. I just need you to understand the severity of the situation. Interview suspended at 11:14 a.m."

After they left, Laura transitioned from belligerent to scared as she paced the room. When she sat heavily in the chair and slumped forward over the table to rest her head on her arms, I quietly left the room and quick-stepped down the hall to the precinct room.

"So what's happening?" I asked anxiously.

"We're waiting for the public defender. Laura's been charged, but she invoked her rights, so we can't question her yet," Jack said. "In the meantime, Travis, let's put all the evidence in a box, check on the status of the phone records, and see if the test results on Alex's cup and the pills we found have come back. Also, follow up and try to narrow down when the art appraiser will get here to evaluate the painting."

"Got it," Travis said, as he moved into the room, pulling out his cell phone while grabbing the evidence box.

"It's a pretty airtight case, at least for the theft of the painting and the threat against you. We have to find more to nail her on the murder. Right now, it's all circumstantial."

"What about the evidence from the crime scene?" I asked.

"We've been through it once, but we'll go through it again."

"Can I watch the interview when the attorney gets here?"

"As long as you stay out of the way," Jack said, walking to his office.

I perched on a chair while the activity ensued around me. A little later, a woman entered the room carrying a briefcase. Even though she had pulled her hair into a tidy chignon, she looked harried; her white silk blouse was coming untucked from her tan skirt, her matching tan pumps were scuffed, and a run had formed in her stockings. Had to be the public defender.

"I'm looking for Chief Maddox," she said in a clipped tone.

"In his office." I pointed at the open door.

****

I was once again in the observation room, but this time I pulled up a chair to sit and watch the interview. After proceeding with the official introductions and charges for the tape, Jack started pulling evidence from the box.

"Okay, Laura, let's start at the top. You've been arrested for theft, assault, and murder. This shipping case and painting have Niko's prints on it, as well as yours. We have reason to believe this painting is a forgery painted by Niko. We believe you got into an argument with Niko up at the falls, and you killed him. We know you went to the B&B on Tuesday, after

Niko's body was found, where you claimed you needed to retrieve something of yours from Niko's room. We believe you took this painting and the bottle of pills. We also have a notebook from your room, with the imprint of a threatening note to Alex."

Jack pulled another baggie from the evidence box and put it on the table. "On this pill bottle, we found both your prints and Niko's prints. The testing has been completed on the pills, and these are street-purchased ketamine. Why Niko had them, we don't know, but we do believe you took them from his room, and later used them to dope Alex to get her to 'back off.' So let's back up and start with the painting."

"Niko didn't paint that," Laura said smugly. "It's mine and I wanted it back, so I went to the B&B to get it."

Her attorney leaned over and whispered in her ear, probably advising her to remain silent, but Laura rebuffed her. "I already told you I did *not* kill Niko. When we heard he had fallen to his death, I wanted to get my painting back. So this was not theft. I was just avoiding having to wait to have my property returned to me."

Jack looked at her with skepticism. "So, you're telling me you happened to bring a shipping case with a valuable Murillo painting to this retreat week? And then you just left this valuable painting in your hotel room, unattended, while you were gone all day for the retreat? No, Laura. I think not."

"Get to the point, Chief," the attorney prompted.

"We have an appraiser coming to evaluate the painting. We know Niko was involved in forgeries. So, your client is either looking at theft charges, or she's complicit in forgery."

"That's pretty thin. What else do you have?"

"We have plenty more. We found Niko's phone in your purse, Laura. Did you take it from his room, or did he have it with him up at the falls? We'll be looking at phone records, and we'll see what communication you had with him prior to his death, and if you were attempting to connect with Niko's contact in order to unload the painting."

Laura remained mute while her attorney scribbled notes.

Jack moved the bag with the pill bottle to the center of the table. "Let's move on to these pills. We found Niko's prints on the bottle, and yours, so how do you explain that?"

"No comment," she said, defiantly.

"And this notebook..." He pulled it out of the plastic bag. "See how when you tilt it in the light you can see the indentation of writing? You must press hard when you write. I do that too. There are all manner of words and numbers, but here...here you can see the words 'Back Off.' This was written recently, because these letters crisscross over other letters and numbers."

At this point, he checked that her attorney was paying close attention, then said, "So you see, this makes the assault on Alex premeditated. You are seen on this video going into the Thunderbird Lodge and leaving approximately four minutes later," he said, pulling up the video of Laura entering the Lodge, with the date and time stamp. "Clearly your plan was to return to get the pills and write the note with the intention of trying to scare off Alex. Why is that?"

Laura looked at her attorney, then once again said,

"No comment."

"To sum up," Jack said, "we have you for theft, and if not theft, forgery. You have the victim's phone. You were witnessed having an argument at the Lodge with Niko the night before he died, and we have you for assault. All of this evidence points to you murdering Niko."

The attorney whispered once again to Laura, then said to Jack, "I'd like a moment to talk to my client."

"That's a good idea. It would be advisable for her to tell us her side of the story before we dig it all up."

Jack once again turned off the tape, picked up the evidence box, switched off the intercom, and left the room.

Stepping out into the hall, I asked, "So what now?"

"We keep working on our end, and then wait till the attorney is done advising her."

I went back out to the reception area and approached the coffee table. Today I didn't even think about the sticky mess. I was just grateful for the warm brew. I took it back with me and reclaimed my seat to observe the guys in action. Travis was looking through phone records, Matt was digging into financials, and Jack was on the phone with what sounded like the fraud department in New York. After a while I leaned my head back against the cool cinder-block wall and closed my eyes. I'm not sure how much time had passed when I heard the officious click-click of the attorney's heels as she entered the room.

"Chief, we're ready for you," she called out.

****

With everyone back in place, the interview continued, and Laura's attorney started things off. "My client is willing to talk about the painting and the pills. However, she firmly denies having any part in Niko's death, so she will not be talking about that."

"All right," Jack said, "tell me about the painting."

Laura crossed her arms. "A few years ago, Niko started doing some forgeries on the side. I found out about it when we dated. He ended up cutting me in on some of the business. I would do lesser-known artists, or maybe unsigned pieces attributed to an artist. I also did a lot of sketches. Minor league stuff."

"How did it work?" Jack asked.

"I would give them to Niko and he would supply them to his contact. The ones I did never amounted to much money. Once the contact got his cut, and Niko took his cut, it was just enough to supplement my own painting.

"I decided it was time to show him what I could really do, so I did the Murillo panel. When I told him about it, he suggested I come here as a last-minute addition to the retreat class and then we could work out the details. I showed it to him at the Lodge, and he took it to offer to his contact, whom he said he was meeting after the retreat.

"When I found out he was dead, I had to get it back, so I went to the B&B and got it from his room. That's it. I did not kill him. I had no motive to kill him."

"Well, maybe you wanted a bigger piece of the action. You were seen having an argument with him Monday evening at the Lodge. Maybe he pushed you too far, and you wanted to cut him out and take over."

The attorney interjected here. "As I stated, I've advised my client not to talk about the murder, and everything regarding that is clearly circumstantial and you know it, so please stick with the agreed-upon topics."

Jack put up his hand and said, "Okay, okay. Let's move on to the pills. They were Niko's, right?"

Laura looked disgusted. "Yes. He got those through a street connection as a painkiller after he hurt his back. Then he kept buying them. I didn't like how he was when he took them. They made him erratic. It's one reason I broke up with him."

"And you took them from his room?"

Laura hesitated and looked at her attorney, who nodded. "Yes. I'm not really sure why I took them. I just grabbed them on my way out of his room. But then, I could tell Alex was trying to dig up information, and I knew she was reporting back to you because you came to pull me out for more questioning after each instance of her sticking her nose in. When I caught her snooping in my bag, I knew she was looking for Niko's phone. I wrote the note, crushed up the K and, later, put it in her tea."

"What did you think would happen?"

"I just thought she would pass out upstairs and then find the note the next morning. I didn't think it would hit her so hard. Listen, this is more proof I didn't kill Niko. I just wanted her to back off so I could get out of here with that painting. That's it. If I had killed Niko, I certainly wouldn't risk calling attention to myself."

The attorney once again chimed in. "I think that's enough for now. Are you going to hold my client?"

"Yes. We can hold her for forty-eight hours, and we'll do that. In the meantime, if you are innocent of murder, as you insist you are, then help yourself, and write down everything you know about Niko's forgery business, and your own part in it. Contacts, locations, everything," Jack said, as he slid a legal pad over to her.

Once again, we convened in the hallway. "Do you buy her story?" I asked.

"I'm not sure. I believe her about the forgeries and trying to get you to back off. Her denial of the murder? I don't know. It has a ring of truth, but murder is obviously a much more serious charge, so she could be lying. And her attorney is correct, right now we don't have enough proof. We have to find something to tie her to it."

"Okay. I'm heading to the Workshop to check in on things, and then I'll be back."

****

I looked at my watch as I entered the building. Everyone would be at lunch now, so I headed to the lounge. Today, the group had moved tables so they could all sit together.

"Alex!" Edgar boomed, when I entered the lounge. "Please update us on what's happening."

"Hi, everyone, how are you holding up?"

"We're okay," said Marie. "Just relieved this dreadful business is over. Don't get me wrong, we are devastated to learn Laura did this, but equally relieved it's over."

"Has she talked?" Peter asked.

I pulled up a chair and sat down. "I'm not sure I can answer all your questions, but I am permitted to relay a few things. Between the line of inquiry opening up after searching Niko's room, and the threat against me, it has led them to a possible link to and motive for Laura. The search of her room confirmed this, and charges have now been filed. I'm afraid I'm only at liberty to give you a brief outline of what we think happened."

Everyone was watching me with rapt attention as I recapped the progress of the investigation, and then all eyes shifted to Annie and Spencer when I credited them with unearthing the forgery angle of the investigation.

Annie said, "We'll tell you more about that in a minute. Go on, Alex."

I finished with the threat against me that Laura had admitted to.

"What was she thinking!" Charles exclaimed. "That's just crazy!"

"She says she didn't murder Niko. So while they hold her, they'll be looking at all the evidence again to find the proof they need. That about sums it up."

While the group turned to Annie and Spencer to hear more about the forgeries, Peter pulled me aside.

"You look exhausted, Alex. Maybe you should go upstairs and get some rest. Chief Maddox has got this, right?"

He had an uncanny way of making me feel protected without being patronizing. "I appreciate your concern, but the adrenaline is keeping me moving. I can crash later."

"What do you think? Do you believe Laura killed him?"

"Honestly? I'm not sure. Her story rang true that she had no motive to kill him since she was just working on a bigger deal with him. But, then again, he could have scammed her out of her cut for that Murillo forgery and she killed him in anger. Something doesn't feel right, though." I scrubbed my face with my hands.

"I don't know. I just need to think."

"From what I understand, ketamine is no joke. You're probably still feeling the residual effects of it. Seriously, why don't you go lie down? Even a half an hour will help."

"Maybe you're right. I'll go talk to the class, and then I'll head upstairs."

The group was enthralled listening to Spencer talk about the technical aspects of forging paintings. I walked up to them and said, "Sorry to interrupt, but I need to ask if you all want to proceed with the rest of the day? We can cancel tonight's reception and exhibition if you don't want to finish this out. It's totally up to you, as a group, and I will support whatever you decide."

Monica put her hand up and said, "I don't know…I wonder if we should cancel. Maybe we should all just go home."

"I don't think so," Edgar said earnestly. "We have come this far together. We need to feel some closure and celebrate that we've gotten through this."

JJ chimed in. "And we've worked so hard. I want to see us finish it out."

"I agree," said Peter. "This has been a tough week. Let's end on a positive note."

"Of course," Monica said meekly. "I don't know what I was thinking."

"It's okay," Bitsy said, patting her hand. "It's been a hard week, but we can either lift ourselves up or go home with a lingering cloud. I think it would be nicer to go home feeling lifted up."

"Then we're agreed," Spencer said. "Ryan and I are going to get all your pieces moved up to the exhibit hall. You'll be thrilled when you see the space this evening."

At that moment, Maggie came running into the lounge. "Alex, can you come to the lab?" When she saw everyone else, she came to a screeching halt. "Um, I need your help with something if you have a minute."

"Of course," I told her. "Carry on, everyone, and I'll see you later."

As Maggie and I rushed down the hall to the photo lab, she whispered, "I found something, and you are *not* going to believe it."

"Is it Laura?"

"Just wait…"

Moments later, Maggie and I were bent over the table with a magnifying glass, looking at an image from the falls.

"I went back through the photos from the falls a second time, saw this, and printed it out. Then I enlarged that area and cleaned it up as much as I could," Maggie said, pointing to the two printed photos.

"Oh my gosh!" I said, in total disbelief. I was looking at an image that showed Niko in the midst of a confrontation up at the falls, and the person he was arguing with was *not* Laura.

I grabbed the photos and magnifier and ran up to my apartment. I texted Jack that I had something for him but wanted to check a couple things first, and then perched on the stool at the kitchen counter and opened my laptop to start a quick social media search. After confirming the timeline and sifting through gallery announcements, I knew I was headed in the right direction. Now it was time to take it to Jack.

Chapter 21

"I need to show you something," I said, entering Jack's office.

"I sure hope it's something to link Laura to the murder," Jack said, swiveling around from his desk.

I set my laptop on the corner of his desk and pulled out the photographs.

Jack leaned over with the magnifier to look at the image and let out a low whistle. "What have we here? It's a little blurry, but it looks like they're in the middle of an altercation." He looked up at me. "But that's not Laura. What else did you find?"

I pulled up holiday images and posts on social media, and the newspaper clip with a short article for a gallery show featuring Niko, which fit the timeline.

"This is good, but it's only circumstantial. We need some solid evidence."

I felt frustrated. "I'm sure it won't do us any good, but have you gone through the crime scene evidence again?"

"Not yet. We have the art appraiser here, and we've been swamped dealing with the New York police about the forgeries."

"Can I help?"

"Yes, we'll get through it faster with more eyes. Grab some gloves from the box on the table."

We pulled the clothing out of the plastic bags and

carefully looked at each piece, and then the shoes. Even though Niko was clearly lacking in the character department, it felt invasive to paw through his personal effects. When nothing new emerged, I blew out a sigh, and at a loss for what to do next, started flipping through the small bags that contained rubbish debris from the scene. There were bits of paper, a bottle cap, a pen that had been in the elements a long time, a rusty nail, and a few chips of glass. I froze when I saw a dirt-encrusted piece of metal.

"Did you see this?"

"Yeah," he said. "It was found on the bank quite a ways from the body. It was rounded up with the other debris during the widened search."

"Can you still get prints off this?"

"It might be possible. I'll get Matt to check. What is it? It just looks like scrap metal."

"I think it's from a bracelet."

Twenty minutes later, Jack and I were sitting in his office chewing over various hypotheticals when Matt stuck his head in. "I was able to pull a partial print, but it wasn't a match for any that we have for this group. And no match from the database. Sorry."

"Damn it," Jack said. "We have everyone's prints, so I guess it was just part of the debris that someone could have dropped at any point."

"Since you've taken prints, can I see it?" I asked.

"Sure," Matt said and handed the plastic bag to me.

I looked at the cleaned piece of metal, turning it over in my hands. "I swear I recognize this, but it's odd there wasn't a print match," I mused aloud. Then the lightbulb went off. Jack looked over at me, and I explained my new theory. We went round and round a few times, my fingers flying on the laptop sifting through more social media.

Jack stepped out to talk to Travis, then came back in and said, "Time is running out. We need to put this all together."

I nodded my head in understanding while taking the last couple of screenshots, and after emailing everything to Jack, I said, "Okay, let's go."

****

As we passed the front desk I looked up at the clock. We were cutting it close. The class would be breaking for the afternoon any minute now. My hands felt clammy, and my stomach was flip-flopping when we reached the room. The participants were washing brushes, cleaning up their work stations, and packing up supplies. Each had left what they wanted to exhibit on their easel. As everyone worked, there wasn't much chatter going on, but the atmosphere was serene.

"Excuse me," Jack said. "Monica, I need you to please come with me."

Monica looked up from drying a brush and blanched. She started backing away from us. "What do you want with me?" she said in a meek voice.

Everyone looked at Jack with confusion on their faces.

"Why do you need Monica?" Edgar asked, in a protective tone.

She sat down on the stool by her easel and, with a shaky hand, set her brush on the table.

I went over to her and laid a hand on her shoulder. "Monica, it would be easier if we could talk privately."

Edgar came to her side, and she looked around at all the concerned faces in the room. "No, I want to stay here, with them."

"As you wish," Jack said. He ushered Edgar back to the others, pulled a stool over to sit beside her, and spoke in a gentle voice. "I need to clarify a few things. Is that okay?"

She nodded.

"Even though we're just talking, if you'd like to have an attorney present, we can move this down to the station and wait while you call one."

Monica nervously looked around the room. "No, I can't fathom why I'd need an attorney."

He pulled out a voice recorder and said, "I'm going to record this, okay?"

She looked at him with wide eyes.

"Don't worry. All interviews are recorded, just as we've done throughout the week when we've talked to any of you." Jack set the recorder on the edge of her worktable, and after carefully sliding her painting over, he pulled out the photos from the falls and placed one on her easel.

"This was taken the morning the class was at the falls. As you can see, in the left corner there is a blur of two people." He then pulled up the second photograph of the enlarged corner. "This is clearer, and if you use this magnifier...well, I think you know what you'll see." He handed her the magnifier, and she timidly leaned forward to look.

Monica abruptly sat back, her pale skin a stark contrast to the sudden flush of red on her cheeks. She opened her mouth but didn't utter a word.

"Can you explain what was happening here?" he asked, pointing to the photo.

She remained mute.

"All right, I'll continue." Jack pulled out a small plastic bag and removed a silver charm. "This was found down on the riverbank near Niko's body. May I please see your bracelet?"

She reluctantly held out her right hand. The bracelet reflected the light from the easel lamp as the little charms swung from the motion of lifting her arm.

Jack looked at me, then returned his attention to Monica. "Would you please remove your bracelet?"

Everyone was stunned. Marie had grabbed Edgar's hand. Paula looked on with sadness in her eyes. Annie, JJ, Bitsy, and Spencer were all looking at each other in disbelief. Peter stood up, sensing we were moving toward a critical moment. He shifted a little closer and leaned his shoulder against the wall.

As for me, I was surprised Monica didn't realize what was happening and that she didn't actually have to talk to Jack. At this point, it was still a voluntary interview.

Jack motioned me over to examine the bracelet. He put Monica's on her worktable and then placed the charm above it. He got up, and I took his seat on the stool next to her. I gently moved the charms on Monica's bracelet until I found the one I was looking for: a silver half heart with a jagged puzzle cut. I took the crime scene charm and laid it next to the half heart. The pieces fit together, and I read the inscription aloud, "Always Sisters, Forever Friends." It was one of those interlocking charms that can be worn on a necklace or bracelet.

I picked up the charm and spoke quietly to Monica. "This isn't yours, is it, Monica? This belongs to your sister Bianca. Right?"

She jerked her head up to look at me, which told me I was right. She remained mute, but I sensed her body tensing, so I proceeded with caution. "Bianca was here, wasn't she? And that photo shows Bianca having an altercation with Niko up at the falls, not you. Her charm must have fallen off in the struggle."

I looked at Jack, and he gave the slightest nod for me to continue. "You had no history with Niko, but your sister did. I went back through your social media. You posted about a trip the two of you were taking. That trip coincided with a gallery show Niko was in, in the same city. I then checked Bianca's socials, and there was a photo of her with Niko at the gallery and quite a few more of just the two of them over a period of days. My theory is that something transpired on that holiday to provoke what happened here."

Monica was looking down at her hands and made no reaction.

"As a matter of fact, when you talked about your sister this week, you never mentioned that she and Niko knew each other. I find that odd. That would have naturally come up in conversation. So that tells me you had a plan before you came. I think maybe you attended this retreat because Niko was going to be here. You've told stories from childhood when you and your sister traded places to prank people, and the two of you hatched a plan to do that here."

"No, you're wrong. I don't know what you're talking about," she said, quietly but firmly.

"As adults you each have your own style, but it wouldn't have been hard for her to alter hers to look like you. And Bianca's an aspiring artist herself, so she could pull it off. Plus, up at the falls, she wouldn't have to interact too closely with the others. Why did she want to see him? Was it just a lark or did she intend to kill him?" I grasped her hand reassuringly, and said, "I'm so sorry, Monica. I'm sure you had no idea what would happen."

Monica pulled away from me, sat back in her chair, and crossed her arms. When she spoke, it was with venom. "You think you know everything. All week you've been asking your questions, thinking you're so smart, and now, you think you know *me*. You still don't get it."

"What don't I get?" I asked, startled by the sudden shift in her tone. "For whatever reason, you created an elaborate scheme to swap places, and Niko ended up dead. When the group came back for lunch, Bianca rushed back to the Lodge on the premise of changing muddy boots, but it was really to switch places back with you. She's the one who killed Niko, and then you covered it up."

"Niko was a horrible person! He got what he deserved. But we didn't do anything, and you have no proof that we did!" she shouted, her face distorted with anger as she wildly looked around the room at the shocked faces of her classmates.

Jack's phone dinged with a text. After checking it, he tapped me on the shoulder indicating he was taking over. I was blindsided by her outburst and numbly stood aside.

"Monica, that is either *you* having the altercation with Niko or your sister. Which is it?" He pointed to the charm and said, "Your half of the charm is on your bracelet, so the logical conclusion is that Bianca was here, this charm is hers, and she was up at the falls.

From your sister's posts, it's clear she knew Niko, but you withheld that information during the investigation. Why would you do that if you or Bianca weren't somehow involved? So what was the nature of their relationship?"

"All right," Monica said petulantly. "Bianca met him last year while we were on holiday. I had to go back home for work, but she stayed on holiday longer and met him after I left."

"How did she meet him?"

"At the gallery. He set his sights on her and showered her with attention. Bianca is a really good artist, and he told her he could introduce her to some dealers and galleries. He said he would help pave the way for her and even help me get into an art school. They spent a few days together, and she texted me how great he was and this would be our way out so we could live the life *we* wanted."

"I can see how that would be alluring," Jack said, in an effort to keep her talking.

She eagerly nodded. "Right? Anyone would have been over the moon!"

"So what happened to make you pull this prank?"

"The last morning she talked to him about the future and the things he had promised—she told him she could quit her job and go with him to New York. He suddenly turned cold and laughed at her. He said they'd had some fun, but it was time to move on and she needed to leave. When she tried to reason with him, he actually threw her out of his hotel room. Can you believe it?"

"So she came here to seek revenge?" Jack suggested.

"No!" Monica said, emphatically. "Bianca and I decided to switch places so she could talk to Niko herself. She deserved that opportunity. He made promises, and he only did it to manipulate her, which devastated her. *Us.* So we wanted to shock him. We thought the threat of outing him for the cad he was to his colleagues and the class would make him follow through on his promises." She looked at her classmates. "I'm sure you all agree. Someone like Niko deserves a little comeuppance every now and then."

Jack pulled her attention back to him. "Weren't you concerned Niko would recognize you and think you were Bianca?"

"Bianca dresses and styles her hair differently than me, and she's more extroverted. At first, I was a little nervous he might recognize me, but then it just made me mad that there was no hint of familiarity. Of course, she cut and dyed her hair to look like me so we could swap places here, but when she revealed herself, he barely remembered her and refused to admit he owed her anything. So yes, they argued, but Niko falling was an accident. No doubt about it."

Jack said evenly, "Bianca shoved him from behind, Monica. Your charade turned deadly. Maybe something more serious happened than Bianca indicated to you."

"No, it was an accident," she said through gritted teeth. "When she confronted him, he just laughed. She told him he wouldn't get away with it, at which point he grabbed her wrist and told her to leave him alone. That's what you see here," she said, pointing to the photo. "He twisted her arm, hissing at her to go back where she came from, that he couldn't be bothered with her silliness.

"*And* he was going to have me removed from the class. He was going to publicly humiliate us! Bianca wrenched to get out of his grasp, and he lost his balance. He couldn't catch himself and went over the edge." Monica shrugged her shoulders and shifted to a blasé tone. "You might even say it was self-defense. But ultimately, it was an accident. These things happen."

Okay, this girl was unhinged. How did we miss that? I looked over at Spencer with wide eyes and the slightest tilt of my head. He got the message and quietly attempted to move the class toward the door.

Jack calmly continued, "Monica, there were bruises on Niko's back—two sets of bruises that indicate a strong shove. That means his back was to her. He had turned his back to her, and she intentionally shoved him off the edge of the cliff. This was no accident."

Jack's phone pinged again with a text. He read it, then gathered the photos, charm, and bracelet. "I was notified earlier that Bianca was located at a motel on the edge of town and again just now that she's being brought in for questioning. So I think it's time we head down to the station."

Monica stood up and looked wildly around the room, yelling, "She didn't intend to kill him, but he continued to mock her. Bianca couldn't stand it anymore and lost her temper. It could have happened to anyone. You all know how he was!"

Everyone stared at her in disbelief.

Monica's behavior had become unpredictable, so Jack discreetly reached for his cuffs, but then hesitated. She had actually confessed that Bianca killed Niko, so I assumed he was waiting, knowing every word she said was going to help build the case.

Monica took a moment to wipe her mouth with the back of her hand. When she saw her outburst didn't garner her the sympathy she expected from her classmates, she returned their stares with a look of disdain.

"It took everything I had to sit here all week acting weepy and meek when on the inside I was cheering that he was dead. And if not for that damned photograph, we could have gotten on with our lives."

"You would have let Laura go to jail for murder?" Charles asked, in a shocked voice from the other side of the room.

She turned to him with a sneer. "Well, as we know, she isn't a saint. She was in cahoots with Niko. Besides, I'm sure she would have gotten off for the murder. They didn't have any evidence.

"But I guess I should thank her for providing a distraction. We were worried when Bianca went back to look for that damned charm and had the close call running into Alex up at the falls. But clearly, Laura was paranoid that Alex was onto her little side business, and drugging her just further shifted attention away from me. And while the police focused on Laura, it left me free to play the helpless waif until I could leave and go home."

I heard gasps in the room, and I said, "Well, Monica, I guess your plan didn't work. You aren't going home any time soon, are you?"

The next thing I saw was a fist, Monica's fist, coming toward my face. I dodged as quickly as I could, but the blow landed on the side of my left eye. I saw little blinks of light and felt myself reeling.

Chapter 22

"Awwww, what the hell! Not again..." I moaned, as I felt myself slipping to the floor.

Jack moved swiftly, grabbing Monica's arm with one hand while applying the cuffs with the other. I vaguely heard him charge her with accessory to murder, followed by, "You have the right to remain silent..." and then I focused on my overwhelming desire to lie on the floor.

Peter rushed over and put his arm around my waist to pull me up, then he lowered me into a nearby chair, saying in a soothing voice, "Here we go, you're all right. Just sit still. Annie, come hold on to her, and I'll go get some ice." He dashed out of the room.

Jack bellowed at me, "Are you okay?"

"I'm fine, I'm fine." I started to slump down in the chair and as Annie righted me, I said, "Whoops-a-daisy," with a lopsided grin.

Jack shook his head and did an eye roll, then he marched Monica to the door, saying through a clenched jaw, "Let's go. You waived your right to an attorney earlier, but I suggest you rethink that now."

****

Everyone had moved to the lounge to digest what had just transpired. When I entered the room, Peter gave me his chair and turned it around so I could sit saddle-style. With my elbows propped on the back of the chair I could hold the towel-wrapped plastic bag of ice firmly against my eye.

"Well, this was quite a turn of events," I said.

"Holy cow, Alex," Annie said. "Are you sure you don't want to see a doctor?"

"No, I'll be fine."

"You're going to have quite a shiner," Ryan said, grinning.

"Yeah." I sighed. "I guess I will."

"I can't believe she fooled us," Marie said, still somewhat stunned. "And why not just confront him? Why the game of swapping places? It was so pointless."

Bitsy, sitting cross-legged on the floor, added, "I know! I feel so stupid for not seeing it. Part of my job is handling the complexities of unstable people, and I did *not* see that coming!"

"Well, I feel betrayed," Edgar said. "I took her under my wing, and she took advantage of me. And to see it unravel like that was scary."

JJ sat up with a jolt and said, "Oh my gosh, I just remembered the card reading I did for Monica during the game night! I sort of glossed over having her reshuffle and draw a second set of cards, but in truth, it was because the first set of cards were quite dark. Those cards actually did portend the depths of deceit, but they were totally out of character for the Monica we knew, so I wasn't suspicious. I figured there might be some minor underlying personal issues we didn't need to get in to, but not this..." She trailed off.

Charles interjected, "And I remember how she was so confused by the threat against you, Alex, and by Laura being arrested. Of course she was confused. She didn't know about the forgeries and couldn't figure out what was going on since Bianca was the one who killed Niko."

Spencer shook his head. "And she kept wanting to go home. Yeah, she just wanted to get out of here."

Paula and I exchanged a glance. We'd totally misjudged this one. The signs had been there, but they were so subtle we hadn't dug any deeper. This was a case of the slow simmer building to the blow.

After a little more back and forth about it, Spencer once again took the reins as class leader. "Okay, folks. I feel some déjà vu here, but I must ask you if you want to continue with the reception tonight. People from the community will be attending, so if as a collective we decide to cancel, then we need to do it now. What do you think?"

The group looked like they'd been "drug through the wringer," as my mom used to say, but they felt a need for the camaraderie of each other and to be around ordinary everyday people. So onward we would go.

Annie pushed herself up from the floor. "Let's all take the next couple of hours to get some rest or take a walk, whatever will help you restore some balance, and we'll meet back here around six thirty so you can see the exhibit before it opens at seven. Spencer, do you and Ryan need any help getting things moved and set up?"

"Nope, we're good. I already plotted out where everything will go, so we'll make quick order of it."

After a round of hugs and small talk, the group went their separate ways, and I headed upstairs to decompress.

****

The "By the Seaside" ring tone of my alarm

brought me out of a deep nap. I reluctantly pushed myself up on the couch and sat for a minute looking out the window. I brushed my hair back off my face, flinched when my hand made contact with my eye, and got up to survey the damage.

I groaned when I looked in the mirror. The bruising had already begun; the corner of my left eye to the temple had a dark tinge of grayish-purple to it. I took a long hot shower, washing my hair twice to prolong the warm envelope of steam, and I already felt better as I wrapped the thick towel around me and padded to the closet.

What to wear, what to wear...I mused, flipping through hangers. *Ah, perfect.* My old standby: a lightweight gray wool sheath dress. It was comfortable, with a little stretch, and I figured the gray would pair nicely with my bruised eye. Along with my favorite black T-strap pumps and some understated silver jewelry, including the amethyst necklace JJ had loaned me, the wardrobe part was done.

The makeup took a little longer. I had to wipe everything off and start over when an attempt to fully cover the bruise made it look like a theatrical makeup mishap. The second attempt was better, with just a little additional powder to lighten the bruise, and voilà! Good enough.

A few minutes later, I was leaning against the kitchen counter, cradling a cup of coffee, when I heard a soft knock on the door.

"Want a cup?" I asked Jack, walking him toward the kitchen.

"Nah, I don't have that much time. I just wanted to drop by to see how you're doing and give you an update," he said, tilting my chin back to examine my eye. "You'll be fine. It'll be quite a sight in the coming days, but eventually you'll have your normal ugly mug back."

I slapped his arm and said, "Thanks a lot...jerk."

He rewarded me with a warm smile. "Seriously, how are you holding up? I'm sorry I didn't cuff Monica sooner. I just wanted her to keep talking."

"I'll be all right. It was kind of my own fault for taunting her there at the end. But boy, that was chilling, and I'm glad you got it all on tape. I've never seen anyone shift personalities like that."

"Still waters run deep. Repression, suppression— whatever the clinical term is—of the life they wanted to live versus the life they felt trapped in, coupled with entangled twin minds and a dose of mania. It created an eruption."

"I guess so."

"Listen, I can't thank you enough for your help. We would still be spinning our wheels if you hadn't noticed that charm and recalled seeing one on Monica's bracelet."

"I'm glad I was able to help."

"But don't let it go to your head. You got lucky. And you could have really been hurt...both with the drugging and that punch. So it's back to the background for you, right?"

"I agree." But did I really? I wasn't going to admit it to Jack, but I kind of liked the adrenaline rush of this investigation.

"Okay. The update. Bianca was tracked down at a motel on the edge of town, where she was waiting for Monica to join her. I've interviewed her, and she mirrored Monica's statement, although she still says it was an accident. The DA thinks she has enough to move forward with the charges."

"Will the charges stick?"

"They'll do their little dance and try to get Bianca to agree to a deal in order to avoid a trial. There's more than enough evidence for a second-degree murder charge, but it will be difficult to prove she went to the falls with the intention of killing Niko. So they are better off making a deal."

"What about Monica?"

"Monica will be facing a number of lesser charges, and I think when they're both hit with the reality of what's ahead of them, they'll each confess and take a deal. They were pretty devious in both the plan and the cover up. Thinking back, even Monica's detailed report of the guy on the trail watching the group was just misdirection."

"They sure were able to be calculated under extreme stress. What about Laura?"

"The FBI has already dispatched someone from the fraud department to interview her. It sounds like they'll probably strike a deal with her in exchange for information. There was even talk of using her for a sting operation. If you can believe it, she was more forthcoming with me because I told her they praised the quality of that Murillo forgery she did."

"It appears a validation of her abilities is her Achilles' heel."

"Of course, she still has the charge for drugging you. We'll have to see if that gets rolled into the other deal."

"Unbelievable. That could have been serious. But I

think I would rather be able to move on and put this all behind me, so if she's beholden to the FBI, that's good enough for me because that means they'll be watching her."

"That's what I thought you'd say." He leaned over to give Baxter an ear rub, then walked to the door. "I gotta get back to the office. We'll talk more tomorrow. Good luck with the reception."

"Thanks," I said to his departing back, as the door softly closed behind him.

****

At a little after six I walked from my apartment across the landing to the exhibit space, where Ryan and Spencer had done a beautiful job displaying the art.

There was a profound confluence of senses in a museum or gallery, particularly when no one else was there. The art sent out an energy of its own. Each artist's voice wordlessly communicated metaphysically, yet you felt as if it was tangible, with each piece's energy surrounding you. I surveyed the exhibit, with the soft-hued task lights highlighting each piece, and for that moment, I could focus solely on the art and nothing else.

A sudden burst of sound interrupted my reverie, and I turned to see Aunt Claudia and Jeff enter from the service elevator with a rolling cart piled high with coolers and trays.

"Oh, Alex," Aunt Claudia exclaimed, enveloping me in a bear hug.

My voice was muffled as I tried to speak from the depths of her embrace. "I'm fine!"

"Let me look at your face," she said, pulling back to examine my eye. "It reminds me of when you and

Jack were kids and you'd get banged up climbing and falling out of trees. You're tough; you'll be okay, kiddo," she concluded. Then her expression changed, and she gave me some stink eye. "But shame on you. You told me you weren't getting involved in this and now look at you. You get drugged and then punched! I guess you haven't learned the art of restraint yet, have you?"

"I guess not," I acknowledged, putting my arm around her to lead her to the buffet table. "Can I help you set up?"

"Sure. You can put out the tablecloth and trays, and we'll load them up. The paper doilies are in that bag," she said, pointing to the cart, "and the wine and punch goes on the side table."

In short order, the trays were filled, and vases with blush-colored dahlias, paired with a variety of greenery, had transformed the tables from ho-hum to lovely.

Near the entrance, on the large monitor mounted to the wall, Maggie had the slideshow up and running. It was on a shorter loop because she had removed images of Laura, Monica, and Niko. We all agreed it was a no-brainer to leave them out of the exhibit altogether and only highlight the remaining group.

Within minutes, the class arrived, with Spencer, Annie, Maggie, and Ryan leading the way. I motioned for them to congregate near the front of the room. Everyone had transformed themselves for the evening reception.

The men looked like they had all shopped together, wearing chinos or jeans, a button-down shirt, tie, and jacket. The women, by contrast, displayed a wide variety of colors, patterns, and styles. Bitsy, of course, took the prize with a stunningly beautiful headband consisting of a cherry blossom vine with delicate flowers, and two gray-and-white birds with partially opened wings. In contrast to her usual bold colors, she had on a pale pink flowing silk blouse over flared black slacks. She looked ready for a Paris runway.

"Do you have an update for us?" Edgar asked.

"I do," I said and gave them the recap of what Jack had given me permission to relay. When I finished, I turned on a smile to change the subject. "We have a few minutes before the exhibit opens, so feel free to wander around and look at your wonderful works of art. We also have a quite a few of Spencer's and Annie's up, too. And I would like to add that, due to the extreme circumstances during this week, I'm extending an offer for you to return any time you wish to participate in another retreat, free of charge, of course."

The offer was enthusiastically received, and once everyone dispersed, Spencer and I took up posts by the entrance to greet the public. There was a higher-than-normal turnout, and we surmised this was because of the news of Niko's murder. The atmosphere in the room quickly ramped up, though, from politely cordial to festive, and the evening was off to a good start. I was happy to see most of our artists from the Workshop along with quite a few students from our classes had also come.

When Brenda and Lyle Danby came in, Lyle headed straight for the buffet table, but Brenda pulled me aside to ask for an update. Since they had to put up with some of the fallout from the week, I obliged.

A little later I saw Ari shyly enter the exhibit. I gave her a quick hug, relieved to see she had some color back in her cheeks. She looked healthy, and dare I say, happy. "You look great. How's everything going?" I asked.

"Good. Real good. Thanks to you and Jack, I've contacted an attorney in New York to help with settling Niko's estate. I'll make a quick trip there next week, and then I'll go back later to take care of the bulk of things, like packing up his studio and apartment. By then the FBI will have taken anything they need. There will still be some red tape regarding his bank accounts, but eventually that will be resolved."

"Sounds like you have things under control, and you seem to be holding up well."

"It's an odd thing. Of course, I would never have wished Niko to be murdered. Never. But I do feel like I'm suddenly back in charge of my life again."

"Well, it's good to meet the *real* Ari," I said.

An hour later, I was finally able to take a break from hostess duties. I grabbed a glass of punch and walked up to Paula, who was standing near her pieces. She'd chosen her small painting from the falls and the drawing she had done of Maggie's hand. They were both delicate and refined. Through subtle shading she managed to tell a story. The finished products were exquisite, and I told her so.

"Thank you," Paula said shyly, but with a hint of pride, as she smoothed down the front of her tailored coat dress. "Aside from the obvious, it's been a wonderful experience."

"I am so sorry for everything you guys in the class had to go through. I can't believe how blind I was to Monica's deception."

"We all were. But from my own experience, it

sometimes happens, and you just have to brush yourself off and go on. Beating oneself up does no good."

"You're right, and I'll try," I said, with a smile of gratitude.

We stood in a comfortable silence, looking at the artwork, and then she leaned toward me and said, "I have a sneaky suspicion Marie and I will take you up on your offer to return at some point for another class."

"That would make me very happy. I would really like to get to know you better."

"Then it's settled. We shall see you again."

I continued on my way around the room and saw JJ's watercolor from the falls, and Bitsy's painting that featured Maggie from the waist up in her forties outfit. They each had their own style. JJ's work had a freedom to it, and you could feel the joyful abandon emanate from the wash of color. Bitsy's hand was more controlled as she meticulously stayed true to the subject, with attention to detail on Maggie's blazer and fedora.

Peter's painting was on this wall as well. His painting of the falls was more broad-stroked, and almost impatient in its expressionism, but it had a certain allure in its bold colors.

Annie came around the corner of the center display and said, "Have you seen Charles' piece yet?"

"No, I was interrupted before I could look closely at everything."

"Come on, you've got to see this. It's really good."

We walked to the righthand wall where Charles' painting instantly drew the eye. It was from the falls, but he'd added a dimension to it beyond what the eye could have seen on that day.

He created atmosphere by altering the sky to create a brooding image of color and clouds, as if a storm were brewing in the distance. The light filtered down to glisten on the water cascading to the river below. You could almost feel the mist gently wafting up from the water. There were undefined figures walking along the paths, and a few seated figures at easels, just as the class had been doing on Tuesday.

I walked up to look closely, taking in every detail of his mastery, when I noticed a lone figure standing on the edge overlooking the falls. Even though the figure was undefined, I knew who, and what, it represented.

Charles walked up to me and I said, "This is really magnificent, Charles."

"Thank you. It's an important work for me."

"That's Niko, isn't it?" I asked, pointing to the lone figure.

"Yes. And it serves as a reminder for me. I've seen some things this week…things I didn't like in others that I started to see in myself. This will be a reminder never to go down that road again."

"Well, not only is this spectacular, but you've also become someone I've very much enjoyed meeting, and I wish you all the best for your future. I truly feel it will be a bright one."

We clinked glasses, and I moved away to look at the front of the portable zigzag wall in the center of the room. There I saw Marie's painting of Pookie, next to Edgar's sketch of a full-length Maggie. He had also included his small painting of a pear with a bowl and paring knife, from the still life class. Each of these, while maybe not at the top of the class, were undeniably quite good.

I could hear Marie before I saw her. She was in full-on swoosh-and-jangle mode. Her chiffon top and circle skirt flowed effortlessly around her, and everything from her glasses chain to her necklace and bracelets emitted a sound as she moved her hands in grand gestures while animatedly talking to JJ. She was quite a character, and I sincerely hoped she and Paula would come back one day.

I continued to the left side wall where most of Annie and Spencer's works were displayed. Annie had chosen a selection of neon signs, and three of her more whimsical pieces; the personality of each was boldly eye-catching. Spencer's selections were more subtle, smaller in scale, with minute detail. I had leaned forward to look at each component in one of his when I sensed a presence behind me.

I turned to see Peter/Walter watching me from a few feet away.

"It's quite a show, isn't it?" I asked.

"That it is. Your team has managed to highlight our work in a way that elevates it way past our actual abilities." He moved forward to stand next to me.

"Oh, I wouldn't say that. You all should be proud of what you've accomplished. Particularly with the challenges of the week. Besides, everything, even great artists' works, looks better when displayed properly. Good lighting is an artists' best friend."

"Well, you're generous in your estimation of our accomplishments. But I do have to say it is gratifying to see our works on exhibit next to Annie and Spencer's. Just having ours in the same room makes us feel better about ourselves."

He turned to face me. "You look lovely, by the

way. Quite a feat considering your afternoon. How's your eye doing?"

I self-consciously put my hand up to my face. "It doesn't hurt too much right now, but that may still be the adrenaline. How bad does it look?"

His eyes twinkled when he smiled, and he said, "Not too bad. Your dress matches it nicely."

I let out a hearty laugh. "No one else has noticed that, and I chose it on purpose!"

"Nicely done. So, I would imagine you're glad this week is over."

"You can say that again. I'm exhausted but also incredibly relieved it was resolved before tonight. I'm not sure how we would have handled things if everyone had to remain here past today. Thankfully, we didn't have to figure that out."

"Yes," he said. "The timing was critical, and you all solved this in the nick of time. I'm still a bit thrown by Monica. Laura was not such a surprise, but Monica...well, that hit everyone pretty hard."

"When in close proximity to each other for so many hours every day, you can't help but develop a bond with each other."

"Plus, the retreat is just that—a retreat from the everyday world, so the usual radar we draw upon to trust people is suspended due to the common bond that brought us here. So it was a slap of reality. But fortunately we have tonight to lighten the mood before we head back to our individual realities."

"And what does your reality look like?" I asked.

"Well, I'm off to London in a few days for a consulting job. Then I'll figure out where my home base is going to be. And I'd like to come back and have that conversation with you, if you are agreeable to it, that is."

I looked at him for a moment, then said, "I'll look forward to it."

"Good. In the meantime, shall we rejoin the festivities?" he asked.

"Absolutely."

The rest of the evening was a blur of conversation and laughter. At the close of the reception, Spencer made arrangements with each participant to pick up or ship their pieces, and after a round of hugs and commitments to keep in touch, the class made their way out. Our crew—Maggie, Ryan, Spencer, Annie, JJ, Bitsy, and I—made quick order of the clean-up, and all agreed a drink out in the courtyard was in order.

I walked across the landing to my apartment for a quick change and to get Baxter, and as we descended the stairs, the familiar sight of the lobby and front desk sparked a recognition that the earlier tightening of senses was dissolving. The emotional warmth of the Workshop was coming back, and my shoulders dropped a notch. We had weathered this storm, and we were going to be fine.

Out in the courtyard, the gang was all assembled. Gone was the heightened tension. Now, feet were propped on chairs, legs were casually crossed, cold beer was passed around, and bottles were clinked for a congratulatory toast. Even Baxter was relaxed, milling around, going from person to person for a pat on the head.

I pulled over a chair and leaned back with a sigh of relief. We all seemed to tacitly agree to leave the talk of Monica and Laura for another day, and instead, the conversation was kept light with stories from the reception or snippets from the prior week. The focus was no longer all about the murder. I knew it would take time, but I also now knew we were going to be able to get past this.

The door from the lobby clanged open, and I turned to see Peter walking over to us.

"Peter! What are you doing here? Did you forget something?" Spencer asked jovially.

I got up to meet him before he reached the group. "What are you doing?" I asked, in a hushed voice.

"I decided it's time I meet everyone. Better now than later, right?"

I looked at him, knowing he was right, but I was not looking forward to another round of shock and questions. "Okay, let's go," I said, with resignation.

We approached the group, and he pulled up a chair and sat down as if he was perfectly comfortable here.

I looked at the circle of expectant faces, and said, "Everyone, I'd like you to meet Walter Sarnov."

Over the next couple of hours, Walter effortlessly engaged my group of friends and seamlessly fit in. The more I got to know him, the more intrigued I became, and I was surprised to find myself hoping he would be back soon.

A word about the author...

Sydney Abrams is a debut author, and her arts and crafts cozy mystery series is steeped in a life's experience in the arts coupled with a love for mystery books. She was immersed in both these worlds from childhood, and that influence stayed with her as an adult. Sydney has created artwork for auctions and commissions, and has been part of an art group of professional and amateur artists for twenty years. Literature and the arts go hand in hand, but these worlds collided when Sydney realized that her art group offered up the perfect cast of characters for a cozy mystery.

Still Life, Still Dead is the first book in her Arts and Crafts Mystery series.

To learn more about Sydney, please visit https://www.sydneyabrams.com/